A Fallacious Seduction

by

Virginia Barlow

A Fallacious Seduction

Cover Art by *Jennifer Greeff*

The Wild Rose Press, Inc.
PO Box 708
Adams Basin, NY 14410-0708
Visit us at www.thewildrosepress.com

Publishing History
First Cactus Rose Edition, 2020
Print ISBN 978-1-5092-3209-3
Digital ISBN 978-1-5092-3210-9

Published in the United States of America

"I know you remember. Quit playing games, Jenna, and answer the question." He let the hammer down slow on his gun and put it back in its holster. "Tell me what I want to know, and I won't hurt you." His voice was smooth as Tennessee whisky. It wrapped around her and settled in her stomach. His blue eyes gazed into hers, and Shanna nearly swooned on the spot. With his gun safely in its holster and no longer distracting her, she realized he was more than handsome. He was perfect.

Her mouth dried, and her palms started to sweat. She must have hit her head hard. She dropped her gaze and sucked in some air. She couldn't remember what she was saying. *This is crazy! Who the hell is this man?* "I don't remember you because I don't know you." It was the truth. She would have remembered a man like him.

The man laughed.

Shanna turned away from the husky sound of his voice. It warmed her through. The last time a handsome man paid attention to her, she jumped in with her whole heart and both feet. She almost drowned. Best get some distance between her and the stranger before she did something she regretted.

Another Book by Virginia Barlow

My previous release is *THE WICKED SISTER*, a novel set in the distant past. It contains danger, excitement, betrayal, and a happily ever after.

Dedication

To George,
George Jr, Lyndon, Melvyn, Grant, Logan and Hugo,
you are my inspiration.

Chapter 1

Somewhere in Wyoming Territory, July 1870

Shanna Marie Johnston would remember this day forever after, as the day her life exploded. Everything changed. As a rule, her life was bland. She got up, walked to work at Tanner's Mercantile, walked home, did her chores, and went to bed. Once a year she took a train ride from Pine Bluffs to Omaha for a week to see Mama. That was as exciting as her life got, until today.

The day started simple enough. She rose, dressed, and helped Mama get breakfast. She packed her traveling case with the few things she had and joined Mama at the table. While they ate, Shanna broached the subject of staying in Omaha instead of going back to Rock Creek. Shanna didn't want to be alone anymore. She wanted a family. She wanted to belong. She wanted a sister or a brother, Christmas presents under the tree, Sunday dinners, picnics, walks by the river, and nights in front of the fire playing checkers. She wanted someone to love and to be loved in return. She wanted to be with Mama.

Mama smiled and shook her head. "It's too dangerous, darling," she said and rubbed a hand wearily through her thinning dark hair. "I do not dare have you here for more than a few days once a year. Someone might see you and recognize you. It's safer for both of us if you go back to Rock Creek with Joseph and Sara. Thank God you don't remember the terror, darling, but I do. I miss you dreadfully, but it's better if you stick to the yearly visits."

Shanna rubbed her sleeve against the little window of the Overland Express as it chugged its way toward Pine Bluffs. She peered through the cloudy glass hoping to see out. She wanted to look at something else besides the happy couple in front of her. Or the young family sitting two rows back. She pretended she didn't notice the two brothers who sat shoulder to shoulder to her left, or the elderly couple whispering together in the far corner. Everyone had someone. Everyone but her. Shanna blinked back tears. She thought that this year she could stay in Omaha. She counted on it. She didn't want to go back to Rock Creek and face Daniel Anderson. Not after he broke their engagement and humiliated her in front of the whole town. She didn't want to face Delphine Otis, either. Delphine lived to torment her. She did a pretty good job of it, too. Shanna sighed. She would rather take on whatever terror frightened Mama, than face the people of Rock Creek.

The little boy two rows back dropped his ball. It rolled toward Shanna and stopped by her feet. Smiling, Shanna bent to retrieve it. She looked into the little boy's chocolate brown eyes and everything went black.

Shanna regained consciousness sometime later. She could smell dirt and smoke. There was no sound except the beating of her own heart in her ears. Nothing stirred. Nothing moved. She winced at a blinding pain in her head. God, she hurt. Where was she? Where was the smoke coming from? She blinked her eyes trying to see. Someone's hands rolled her onto her back.

A smooth, husky voice murmured, "You're okay. I've got you."

Shanna threw an arm over her eyes to protect them from the sudden glare of the sun. Did she know a man with a husky drawl? She didn't think so. She moved her arm to get a peek at him and winced. She caught sight of a bulky figure before the sun blinded her, and her eyes watered. Hastily, she covered them again. She didn't want to move. She listened. Everything was quiet. Did the man go? She decided she didn't care. She was hot as all get out, and sticky. Her head throbbed. Every part of her body ached. Shanna wrinkled her brow. *Where the hell am I?* She blinked and reached tentative fingers to the sore spot on her head. She wasn't bleeding. A movement above her caught her eye. So, the man hadn't gone away. She could hear him moving in the grass beside her. She heard a metallic click as the hammer of a gun was pulled back right above her. Shanna moved her arm and looked up. She gazed into the barrel of a pistol. It loomed in front of her face. It looked about ten feet long and six feet wide with a gaping black center. Her heart stopped. Funny how guns looked bigger than life when they were pointed at you. Shanna's mouth went dry. *Who the hell would want to shoot me?* Cautiously, she moved her arm away from her face and gazed past the gun at the giant man holding it. She met the ice blue stare of a scruffy, blond-haired man. He knelt by her side frowning ferociously. He must be the owner of the smooth, husky drawl.

Shanna swallowed. "Who are you, mister, and why are you pointing your gun at me?" She gazed at him trying to remember who he was, or why he wanted to shoot her.

"You know why, Jenna," the man answered. His eyes narrowed on her face. Shanna's throat tightened. He stared at her for a long minute, and then he got to his feet. He searched the area around them on every side. The pistol moved with him. She let out a shaky breath when he moved his gun away from her. Her heart started to beat again. Shanna sat up, keeping her eyes on the stranger. He was wound as tight as a rattlesnake ready to strike. Dizziness forced her to drop her head for a minute. The man turned slowly in every direction. He surveyed the area carefully, his gun still cocked in his hand. Cautiously, Shanna slipped her hand into the pocket of Aunt Sara's old dress and through the hole in the bottom. Her hand closed around the ivory handle of the knife she wore strapped to her thigh.

She frowned up at the man, hoping he didn't see her hand moving inside her pocket. She had no idea where she was, or why this stranger had his gun pointed in her direction. There was no way in hell she was going down without a fight. He stared down at her. He pointed the gun at her head, again. It was still cocked. Shanna quit breathing.

"Where are they, Jenna?" the man asked.

"Where are who?" she answered slowly inching her knife forward.

"Your men. Where are your men?"

"What men?" She moved her knife to the opening in her pocket.

He waved his gun in her face. "You know what men. Answer the question." The big man said the words between clenched teeth. He leaned toward her until the barrel of his gun touched her nose. He was angry if the muscle working back and forth in his jaw was any sign.

"I don't have any men," she answered without blinking. Her mind searched for any memory of him, or a woman named Jenna. She drew a blank.

He stood up and scanned the area around them, again. He took his revolver with him. "I know they're here somewhere," he said. His gaze swiveled back to her. He leaned forward, caught her wrist in one big hand, and squeezed. "You still have a knife strapped to your thigh?" he asked. His eyes narrowed on her face.

"No," Shanna lied. She barely had time to shove it back into the scabbard before he pulled her hand out and glared at her empty fingers. How the hell did he know about her knife? Her blade was the only defense she had.

The big man stared at her for several minutes. "If I find out you're lying to me, you'll regret it," he threatened.

Shanna held still for a few minutes. Who was he? How did he know she wore a knife on her thigh? She glanced at his pistol and swallowed. She decided to stay quiet until she figured out who he was and what he wanted.

"How long have you been this far west?" he asked studying her face. "Why are you here?" He narrowed his gaze on her. "What could you possibly want in the middle of Wyoming territory?" he murmured. His sharp gaze swept over her again. "Tell me what I want to know, and I'll tell the judge you cooperated. It's the best offer you're getting from me."

Shanna didn't answer. The man was out of his mind. He wasn't making any sense. She wiped the perspiration from her forehead and took the opportunity to stare back at him. He was handsome with dirty blond hair, a coating of whiskers, and piercing blue eyes. He wore a dirty blue shirt stretched tight over his broad shoulders. One sleeve was missing, revealing a large bronzed bicep. Her gaze caught on the bulging muscle. His skin looked as smooth and golden as melted caramel. She licked her lips. *He sure is big.* Shanna's gaze traveled over his flat stomach and focused on the missing sleeve tied around his massive thigh. The giant man was injured. The sleeve around his thigh was bloody.

"I'm in the middle of Wyoming Territory because I live here. What I want is to go home. I don't know why a judge would care where I am or what I'm doing." Shanna locked gazes with him. "I think you hit your head, or you've gone loco in the sun. You're not making any sense. Now, let me go."

He glared at her. He didn't believe her. She could see it in his expression. She got unsteadily to her feet. Every part of her ached. Shanna swayed. She put a hand to her head to stop the dizziness.

"Where are they? I won't ask again, Jenna," he said softly.

Shanna shivered. When he spoke soft, it scared her to death. "I don't know what you're talking about, mister. I do not know you, and I do not have any men. You've got the wrong girl. My name is Shanna, not Jenna. I haven't done anything wrong." She hoped she sounded stronger than she felt. As soon as her head quit spinning, she'd figure out what to do with him.

"I know you remember. Quit playing games, Jenna, and answer the question." He let the hammer down slow on his gun and put it back in its holster. "Tell me what I want to know, and I won't hurt you." His voice was smooth as Tennessee whisky. It wrapped around her and settled in her stomach. His blue eyes gazed into hers, and Shanna nearly swooned on the spot. With his gun safely in its holster and no longer distracting her, she realized he was more than handsome. He was perfect.

Her mouth dried, and her palms started to sweat. She must have hit her head hard. She dropped her gaze and sucked in some air. She couldn't remember what she was saying. *This is crazy! Who the hell is this man?* "I don't remember you because I don't know you." It was the truth. She would have remembered a man like him.

The man laughed.

Shanna turned away from the husky sound of his voice. It warmed her through. The last time a handsome man paid attention to her, she jumped in with her whole heart and both feet. She almost drowned. Best get some distance between her and the stranger before she did something she regretted. She needed to head for home as soon as she figured out where the heck she was. Shanna turned around. Her eyes widened when she spotted the mess. A train lay on its side not fifty feet away. Debris and twisted metal were everywhere. It looked like an explosion split the train in two and scattered pieces of it all over the countryside. Black smoke billowed from a roaring fire licking away at the cars. Now she knew why she hurt so badly. She remembered everything, her mother, the train ride, the little boy and his ball, and the explosion. Shanna choked back a sob. The last thing she remembered was handing the ball back to the little brown-eyed boy. She thought of the other passengers.

"Did anybody else make it?" Shanna whispered.

"No." His words were clipped. He stared at her. "I don't know how you sleep at night after the things you've done. Most people couldn't."

Shanna looked over at him. "I sleep fine," she lied. She would if her life wasn't so complicated.

"You're going to prison if it's the last thing I do on God's green earth," he promised.

Shanna stared at him in disbelief. The man was several bullets shy of a loaded barrel. Then she frowned. It occurred to her this delusional man might have a reason for being so aggressive. He might be connected to Mama. Was he part of Mama's secret?

"Do you know Mary Johnston, from Omaha, Nebraska?" She watched him intently, searching for recognition. Was he the reason Mama sent her back to Rock Creek instead of letting her stay in Omaha? Was Mama's secret the reason he pulled a gun on her?

The man's gaze narrowed. He looked at Shanna suspiciously. "Who the hell is Mary Johnston?" His hand dropped to the butt of his gun, pulling it from the holster. He scanned the area around them again.

Shanna shrugged. *It was worth a shot.* The man looked as surprised by the name as she was when she opened her eyes with his pistol pointing at her. He probably didn't know who his own mother was, let alone hers. She looked toward the train once more, and suddenly it dawned on her. She was stranded out on the prairie, alone. Well, except for the giant cowboy with the delusional mind and smoky voice. Granted, he was handsome as all get out, but he was also too gun happy.

It took the edge off his good looks. Shanna kicked at a clump of sagebrush and then looked at the sky. It was late afternoon and high time to skedaddle. Nobody would be coming to look for her, so she'd best get a move on. Uncle Joseph and Aunt Sara would throw a party if she didn't show up. They didn't like taking her in any more than she liked being there. And Daniel Anderson? Daniel would make some mean comment, and then he and Delphine would laugh. Delphine. Shanna frowned. Delphine Otis would gloat over her demise. She'd think she won, too. The thought stopped Shanna for a second or two. She didn't know why she cared. Delphine Otis could take a wild train ride to Hades.

Then she thought of Rose. Rose would worry. Shanna smiled. Rose Tanner was her best friend and the only good thing about Rock Creek. If Shanna didn't make it home, Rose would scare up a search party and come looking for her, one way or another. Shanna turned toward the wreckage. She had a long way to go before she got back to Rock Creek, and on foot, it would be infinitely longer.

"Who is Mary Johnston and how does she tie in with you and your men?" the man asked again.

"She doesn't. Forget I asked," Shanna said, walking away. She had too much to do and a long way to get there.

****

Reese grimaced in response. "That's the last damn thing I'm going to do!" he called after her. She didn't turn around. He watched her for several minutes. Who would have guessed Jenna was still alive? Seven years ago, he was unable to stop her from opening the door to the train car. He witnessed the explosion. She was right there. So how was it she escaped without so much as a scar? He had no idea when he got on the train this morning, providence would smile on him, and drop Jenna into his life one more time. One minute he was having a little nap while the train rumbled toward Pine Bluffs, the next he was waking up on the floor of the train car with an eight-inch gash in his leg. *What was she up to?* Why did she go by Shanna?

She was the only person he found alive in the train car. He carried her away from the carnage and laid her down. When he turned her over, he got a good look at her. He almost choked when he recognized her and sat back hard on the ground. She was the last person he expected to see. He remembered every facet of her beautiful, deceitful face. He never considered he would see it again. And yes, he'd like to shoot her. Shoot her right between her lying, scheming eyes, or her heart. Yeah, he could shoot her in her cold, shriveled heart. It would make a mighty little target, but hell, he was the best marksman in the western territory. Nothing would make him happier right now then to put a bullet through her blackened heart, even if it was the size of a pea. Then again, maybe he should snap Jenna's neck. He wouldn't need a gun to do it. He would use his bare hands. Reese savored the picture he created in his mind. Then he frowned. Without hard evidence, he couldn't do any of it. He wished he could handcuff her, at least. Anything to show her how much he enjoyed running into her again after all this time. Her betrayal nearly destroyed him. He believed she was dead, and now he knew she wasn't, he'd make sure she atoned for the wrongs she committed.

Reese frowned again. *Who the hell is Mary Johnston?* He'd be looking into the name, whoever the hell she was. He wasn't letting anything go, not by a long shot. "Tell me where your men are hiding, Jenna, and I'll see you get a fair trial," Reese called after her, again. If Jenna was here, her men were, too.

Shanna turned to stare. "A fair trial? For what? Being in a train wreck? I do not know this person Janie, or Jennie or—"

"Jenna." Reese supplied.

"Fine, Jenna. For the last time. I do not know you. I do not know Jenna. I do not have any men. If I did, they would have rescued me from the train. They would find a way to transport me to my destination, not leave me stranded with a twat for company. And one more thing, I haven't done anything wrong. So, you'll have a hard time convincing some sheriff to lock me up. Now if you'll excuse me." She ticked the items off on her fingers as she talked. When she was done, she turned and walked toward the train once more. Her long, blonde hair blew in the slight breeze as she walked.

Reese caught her by the arm. "Where the hell do you think you are going?" he asked. Chicago was east. The loco woman was going the wrong way.

Shanna pointed at the train. "I'm going to see if there's anything useful in the baggage car."

"Why?" Reese asked.

"What's it to you? I don't explain myself to strangers but if you must know, I could use some supplies. I didn't come prepared to make camp, and I have a long way to go. Now, let go of my arm." She stopped.

He didn't loosen his grip. *But I am not a stranger.*

He figured they knew each other as well as any two people alive. Those two months in bed together had been some of the most memorable of his life. Anger tightened his hold. He loved her dammit and thought she felt the same way. She didn't, not if she could betray him the way she did. "Why?" he insisted. She was up to something, and he aimed to figure out what it was.

****

Shanna's anger rose. *What the hell is his problem? What difference does it make where I go or what I do?* It was easy to see why the man was single. No woman in her right mind would put up with the idiot, even if he was handsome as hell. This Jenna must have figured it out and left him. Was the man sore about Jenna leaving him, so he threatened to lock Shanna up because he hated women? "Okay, mister, I'm going to use simple sentences so you can understand. We have been in a train wreck. We are stranded. We will be walking. It's going to be dark soon. There are dead bodies all around us. There are wolves living here. I do not like wolves. I want to go. *Now!*"

He frowned. "Where are you trying to get to?"

Shanna rolled her eyes. At least the simple sentence thing worked. She was finally getting through. "Pine Bluffs," Shanna said. She jerked her arm from his grasp and started walking.

The man frowned. "What's in Pine Bluffs?" Her answer took him by surprise, judging from the look on his face.

Shanna stopped. The man was lucky his Jenna didn't shoot him right between the eyes for being so annoying. Shanna toyed with the idea and then discarded it. As appealing as the notion was, she didn't have a gun. Shooting him would make more blood. More blood meant more wolves. More wolves meant she needed to get the hell out of here. "Someone has to tell them about the train, and I need to get home." Shanna explained slowly so the man would understand.

He narrowed his eyes at her. "Where's home?" he persisted.

Shanna could see his mind working over-time. "What do you care? Are you planning on following me all the way? Listen, mister. I told you. I am not this Janie, Jennie woman. I have no idea who the woman is. My name is Shanna. Where I go, and where I live is none of your business. So, let go of my arm, and go threaten somebody else." Shanna stood toe to toe with the giant. She had to tilt her head all the way back to look into his eyes. It took the wheel off her wagon when she realized how much bigger he was than her. So, she focused on the top button of his denim shirt instead and gave it a good glare.

The man stared at her. Shanna fancied she could see the cogs turning in his head.

He pulled his gun free from his holster and shot at her feet. His gaze never left hers.

Shanna jumped so hard; she was afraid she dislodged something.

"Where is home?" he persisted, his gaze boring into her.

Shanna glanced down at her feet, and her knees buckled. A dead rattlesnake lay curled next to her boots. She looked back at him in disbelief. She had never seen anybody so good with a gun. The man didn't blink. If he wanted her dead, she would be. She hadn't seen him move. Shanna decided she best answer his questions.

"Rock Creek," she whispered. "Is there anything else you're wondering? I don't even know your name."

"You know my name. Quit pretending you don't," he said.

The dizziness returned, and the world began to spin. Shanna shook it off. "Are you planning on shooting me?" she asked, indicating his gun. He glared at her. Shanna swallowed hard and turned her back on him, hurrying toward the train.

****

Reese glanced down at his hand. *Damn!* He still held the pistol. He holstered his gun. *Shanna*, he smiled as he watched her walk toward the train. Where'd she come up with the name? He knew where her home was. Home was Chicago. What interested him was what lie she would concoct to explain her presence in Rock Creek. Look how she lied about her name and everything else since he first slapped eyes on her. She knew him, knew his name, knew everything. He was out of patience. Her slow answers were not helping his irritation any, either. Reese stared after her again. *What the hell did Jenna want in Rock Creek?*

Rock Creek was a little town in the middle of nowhere, Wyoming Territory. The only thing interesting about it was the recent arrival of the Turley Gang. As luck would have it, Sheriff Holden of Rock Creek sent for the best US Marshal in the territory to help catch the Turleys. The best was Marshal Reese Calhan. Rock Creek was his destination as well as hers. He smiled. Providence was on his side this time. Look how it brought the two of them together after all these years. They were on the same train, in the same explosion, and headed to the same little town in the middle of nowhere. The sun shone down on him. It was going to be a good day after all. If Jenna and the boys were up to something, he would catch every one of the sons of bitches and throw them behind bars where they belonged. Reese rolled his shoulders in anticipation. Lady luck finally smiled his way.

Chapter 2

He caught up to Shanna as she neared the train, whistling a jaunty tune as he walked.

"Where did all the cattle come from?" she asked.

He looked at her in surprise. "The train pulled livestock cars as well as passenger and cargo cars. Didn't you see them when you boarded? Or did you miss that little detail when you and your boys planned the explosion?" the man asked, his eyes on her face.

Shanna dropped her head. She'd been too busy watching Mama until the last second to pay attention to anything. Shanna turned away to hide her tears.

He smiled. "Why did you blow up the train? Was there something special in the cargo car?" the man asked. "It must have been some haul for you to miss the livestock. The smell alone permeates miles of prairie in this heat."

Shanna stared at him in unbelief. *Honest to God the man needs to find somebody else to bother. He has an incredible imagination.* "Now you think I blew up the train?" *I should go back to simple sentences. I'd been making progress.*

"No?" he asked one eyebrow cocked in disbelief

"*No!* Why would I blow up a train I was riding on? I could see you doing such a thing with your simple mind, *but I happen to believe in self-preservation.*" The man may be good looking, but that's all he had going

16

for him. He had the personality of a rock.

Shanna turned away and stomped into the cargo car. She looked around for anything to help get her to Rock Creek. The bothersome man could follow if he wanted to. He was too big for her to deal with. She supposed she would have to put up with him following her around. She glanced backward to see if the man was still there. *Yup, he was.* She gazed at his bulging biceps and massive thighs. She should feel safe with such a large man nearby. This man would hold his own no matter what the situation was. Look how he shot the snake without even looking at it. She supposed she should have thanked him for saving her life, but she didn't feel grateful. Instead, she was angry, and frightened. He wanted to punish her for something someone else did. Shanna turned away. She didn't need the complication. Her life was crazy enough as it was. She bent and sifted through the heap of baggage. Shanna found her suitcase amid the rubble and pulled it free. She brushed dirt and ashes from the hard case and set it by her feet. *This would help.* She always carried extra things in case she needed them. Shanna pawed through another heap, her eyes on the fire behind them. The heat inside the baggage car was excruciating, and Shanna decided her suitcase would have to do. She didn't want to waste any more time rummaging so close to the fire. Shanna climbed out of the car and headed west, carrying her suitcase with her.

****

Reese snorted as he went back over their conversation in his mind. Self-preservation and Jenna were synonymous terms. One thing Jenna was extremely good at was self- preservation. He gazed at her thoughtfully. She was right. Jenna would not be on a train she planned to blow up. So why did she look so damn guilty? If she didn't do it, then who the hell did? Assuming she was telling him the truth, which Reese doubted. When had Jenna ever told the truth? Maybe it was a ruse, like her name. Her smug voice played in his mind. Sooner or later Jenna would mess up, and he would be right there when she did.

He followed her into the baggage car. He was curious about what she wanted there. He didn't believe her nonsense about looking for something useful. He was pretty sure she either went to make sure her boys got whatever they were after or went to get it herself. It was one or the other. Only a fool, or someone looking for something valuable, reentered a burning train. He was not convinced Jenna was innocent, any more than he believed she'd lost her mind, and now answered to Shanna. He thought about the passengers. None of them deserved to die. He was going to see whoever was responsible, hung for it. He had a hell of a lot of unanswered questions.

Reese rummaged around and found a bedroll and a box of matches. He kept Jenna in sight the whole time. She pulled a suitcase from the wreckage and climbed out. He was right behind her. Jenna headed west. He hurried toward what used to be the livestock car. *Maybe Pegasus survived.* He needed the horse. He did not intend to be caught on foot with Jenna and her crew around. Reese found his stallion a few hundred feet away, spooked but otherwise fine.

He ground-tie trained the horse when he was a colt. As a result, Pegasus stayed put when Reese was close by. He found a saddle and strapped it on Pegasus. He tied the bedroll behind it, dropping the matches into his saddlebag. He stepped into the saddle and started after the she-devil. It would be hours before anyone realized the train was not coming. Hours before the bodies were gathered up and buried. Jenna was right about one thing. The wolves would come calling as soon as the sun went down.

****

Shanna walked along lugging her suitcase. Her mind was preoccupied with remnants of their conversation. *Who was the stranger, and why did he insist on calling her Jenna?* She knew no one named Jenna. The man was delusional if he thought she would blow up a train. *What about all the innocent men, women, and children aboard? Only a monster would do such a thing.* She never met this man before. She would have remembered him. So, why did he insist they knew each other? It was probably the bump on his head. He must have knocked something loose when he hit his head following the explosion. The funny thing was he claimed to remember her from somewhere. Men did not remember her. She knew it for a fact. After all, her fiancé Daniel forgot they were engaged the second Delphine Otis rolled into town. Daniel forgot all about their kisses, his promises, and everything else they shared. So why should *this* man claim to remember her? Then again, he knew about the knife on her thigh. Shanna frowned. He worried her a little. No one knew she carried it except White Eagle and a couple of intoxicated cowboys who got too friendly. How did the stranger know?

The object of her disdain appeared by her side, riding a large bay stallion. Shanna glanced at him. His leg was bleeding again. She rolled her eyes. Maybe she should rethink his ability to be self-sufficient. The man needed a nanny, full time. He should not be out on his own, alone. Shanna walked along in silence, studying the foliage she passed. She stopped when she spotted the plant. Setting her suitcase down, Shanna gathered a handful of leaves from the yarrow plant and smashed them with her hands. She walked toward the man; her eyes narrow with intent. He stopped when she did, watching her with hooded eyes.

"Let me see your leg," she commanded.

He glared. "Why?"

"This will help with the bleeding, make the swelling go down, and keep infection out until you get to a doctor. Now, let me see your leg." She held his gaze with her own. Neither one backed down. She wasn't about to let anyone else die.

The man held her gaze for another long minute, and then looked behind her. "What is it?" he asked at last.

"Yarrow," Shanna answered. Her patience ran out. She reached for the bandage, but the man caught her hand, his grip hard around her wrist.

"What are you up to?" he asked softly.

"For the love of God, I am only trying to help you, so you don't catch an infection and die! Are you going to untie it or not?" Shanna asked with exasperation. The man was so damn annoying most people he met probably *did* try to kill him within the first several minutes of making his acquaintance. The good Lord knew she was a sweet good-natured girl, and she had already considered it. Shanna glanced at the bloody sleeve tied around his thigh and sighed. How was she going to get around the man's suspicious nature and help him before he bled to death or got gangrene? A sudden thought struck her. "Consider it repayment for rescuing me from the train. I help you with your leg, and we are square, even. I don't owe you, and you don't owe me." She tossed it out there like a bone to a hungry dog and waited.

He circled the bone as if afraid it was laced with poison.

"What's your options?" Shanna asked, completely out of patience. "If I don't help you, your leg will become infected, and then, you will have to have it amputated. Is this a risk you are willing to take? I have a healthy dislike of strangers too, but you have no choice. At least I'm not holding a pistol to your head like you did me and asking crazy questions." Shanna stared into his beautiful blue eyes, daring him to accept her challenge. Men were such babies when it involved pain. Like it or not, she would do what she could for his leg. White Eagle expected it of her.

****

He stared at her for several minutes. She wasn't going to give in, if her hostile expression was anything to go off. She made a valid point about his leg becoming infected. The way he figured it, there was enough dirt and grime inside his wound to cause real damage. He needed help, and soon. He gingerly untied the sleeve from around his thigh. The wound gaped open. It was ugly, bloody, and bright red. Not a good sign. He stared at Shanna from under hooded eyes. His leg hurt like hell, looked like hell, and smelled worse. He waited for her to turn away and puke, or faint at the sight of so much blood. She did none of it. She leaned toward the wound and probed it gently with her fingers, looking for debris amid the blood and pus. She grunted when she was through poking around.

He gritted his teeth against the pain and winced, as she placed the crushed leaves against his wound, spreading it evenly with her finger. Then, she swiftly retied the sleeve making sure it completely covered the jagged edges of his torn flesh. When she was done, Shanna turned, picked up her suitcase, and started walking again.

He was dumbfounded. *What the actual hell was going on here?* Jenna knew nothing about plants or wounds. She was a city girl. A big city, spoiled, rich girl, and she applied smashed leaves to an ugly wound without even flinching. A bloody, ugly wound, and then retied his bandage as if she had done it a hundred times before. Jenna hated blood, hated wounds, and broken flesh. It made her want to gag. This Jenna didn't even spare it a glance. Something wasn't right about this day, this situation, and this woman. *Since when did Jenna give a damn about anybody?* It was out of character for her to want to help, especially him. Maybe she was trying to poison him.

He nudged Pegasus forward. He was going to find out what was going on, and what the hell happened to make Jenna forget she hated the sight of blood. Reese stared hard at Jenna's profile. Dammit, he would know her face anywhere. *This was Jenna.* The same Jenna who shared his bed, the same Jenna who swore she loved him more than life itself. The same Jenna he'd asked to marry him, and the same Jenna who turned traitor, leaving him to face the Chicago police all alone after all the lies, all the thefts, and after the massive explosion he believed took her life. Now, she claimed to be a woman named Shanna. Somehow, it was an act to throw him off the scent. It had to be.

"They hang horse thieves in this part of the country," Shanna said casually, breaking the silence.

Reese frowned. "This is my horse."

"I hope you have a way to prove it because if someone else can claim the horse, they won't waste time asking questions. They will string you up," Shanna said cheerfully. She almost sounded hopeful.

"Pegasus is my horse, and I don't have to prove a damn thing to anybody," he said furiously. He was angry again. She was the thief, not him. If anybody got themselves strung up, it would be her.

Shanna merely shrugged as if to say, *yeah, we'll see.*

He nudged Pegasus with his heels. "No one will question me. No one will dare. Do you want to know why?" He didn't give her a chance to respond. He jabbed at his chest as he said the words to give them more emphasis. "Because, I'm the law here. I make the rules. I decide who's innocent, and I decide who gets hung." He glowered down at Shanna. The damn woman, she knew how to provoke him like no one else he ever met.

Shanna shrugged again. "You can be whoever you want to be and decide all you'd like, until you come face to face with a real sheriff. Then things might be a little different than you suppose."

He stared into her eyes when he said the words. He wanted her to feel them to the bottom of her rotten soul. "I'm not an officer anymore, Jenna. Not like I was when you knew me last. Now, I'm a US Marshal.

Marshal Reese Calhan. It has a nice sound to it, doesn't it? I have total jurisdiction in this part of the country. I have the right to decide who's innocent. I also have the right to decide who hangs. *Every* sheriff this side of the Mississippi must obey my orders. So, you see, my dear Jenna, or Shanna. Whatever you call yourself doesn't matter. I know you for who, and what, you are. I will see you get justice one way or another."

Reese smiled when she started over his comment. Maybe she was surprised he'd been promoted with all the things she had done to drag him down, and she would be right. He'd worked his ass off following her betrayal, but he was here now, and she was going to pay.

Shanna glanced at him warily and shivered. Reese smiled with satisfaction. She needed to worry about his intentions. She needed to fear what he could do, because he intended to do all of it.

Chapter 3

The first of the rain hit right as the sun went down. A rogue cloud appeared and dumped torrents of freezing rain on them as they walked along. The wind picked up, and Shanna leaned into it to keep going. She set her case down and rummaged around until she found her shawl. She packed one wherever she went. Wyoming weather was too unpredictable to be without one. Wearily, Shanna threw the shawl over her head and tied it around her shoulders. She picked her case up and continued walking. Her progress was slow. The mud and wind made it hard to keep up her earlier pace. Shanna looked around for a place to camp for the night. She was tired and walking for miles lugging her suitcase, was beginning to take its toll. Shanna was cold, wet, and hungry. She surveyed the open prairie with distaste. Prairie grass and a few scant bushes here and there, was not much protection to speak of. What she needed was a cave or a good tree to protect her back. She could hack down some branches to make a shelter. Shanna glanced sideways at Reese. One would think having a large muscular man in company would be protection enough, but it wasn't. *Who is going to protect me from him?* She knew who Marshall Reese Calhan was, hell everybody did. He had a reputation as the best US Marshall around. She knew Sheriff Holden sent for him to take down the Turleys. The whole town did. The thing worrying her the most was the marshal's confusion over her identity. He couldn't prosecute her without proof, could he? She shivered. He was pretty convinced she was Jenna. He sounded as if he was just waiting for the right occasion to arrest her. The best thing to do would be to lose him between here and Rock Creek. With any luck she would be able to stay out of his way. She wished she hadn't told him where she lived, because now he knew where to look.

Shanna was glad for the silence as they walked. It gave her time to think. Never in her deepest imagination would she have guessed she would be walking beside Marshal Reese Calhan tonight. Every woman in the western part of the United States hoped to meet up with the marshal. His reputation was larger than life, his prowess as a lawman second to none. He was rumored to be as handsome as the devil, hell on wheels with a gun, fast with his fists, a better tracker than most guides, and single. He seemed a safe avenue for the fantasies she told herself late at night when she wept into her pillow. She wondered what it would be like to be wanted and needed. She wondered what it would be like to have such a powerful man love her. Men as famous as the marshal never rode into Rock Creek. It was too little of a place to gain much attention. So, she'd given her imagination free reign. It was a little different than this when she dreamed, though. For instance, in her dreams, the marshal wanted her with a passion which could not be denied. He followed her everywhere, driven mad with love. He bought her flowers, offered her chocolate, and took her driving every Sunday afternoon. Here he was in real life, following her around, but the passion he had wasn't to take her in his arms, but to see her behind bars. In her dreams, Marshal Calhan swore he would love only her and never noticed the other girls in town, especially not Delphine Otis. He didn't even know Delphine's name, nor did he want to. He wanted Shanna and Shanna alone. In real life, the marshal didn't know Shanna's name, nor did he want to. He confused her with another woman named Jenna. It was sobering to say the least. In her dreams, Marshal Calhan got on his knees before the whole town, begging Shanna to marry him and live happily ever after. Shanna sighed. Marshal Reese may go before the whole town with her, but it wouldn't be to place a ring around her finger. No, it would be to place a noose around her neck. So much for fantasies. They were best left alone.

Shanna felt her knife against her thigh. The knife was supposed to keep her from harm. So, why wasn't it throwing itself toward Reese Calhan and burying itself in his black heart? She tugged her suitcase a little higher. It was getting heavy. She had no idea how far she was from Pine Bluffs. The problem was there wasn't a good place to make a camp. White Eagle would scold her for not being more observant. Maybe if she hadn't been so preoccupied with Reese Calhan, she would have seen a good spot. She had to get to higher ground so she could inspect the terrain. Only there wasn't higher ground, or even a tree to climb up to have a look around. Shanna set her suitcase down and held her hand to her head to shield her eyes from the rain. She looked around them in every direction.

Reese's eyebrow rose. "What are you doing?"

Shanna glared at him. "I'm looking for a place to make camp."

"This should be entertaining," he said with a chuckle.

Shanna ignored him. She spied a large rock. It would be better than nothing. At least, it would shield her back. Shanna picked up her case and headed in the direction of the rock.

"Pine Bluffs is a little over an hour away. I could let you ride with me on Pegasus, and you could sleep in a bed tonight," Reese said.

His offhand comment stopped her in her tracks. Shanna turned in surprise. "You're offering to give me a ride to Pine Bluffs? Why?" Shanna stared up at him. *Why is he being nice suddenly?*

Reese shifted in the saddle at the accusation in her voice. "So, I can keep an eye on you. Why else?" he said, whether for her benefit or his own it was unclear.

Shanna nodded. This was something she believed. She ought to tell him to leave her be, but she was tired, and a bed sounded awfully nice. Besides, every part of her ached from the train wreck. She was soaking wet and freezing cold. She didn't want to walk any further. "Okay." She held her suitcase up.

****

Reese's eyes narrowed. She gave in way too easy. He made a quick assessment of their position from every side to make sure he hadn't missed something or someone. He took the suitcase and then glanced back down at her. It was heavy. *How the hell did she walk all afternoon carrying this thing?* Suddenly, he felt like an ass. He could have strapped it on his saddle hours ago, but he hadn't. He should have offered her a ride when it started to rain. He expected her to complain, but she didn't. She took a shawl from her case and kept on walking. He wanted to watch her struggle. He wanted to see how long she could maintain the innocent act she was putting on, but she hadn't faltered. She plodded on all afternoon and evening, never letting on it was heavy, nor giving any indication she was tired at all. And she must be. He hurt like hell, and he'd been letting Pegasus do all the work.

He was a nice man by nature. His mother raised him to be a gentleman. In a normal situation, Reese would have offered a lady a ride, taken her suitcase, and saw to her comfort. But this situation was not normal, and Jenna was no lady. It was she who brought out the meanness in him. Reese held his arm down and lifted her up onto the saddle in front of him. He settled her on his lap and nudged Pegasus forward. He wrapped his arms around her. She was cold. She shivered against him. Her head was down to keep the rain off her face. She was silent.

She was asleep before they had gone twenty feet. She was relaxed against him, her breathing, slow and even. She looked as innocent as a patron saint, but Reese knew better. This woman looked like Jenna, talked like Jenna, and walked like Jenna. It was safe to assume she was Jenna, despite her denial. Yet, there was something different about her he could not figure out. There was something not right, which bothered him. He looked at the situation from every angle. He still had no good explanation for Jenna to be alive and this far west.

In Chicago, the opportunity to make a substantial heist was at least ten times what it was out here. Jenna only bothered if the take was in the tens of thousands. So, why was she *here*? The only thing he could think of was Fort Buford. The army payroll wouldn't be delivered to the fort for another month or two. Jenna and her men had their system down to a science. They wouldn't need two months to plan a heist at Fort Buford. They would need extra men, though. Fort Buford was large, and several companies of soldiers were stationed there. Jenna and her dozen or so riders would be no match for an army. He didn't figure a low-level gang like the Turleys would hold much appeal to Jenna and the Delaneys...unless she planned on using them, and then letting them take the blame.

Reese glanced at Shanna. He'd underestimated her once before. He wouldn't make the same mistake this time. He frowned. He knew this woman, knew everything about her, and knew what she was capable of. He knew the ugliness of her soul as no one else did. Today was different. Today he witnessed her perform an act of kindness despite the ugliness and selfishness of her soul. Jenna had changed. Whatever was different with her must have happened in the explosion seven years ago. He wasn't going to be caught off guard again. He nudged Pegasus into a trot.

Chapter 4

Shanna opened her eyes slowly, her vision blurry from sleep. She was in bed, snuggled under a warm blanket. She sighed and wiggled her toes, closing her eyes once more. It must have all been a dream, a horrible nightmare—the train wreck, the smoke, the dead bodies, Marshal Reese, all of it. She smiled, rolled over onto her side, and sighed again. Maybe she should have tried to dream about him kissing her. She pictured the marshal's well-formed body, his bulging biceps, and thick thighs. She sighed over the blue of his eyes and the way they wrinkled at the corners when he smiled. It was too bad the man lacked intelligence, or he would be perfect. Shanna opened her eyes expecting to see the rough walls of her tiny room in Rock Creek. Instead, she gazed into the hypnotic blue eyes of Marshal Reese Calhan. A frown immediately replaced her smile. It hadn't been a dream after all. *Damn.*

"It's time to go. The mail coach is leaving in ten minutes." Reese was all business.

"The mail coach?" she asked sleepily, trying to understand what was happening.

"That's right, the mail coach. It will take us to Fort Buford. From there, we can catch a ride on a wagon into Rock Creek." Reese poured a cup of coffee from a pot sitting on a little table against the wall.

"The mail coach left yesterday. There won't be

another one for another day or two." Shanna already knew the mail coach traveled to Fort Buford. She rode it every year when she went to see Mama. She figured she might have to wait in Pine Bluffs for a day or two and catch the next one, since the train explosion made her miss the one she originally planned to take.

She didn't like the marshal taking control and making decisions for her. Shanna shoved the blankets down, intent on getting to her feet. When she realized she wore nothing but her underwear, she quickly pulled the quilt back up to her chin.

"The mail coach waited. Men from town rode out as soon as I told them what happened. They were out all night. All the towns in the area were sent a telegram with the news. Now the mail pouches are here, the coach is ready to leave. Get up. We have nine minutes."

"We? Since when is it, we? I am not going anywhere with you. I can find my own way." Shanna turned her back, the quilt clutched tightly against her. She could do without the twat's delightful conversation and company.

"Yes, we. You aren't going anywhere *without* me," Reese threatened as he set the cup of coffee on the table by the bed.

"What about your horse? Why don't you ride him wherever it is you're going, and I will take the mail coach?" Shanna suggested, warming to the idea. "I'm sure your horse will get you wherever you're going much faster than the coach."

"Not a chance. My horse can follow along behind." Reese smiled a smug smile. "Wherever you go, I go. Now get up," he ordered. His hands rested on his narrow hips.

Shanna frowned. Rebellion ran amuck inside her head. There was no way in hell she was going to let him follow her all the way to Rock Creek. The sooner he understood the better. "No. I told you. I'm not going anywhere with you. Now, leave me be, or I'll start screaming at the top of my voice," she threatened. She narrowed her eyes, hoping she looked mean.

He was having none of it. Reese scooped her up out of bed, blanket and all, and set her on her feet. Shanna squeaked in surprise, holding the blanket tight against her chest.

His face was inches from hers. "Scream all you want, no one will care. Now you have eight minutes. Either you can get ready on your own, or I do it for you." The look in his eyes told her he wasn't joking.

Shanna swallowed. *Okay. I will ditch him somewhere down the line, and a mail coach is better than walking all the way.* "If you would be so kind as to leave, I will get dressed," she said, tugging the blanket a little higher. She held it with a death grip, wishing Reese would get out and let her get dressed in peace.

"I'm staying right here. You don't have anything I haven't seen before. So, get moving," Reese said silkily. His eyes roamed over her from head to toe. A knowing smile tugged at his lips.

Shanna's mouth dropped open. Calling her by a different name was one thing, this was another! "I will not! You may have seen what's-her-name, but I'm not her, and you are not seeing me!" Shanna was livid. She shot him a furious look.

A dangerous gleam entered his beautiful eyes. "We both know all I have to do is kiss you, and I can have and see whatever I want, but in the interest of time…"

Reese's gaze heated up as he stared at her chest.

Shanna swallowed, and licked her lips. His gaze rested on her mouth for a few heart-pounding seconds, then Reese turned his back.

"Touch me, and I will carve out your heart," Shanna threatened. *Damn the man.* She shook so hard, she doubted she could hold her knife at all, but he didn't need to know. Reese chuckled at her statement. *He doesn't think I will do it*, Shanna thought. Most men took one look at her and decided she was fair game. The ones who got too close found out differently. The marshal would too, if he didn't leave her alone. Shanna decided she'd better get her clothes on while his back was turned. She might not get another chance. She caught sight of her dress from the day before, hanging over the back of a chair close to the fire. Her stockings and shoes were there, as well. She picked up her case and set it on the narrow cot. She pulled out clean petticoats, a clean dress, and a pair of stockings. She dropped her blanket and dressed hurriedly. *Damn him to hell!* She was obviously more tired than she thought last night. She had no memory of getting undressed. Her eyes narrowed as she considered his statement about having and seeing whatever he wanted. She snorted. *Not in this lifetime.* "Who took my dress off?" she asked suspiciously.

"I did." His voice was smug.

"Why?" she wanted to know. This ought to be good.

"So you could sleep more comfortably." He chuckled again.

"Where did you sleep?" she insisted.

His turned and grasped her by the shoulders. She

had barely done up the last button. "Right here. I slept right here with you all night, but nothing happened. I like my women awake and participating. We both know you're no blushing virgin. I know you remember what it was like between us. I'm willing to wager one open mouth kiss will release all those memories. They're in your head somewhere. I know it." His heated gaze slowly traveled over her from head to toe.

Shanna shivered. "I know nothing about you, mister, and what's more I don't want to," she lied, "so you can go to hell." She jerked away and sat on the chair to put on her stockings and then her shoes. She kept her back turned as much as she could. She decided to ignore him. Maybe if she did, he would go away and leave her alone.

****

Reese watched her through narrow eyes. She was efficient, cold, and quiet. *What the hell is wrong with her?* Normally, Jenna would be trying to entice him to bed her. Jenna liked men, and men liked Jenna. She never wasted an opportunity to flirt or entice a man. It made her feel powerful, a feeling she was addicted to. Jenna also liked to be the center of attention. This Jenna was too quiet. Reese frowned. Nothing about this woman made any sense. Maybe the explosion seven years ago caused her to have amnesia, forgetting everything. Then started a new life with a new name. It sounded good, but it didn't explain why she was here, instead of in Chicago being pampered by her uncle. He figured if Jenna forgot who she was, Adam Delaney wouldn't let her out of his sight. Her charade pretending to be someone else must be a ruse of some kind to get her close to her target. "Are you ready

35

then…*Shanna?*" he asked when Shanna tied her last shoe.

She stuffed her soiled dress and stockings in her case and snapped it shut. Shanna narrowed her eyes at the exaggerated way he said her name but said nothing. She picked up the coffee and drank it down without stopping. "Now I'm ready." She wiped her mouth with the back of her hand and picked up her suitcase.

Reese stared at her, confused. Jenna lived with one of the richest men in the country. She would never wipe her mouth with the back of her hand. *God, she's good!*

"Have you changed your mind…*Marshal Calhan?*" Shanna exaggerated his name the way he did her name moments earlier. "I can find my own way. In fact, it's what I prefer," Shanna said, challenging him.

"No, I haven't," Reese bit out. He opened the door and took her suitcase, or attempted to. Shanna jerked it out of his hands and marched down the stairs. Reese let her go.

They found the mail coach and after tying Pegasus to the back, took their seat. Shanna was crammed between Reese and a foul-smelling little man with a handlebar mustache. The man liked his tobacco and spit out the window every so often. They were jammed together from shoulder to knees. Shanna did her best to scoot away from Reese but there wasn't room. She ended up rubbing up and down his side. Reese threw an arm around her shoulder and pulled her close. He grinned knowingly into her upturned face. "I knew you remembered. If you want me so bad you should have told me before we left the room," he breathed into her ear. His mouth hovered above her neck, wanting to taste her delicate skin. His other hand moved to cover her knee. He knew she would not be able to hide who she really was. A wry smile tugged at his mouth.

****

Shanna became rigid. That was *not* what she was trying to do. If his hand moved any higher up her leg, she would introduce him to her knife. Shanna looked up and met the interested looks of the three men sitting opposite. They must not see many women judging from the way they stared at her. Shanna dropped her gaze and held perfectly still. The last thing she needed was for Reese, or any of the other filthy men in this coach, to think she wanted anything to do with them.

"What's yer name, darlin'?" The man directly across from her leaned forward, boldly looking her up and down.

"Taken," Reese answered. "She's mine." His put his arm around her shoulders and pulled her tighter against him. If he didn't cut it out, she wouldn't be able to breathe at all. *The hell I'm his.* Shanna thought angrily. She turned her head and glared at him. Reese smiled a slow, sexy smile and winked at her. The other man leaned back, but he kept on staring. They were all staring. It was going to be a long, long ride.

When they stopped for the night, Shanna gulped down her stew and hurried outside. The little one-man outpost was hot and humid. It consisted of one room made entirely of adobes. It smelled like sweat and unwashed human, the male portion of the species. It made Shanna sick to her stomach. There was nowhere to escape the smell. She was sick of the stares, too. She stood behind the little outpost, leaning against the outer wall. She let the cool, evening breeze whisper across her face and smiled. It smelled of sagebrush and juniper trees. It was a vast improvement to the smell inside. She stayed for a minute enjoying the breeze, and then she went in search of more yarrow leaves. The marshal's wound needed attention. She could get hot water here. She intended to clean and bandage his leg. If he got a fever and died, she would be stuck with the other four filthy men they rode with. The idea held no appeal whatsoever. So, she decided to keep the marshal alive, at least for now.

Shanna found a nice-looking yarrow plant and gathered the leaves. She was turning to go back, when she was knocked to the ground by a large foul-smelling man. The man deftly flipped her onto her back. He slapped a hand over her mouth and made a grab to pull her skirts up. Shanna brought her knee up hard. The man doubled over in pain. She pulled her knife from its scabbard and threw the man on his back. Her knife was at his throat before he knew what happened. It was the greasy looking man who sat directly in front of her on the coach, the one with the crooked, yellow teeth. "I am good with this knife. If you want to live to see another day, you will high-tail it back inside, and stay out of my way." She pressed her knife a little harder against his neck drawing blood.

The man attempted to swallow.

"Do you hear me?" she asked.

He slowly nodded his head.

"If you ever touch me again, I will slit your throat, and feed you to the wolves. Understand?"

The man nodded again.

Shanna stood and allowed him to get to his feet. He scampered away into the shadows. Shanna sheathed her knife. Men were so dumb. Honest to God, it was a wonder the species continued to exist. She returned to the one room outpost and asked the keeper for some boiling water.

"Where'd you go?" Reese was walking out as she walked in. He must have changed his mind, because he limped back inside.

Shanna ignored him. She crushed the yarrow leaves into a bowl, ripped several long strips from her petticoat, and got her needle and thread from her suitcase. Then she approached Reese. "Sit down, Marshal. I am cleaning your wound," Shanna commanded. She wasn't taking no for an answer.

Surprisingly, he nodded and sat on one of the chairs. He grimaced with pain when he moved his injured leg.

"I need a knife," she told the man who ran the outpost. The one strapped to her thigh was for emergencies and scoundrels.

"Why?" Reese asked. His hand dropped to the butt of his gun. His eyes glared a warning. Shanna rolled her eyes in response. She took the knife the man handed her and cut Reese's pants away from the wound. The man who attacked her earlier chose that moment to come in. He took one look at Shanna standing there with a knife in her hand, turned around, and left again. Shanna chuckled. She handed the knife back to the keeper of the outpost.

"What's so funny?" Reese wanted to know.

"Nothing." Shanna bent her head and started to clean his wound. Dried blood and debris filled the gaping flesh, and Shanna had to clean it all out. "Anyone have some whiskey?" Shanna wondered.

A bottle was thrust into her hands. She poured it

liberally over the wound and then handed the bottle to Reese. He looked like he could use a swallow or two. He was pale and shaking. Once the wound was cleaned and the water ran clear, Shanna reached for her needle and thread.

****

"What the hell are you planning to do?" Reese demanded. The whiskey and the pain made him nauseous. Sweat broke out on his forehead. Reese gritted his teeth and waited. The sewing was a lot easier to bear than her poking around in his wound while she cleaned it. Shanna pressed a damp cloth against his head. "Here, this will help."

He took the cloth and wiped his face. It did feel good. He looked at her in surprise. Then he caught sight of the bruise on her face. Reese sat up. "Where the hell did you get the bruise?" he demanded. Reese looked around. He couldn't let her out of his sight for two seconds. She'd only been outside a few minutes. He'd given her time to see to her personal needs. Then, he'd been going out to see what kept her, when she walked back inside. Were Jenna's men outside? What the hell happened once she left? He looked around at the men inside the room. They were the same men he had been looking at all day. They looked back. No one moved. One man was missing. Had Jenna's men killed the man or abducted him? He started to get up, but Shanna shoved him back down.

"Hold still! I'm not done yet."

"Answer the question. Where did you get the bruise? And what the hell happened while you were outside? I assumed you went to the outhouse, but you look like you got into a fight."

"I hit my head on a tree," Shanna said

Reese nodded his head. His whiskey-addled mind decided her statement made sense. He couldn't remember what else he was going to ask her.

She knotted and snapped the thread. Carefully she covered her stitching with the crushed leaves and wrapped the wound, tying the ends tightly so they wouldn't come undone.

Reese grunted when he looked at her work. It would do. Where did she learn how to do that was the real question? Why was she helping him? The whiskey was starting to make him woozy. He took another swallow for good measure. Reese stood and walked to the corner facing the door. He needed to lie down before he fell. First, he had to make sure Jenna or Shanna, whoever she pretended to be, didn't walk away in the night. He threw out his bedroll and motioned at Shanna. "Come here," he ordered.

She nodded and without a word lay down where he indicated. Reese scooted closer to Shanna, wedging her against the wall. The last thing Reese thought before he drifted off to sleep was there weren't any trees.

Chapter 5

The first thing she was aware of was the hand on her breast. Shanna opened her eyes. Reese was tucked in behind her like two spoons resting in a drawer. His arm was across her waist, and his left hand held her right breast. She was facing the wall, her bottom tucked against his hips, and their legs were all tangled together. Shanna squirmed uncomfortably and moved Reese's hand. She felt his arousal press against her backside and jumped to her feet.

His chuckle followed her outside. She slammed the door shut on her way out, so he'd know she wasn't happy. *Damn him to hell and all the way back!* He sure knew how to make her uncomfortable. She thought it was a nice gesture he protected her while she slept. Anyone who attempted to bother her in the night would have to get through him first. Then he had to ruin it all by poking her in the backside. What was it with men anyway? Shanna grabbed her suitcase from the mail coach and headed for the stable situated next to the little mail station. She searched for her hairbrush. Vigorously, she brushed her hair out and plaited it. Once she got a good chance, she was going to ditch the marshal. His arousal scared her. He was too big to manhandle if he got aggressive. But that wasn't the only reason she was frightened. She was afraid of her own self, too. She wasn't sure she wanted to stop him if he did try something. She'd never let any man get close to her before. She shouldn't have let this one.

"Here, have some breakfast." Reese stood in front of her with a bowl of runny porridge.

She was still irritated with him, so she took the bowl, and turned her back on him. She sat on a bale of hay and started to eat the porridge.

"Know anything about the big man with the yellow teeth?" Reese drawled casually.

"No. Why?" She kept eating.

"No one has seen him since last night. I figured you knew something."

Shanna turned toward Reese. "Why would I know anything about him?"

"You were outside last night when he disappeared." Reese studied her face, "Then there's the bruise on your cheek. You never did say how you came by it.'

"I told you. I hit my head on a tree," she answered, scooping the last of the porridge into her mouth and standing up.

"There aren't any trees," Reese commented. She was lying, and he knew it.

"Mind your own business." Shanna left the stable and ran all the way to the one-room outpost. She handed the keeper her bowl. She stepped back and came up against Reese's chest.

"You *are* my business." He breathed into her ear. Shanna turned on her heel, ignoring him. She ran back to the stable and did up her suitcase. She put it back in the mail coach.

They left several minutes later. The big man with the yellow teeth was gone. Nobody knew where. One of the other passengers rode on top with the driver, so only four passengers rode inside. Reese shared the same bench with Shanna they rode on the day before. Now, it was only the two of them, and Shanna was able to scoot far enough across the seat she wasn't touching Reese. She smiled with relief. The next day, they lost another passenger. Now, there were only four of them. Reese pretty much kept to his side of the seat and conversation was kept to a minimum. When he did talk, he asked her questions about her men, and why she was in Wyoming Territory. He didn't believe her when she answered she didn't know anything. His eyes were always on her, watching everything she did. Shanna grew tired of the interrogation and quit responding when he asked her questions. She couldn't wait until they reached Fort Buford. It was a busy, bustling place. She could disappear without the marshal knowing which way she went.

On the third day, the terrain changed. They were up in the mountains now. The going was slower. They stopped at another mail station at noon to change horses. Shanna took the opportunity to get some fresh air. She excused herself, saying she was going to the outhouse. Once outside, she hurried into the trees. A few minutes alone without the watchful eyes of the marshal sounded like heaven. Shanna slowed down and crept forward until she was sure she was far enough away from the outpost she wouldn't be seen or heard. Sighing, she leaned against a pine tree and closed her eyes. A gentle breeze teased her nose with the smells of the forest, pine, earth, and the fresh scent of freedom. The locusts buzzed in the trees, and the leaves rustled.

A low rumble caught her attention. Shanna's blood

froze. Her breath caught. Cautiously she looked up and met the slanted yellow eyes of a *mountain lion!* He was huge and right above her head. Shanna was rooted to the spot. *Oh God! What should I do?* The cat snarled and crept forward on the branch holding him. Shanna's heart quit beating. She was too far away from the outpost to call for help. She slipped a shaky hand into the pocket of Aunt Sara's dress and fumbled for her knife. Carefully, she stepped from the tree, backing away slowly. She kept her eyes on the mountain lion. The giant cat crouched, getting ready to spring, and his snarls grew louder. The mountain lion gave a loud scream and sprang from the tree toward Shanna. She cried out and stumbled backward, trying to run. The crack of a pistol sounded behind her. The cat crumpled and fell dead at her feet. Shanna stared in disbelief.

"Don't sneak off again." Marshal Reese stood a hundred yards behind her, mad as hell. He walked swiftly toward her.

Shanna shook violently. She stared at him. Then, she turned back to look at the cat on the ground. Her whole life blazed in front of her as the lion leapt toward her. Now, it was dead, shot between the eyes. "How the hell did you do that?" He was too far away to get a clear view of the cat, especially through the trees.

Reese holstered his gun, grinning. "I'm the best marksman in the territory. Come on. The mail coach is ready to go."

Shanna could only nod. For the first time since she met the infamous marshal, she was grateful he followed her around. Rose would never forgive her if she died before she got home. Shanna stumbled as she walked past Reese.

He took her arm to steady her. "I'm not letting something as stupid as a mountain lion keep you from going to prison like you deserve."

Shanna only nodded. She realized she held her knife in her other hand. She slipped it back into her scabbard and jerked her arm from his grasp. She ran all the way back to the mail coach without saying another word. Leave it to the marshal to make a mean comment after saving her life. She was grateful he rescued her, even if he did have to ruin it.

****

Several hours later, Reese caught a glimpse of something through the trees. He pulled his gun from its holster and peered through the window of the coach. Horsemen appeared out of nowhere behind them and beside them. They shot the driver and the passenger riding on top. One of the horsemen jumped onto the coach and grabbed the reins. Reese fired. "Get down!" he roared at Shanna, while he aimed his gun at another rider. The two men inside the coach with them fired out the other window.

Shanna shrank onto the floor of the coach and hid her head. The coach came to a sudden stop. Dust billowed into the coach making it difficult to see. Shanna coughed. The door to the coach was jerked open before Reese was able to get turned around. The man pointed his gun at Shanna's head and cocked it. The bandits ordered everyone out. Then they took everyone's guns. Reese stood quietly beside Shanna, watching the men. They demanded wallets, jewels, money, and watches, anything the passengers carried. Two of the men unloaded the back of the coach, rummaging through the mail pouches. Reese eyed the men, and decided they weren't Jenna's trained monkeys. He eased his other revolver slowly out of its holster. He always kept a second revolver hidden beneath his shirt for situations like this.

The leader, a big ugly brute with a patch over one eye, stared at Shanna. He looked her up and down. He wanted her. Reese could see it plain as day. They shoved Shanna forward until she stood right in front of the burly man. The top of her head barely reached his shoulder. Shanna didn't flinch. The man grabbed the neckline of her dress and ripped the garment in half. Her undergarments ripped with it leaving her naked to the waist. He stared at her full breasts, licking his thick, ugly lips. Shanna didn't move. She stared the man in the eyes without blinking. Reese was almost impressed, but then he remembered who she was, and waited. The big man grabbed a handful of her hair in one big paw and pulled her face to his. Shanna's knife flashed in the sun. The man grunted and sank to his knees.

As soon as Shanna made her move, Reese pulled his spare revolver out and started shooting. He knew Jenna would do something. She lied about her knife. She may pretend to not remember. She may answer to a different name. She may claim no memory of the last seven years, but she was still Jenna.

Once the bandits were all dead, Reese holstered his gun and looked around. The other men got their guns from the pile of loot the robbers collected. Shanna was nowhere to be seen. Damn! Was it a distraction? Had Jenna planned it all to get away from him? Reese started off. The incident with the mountain lion earlier scared the hell out of him. It should have scared Shanna. She surprised him with her silence, but then she'd been silent all day. The old Jenna would have screamed like a banshee once she spotted the big cat. This Jenna backed away quietly. He was still processing what it all meant when the bandits appeared. Now she was gone, again. He would find the little traitor if it was the last thing he did. He rounded the tree furthest away from the coach in time to see Shanna shrug out of her ripped dress. He stopped in his tracks. She was naked from the waist up and rummaging in her suitcase. Reese walked over and leaned against a tree. He folded his arms over his chest while she struggled with her clothes. Shanna turned, and he got a view of her full, round breasts and pink nipples. Reese's mouth went dry, and his manhood sprang to life. *Stop it*, he said to himself. He had to get his wayward mind under control. *This is Jenna. You know what she does.* The problem was he did. She was so sweet when they first met and so loving. She was the perfect woman in every way. And the lovemaking? When he finally took her to his bed, the loving had been heaven on earth, his climaxes explosive. He never forgot what it was like to love this woman.

****

Shanna looked up and met Reese's heated gaze. Damnation! How long had he been standing there watching? She barely got a clean chemise on. Was the man completely without morals? She glared, turned her back, and pulled a clean dress over her head. She reached behind her to do up the buttons.

"Let me." Reese was there behind her, his hot breath on her neck, the backs of his fingers brushing against her skin.

Shanna's breath hitched in her throat, tingles

spread up and down her spine. She shook herself to break the spell he wove around her. "Thanks." She stepped away from him and snapped her case shut.

When she turned to face him, Reese tugged her into his arms, his hot mouth coming down on hers. She gasped, and his tongue swept inside her mouth. His hands were everywhere, molding her slim body to his, searching, caressing, and touching. His hand found her breast, and he squeezed. White-hot pleasure surged through her. She had never been kissed like this before, and her traitorous body responded with a passion which shocked Shanna to her core. His tongue stroked against hers. He drank from her mouth as if he were starving for her touch. Shanna trembled in his arms. She thought she might fall, so she wrapped her arms around his neck and ended up pulling him closer. She leaned in, relaxing her soft curves against the hard planes of his body. He grabbed her head, holding her still as he deepened his kiss. Shanna whimpered in response.

Suddenly, Reese stepped back, his breathing ragged. He stared at her. Angrily, he swiped a hand at his mouth as if rubbing the taste of her from his lips. He removed her arms from around his neck and dropped them by her side.

Shanna stepped back, also. She was deeply shaken. Her self-control was completely gone. She reeled from the storm of emotion Reese unleashed inside her. Tingles raced up and down her back and around inside her stomach. Never had a man taken such liberties, and she not only let him, but willingly participated. The realization set her back. *What the hell am I doing?*

"That was a mistake," Reese ground out, not looking at her. He dragged his hand through his hair.

He was mad as hell. He stood glaring at her; his hands fisted at his sides.

"You got that right," she answered. Shanna grabbed her suitcase and brushed past him. She marched to the coach and after putting her case in the back, climbed inside. She swung the door shut behind her and slid back into the furthest corner. With trembling hands, she wiped his kisses from her quivering lips. What the hell was she thinking to let the marshal paw her? Any other man would be dead on the ground at her feet, her knife sticking out of his chest. She still wasn't sure what happened exactly. One minute she was dressing, and the next the marshal had his hands all over her, his tongue deep inside her mouth. Her stomach tightened at the memory. She should have got her knife out right then and there. Instead, she'd kissed him back. Heat flooded her once more as she remembered how he tasted and how good his mouth felt moving over hers. Men shouldn't taste so good or feel so good. It made her wonder what bedding him would be like. She closed her eyes and brushed her fingers over her still swollen lips. Marshal Calhan was the very devil when it came to women. He made her lose all good sense. One touch of his lips and things got out of hand in a big hurry. The man kissed as good as he looked, damn his hide. The sooner she ditched the marshal and put as much distance between them as she could, the better off she would be.

****

The other two passengers dragged the dead leader away from the front of the coach so they could be on their way. One of them pointed at the knife wound in his chest. "Now look there," the man said, scratching his head.

"Didn't the marshal shoot him? How did he get a knife stuck in him?" the other passenger asked.

Reese overheard the conversation and stomped over to investigate. Sure enough, the man sported a knife wound right above his heart, a deep one. Jenna did what she does best. "It was the girl," Reese answered. "She's mighty good with a blade."

The passengers nodded and continued clearing the way for the mail coach.

Reese studied the wound with narrowed eyes. Jenna usually left the killing to her men. The only time she used her knife was to torture information from someone. She liked to make people hurt. She was an expert at keeping her victims in the maximum amount of pain for extended periods of time. This wound was clean and precise. She executed it with minimal damage. Reese puzzled over this new situation. Had she started doing her own killing in the last few years? Reese shook his head. *Had she learned new skills since he last saw her?* Lord knows he had. She learned to kiss better, if their encounter earlier was anything to go by. This new Jenna put her heart and soul into the kiss, messing with his self-control. It was all he could do to let go and step back. Only the memory of her betrayal gave him what he needed to end the kiss and push her away. So much about Jenna was the same, but as much was different. Was it possible to mess your head up so bad you became an entirely different person? It was a real good question.

Chapter 6

They arrived at Fort Buford late the following day. Shanna stayed on her side of the coach and answered in monosyllables for the rest of the journey. She kept her head turned toward the window and stared out, refusing to acknowledge Reese's presence. She hated herself for giving in to his charm. She hated him even more for treating her like it was all her fault. The marshal glared every time their eyes met; his face a mask of frozen indifference. He shifted away from her when she slid across the seat into him as the coach rounded a corner too fast. She apologized, scooting back to her side. He turned away and didn't bother to answer. Shanna wanted to kick him. He's the one who touched her, not the other way around. So, she returned his kisses with a little too much enthusiasm. Why did it make it her fault? She'd only been responding to something he initiated. If he didn't want her kissing him back, he shouldn't have kissed her in the first place. The tension in the coach vibrated between them. The silence grew unbearable. Shanna breathed with relief when they passed through the heavily fortified walls of the fort. Once she ditched the marshal, she could make a run for it. She wanted to get as much distance between her and the marshal as she could.

Fort Buford bustled with soldiers. Shanna faded into the background once the soldiers realized Marshal

Reese Calhan was within their fort. He was a famous man, and everybody wanted to shake his hand. She kept an eye on the marshal as she wove between the soldiers crowding around him. Shanna hurried toward the supply building inside the fort. She hoped Mr. Tanner would be there. If the railroad sent a telegram about the train wreck to all the nearby towns, hopefully Mr. Tanner knew, and came to meet the coach. She could catch a ride to Rock Creek with him.

Harold Tanner owned the local mercantile in Rock Creek. He often journeyed to the fort for merchandise he shipped in, and supplies. Harold Tanner was also Shanna's boss. He hired her to work in his shop after Uncle Joseph and Aunt Sara ran up a huge bill and then offered Shanna as a means of repayment. She didn't mind most of the time. It was better to be at the mercantile working than out on the claim, despite the dirty saddle-sore cowboys who came in to buy supplies. Shanna learned fast how to deal with the lecherous ones and was friends with the Tanners' daughter, Rose.

Shanna caught sight of the Tanner wagon outside the supply building and quickened her step. She wanted to be on her way to Rock Creek before the marshal realized she was gone. Mr. Tanner waved when Shanna approached.

"There you are! Rose was worried when we got the telegram about the train. We heard there were only two survivors. She wanted me to wait until I found out where you were. I've been here since early this morning waiting for the coach, so I had news for Rose. I am happy you're okay."

Shanna smiled and talked quickly, convincing Mr. Tanner to let her ride in the back, instead of on the seat, claiming fatigue. She climbed in the bed of the wagon and pulled a dust cloth over her to conceal her presence. Two hours down the road, Shanna breathed a sigh of relief. She giggled. The marshal wouldn't know which way she went, and it pleased her greatly. He would be extremely annoyed when he realized she was gone. After a minute, Shanna climbed up on the seat by Mr. Tanner and told him all about her trip to Omaha, her mama, and the train wreck. She didn't mention the marshal. She only wanted to tell Mr. Tanner about the exciting things, not the disturbing ones.

****

"So, you're back."

Shanna jumped when she heard the high-pitched voice.

Delphine Otis stood a few feet in front of her wearing a pink satin day dress and holding a matching parasol. Her red hair gleamed in the sunlight. She looked Shanna up and down with disgust. "It looks like you put on weight while you were gone." Delphine's high-pitched voice got louder.

Shanna grimaced inwardly. "Good morning, Delphine." She continued sweeping in front of the mercantile.

"You know, I've always wondered which one of your parents you take after." Delphine smiled. "Is your mother as ugly as you, or do you take after your father?" Delphine tilted her head and studied her for a minute. "I'm thinking your father. You have such a large masculine look about you."

Shanna continued to sweep. Ever since Daniel broke off their engagement and took up with Delphine, the woman delighted to torment her.

"My mother is beautiful, and I never met my father," Shanna answered.

Delphine laughed out loud. "That explains it. It must be your father. You look so manly and rugged. I swear, it's the reason you wear Sara's old cast offs. No other dress will fit your odd shape. Don't you think so, Daniel?"

Shanna looked up. Why was it these two she met as soon as she got back?

Daniel Anderson stood beside Delphine. He was tall, thin, and good looking, with wavy brown hair and brown eyes. He stared at her. "We heard you were in a train wreck," he said.

"I was," Shanna answered and turned her back on them to sweep the steps.

"Darling, she is the train wreck! Look at her!" Delphine said. They both laughed. Then Delphine turned to Shanna. "It's too bad you were the only survivor," she exclaimed. "Come, darling, let's send this telegram, and go find Daddy." Delphine tucked her gloved hand into Daniel's arm, and together they walked away.

Shanna stopped sweeping and leaned her forehead against the handle of her broom. Her hands shook. She pulled in a deep breath. Delphine loved to make her feel inadequate and inferior. Did Delphine mean it was too bad nobody else survived or too bad Shanna did?"

"Don't ever do that again," a deep voice said next to her ear.

Shanna jumped at least a foot. Great! Now the marshal found her, too! Broom in hand, she turned toward the street. Marshal Calhan stood directly in front of her, hands on his hips, and anger in his brilliant blue eyes. She stood on the second stair down. She was eye to eye with an extremely irritated man. Shanna leaned against her broom handle. "Do what?" She pretended innocence. The man was livid because she escaped him and made it to Rock Creek without him. Shanna resisted the urge to giggle.

"You know damn good and well what," Reese said irritably.

Shanna smiled despite her effort to control her laughter. "Did you just make it into town?" she asked, moving the broom side to side halfheartedly.

"Damnit, Shanna, quit playing games with me. I'm going to figure out what you're up to. You won't escape justice. Not this time," Reese threatened.

"You're mad because I left you at the fort. I told you I could take care of myself. I also told you I would make it on my own." Shanna stopped sweeping and turned her back. She would have walked away, but Reese caught her arm.

"I'm watching you. Every step you take, every move you make, I'm going to be there. When I figure out what you're doing here, I'm going to send your boys to hell and you to prison, where you belong." His voice was silky soft.

Shanna shivered, despite her best efforts not to. *Dammit, why doesn't he leave me alone?* She hadn't done anything wrong, and she was getting tired of him accusing her. "Okay. I give up." She slumped in defeat. "I thought I fooled you, but you caught me." She held her broom toward the marshal, her face turned down in guilt. "Take it. I never should have used it in the first place. You're right. It's a terrible thing to do, and I'm so ashamed." Shanna looked up, her eyes wide and frightened. Her mouth quivered in fear. "What will they do to me for sweeping a porch in broad daylight?"

Reese narrowed his eyes. He took a swat at the proffered broom, sending it flying into the street. "I mean it, Shanna. I'm through playing games. You're going to wish you died on the train." Reese glared at her. Then, he turned and stalked off toward the sheriff's office.

Shanna smiled and picked up her broom. She stared after Reese. She was done playing games, too. She hadn't done anything wrong. It was high time he realized he had the wrong girl.

****

Reese strode toward the sheriff's office. He needed to let the sheriff know he arrived, and he had a question or two to ask the man about Shanna. How the damn woman escaped and made it to Rock Creek without him, still eluded him. She must have run into someone from Rock Creek at the fort and asked for a ride. Otherwise, he would have known when and where she went. The soldiers at Fort Buford were only too happy to give him any information he desired.

Reese stepped up on the boardwalk and reached for the sheriff's door. Folks in small towns always knew everybody else's business, and they usually distrusted outsiders. It would be interesting to see how the folks of Rock Creek viewed Shanna. Reese glanced up and down the street before he walked inside. Once he was done here, he wanted to get a telegraph off to Sergeant Baxter, his old boss in Chicago. Sergeant Baxter would be as surprised as he was with Jenna's resurrection and transformation. He would also be surprised when he heard she lived in Rock Creek and answered to Shanna.

****

Rose Tanner whistled softly between her teeth as she walked up behind Shanna. Shanna turned to see what held her friend's interest and rolled her eyes at Rose's expression.

Rose stared as the marshal walked away. "He is one fine looking man. Who is he?"

Shanna turned to her friend. "He's a demon from hell."

"Well, I guess I'm going to be a big disappointment to my mother and Reverend Wilson, because if hell looks like him, I'm going," Rose said with conviction. Her mouth gaped open. She came close to drooling over the marshal's broad shoulders and sculpted backside. "I think he likes you," Rose commented thoughtfully. "Does he have a brother?" Rose asked, her eyes still wandering over the retreating form of Marshal Reese.

"No, and he doesn't like me. He has me confused with some woman he calls Jenna. He won't leave me alone. He keeps following me around threatening to arrest me. Do you know he accused me of blowing up the train? I had to sneak out of the fort on your papa's wagon for Pete's sake to get away from the man."

Rose turned to Shanna, her mouth wide open. "You had to sneak to get away from him. Are you crazy? Let him catch you! I would. I would have twisted an ankle, had a sudden dizzy spell, or tripped over something so he'd have to carry me. I've only seen men who looked like him in Mama's magazines! Maybe you need glasses, Shanna. Open your eyes and look at the man! You have a living, breathing god following you around, and you're trying to get away? Honest to God, Shanna, sometimes I wonder about your mental abilities."

"You did hear the part about him confusing me with somebody else and wanting to arrest me, right? And he's not a god, he's the devil."

"So, what if he's confused," Rose muttered and then brightened. "I mean, how bad do you think his confusion is? Do you think I might be able to convince him I'm this other woman, so he follows me instead of you?"

"And what? Get arrested? Think it through, Rose."

Rose stood up straight and placed her hand across her heart as if getting ready to recite the Pledge of Allegiance. "I would be willing to take the chance." Rose's smiled deepened. "I am willing to sacrifice myself to this delicious demon." Rose paused, lost in her own imagination, and then added as an afterthought. "Um, for you of course. How could I let me dearest friend suffer without doing anything to help?"

Shanna laughed. Rose could be so dotty sometimes. "I could have used your help a few days ago. The man is determined to prove I've done something wrong. The only thing he talks about is how he's going to send me to jail, and he keeps making comments about "my men," as if I secretly run a gang like the Turleys or something."

Rose turned to Shanna, hands on her hips. "You have men? As in, more than one? How could you, Shanna? I'm your dearest friend, and I know nothing about any of this." Rose started to giggle. "What do you think Daniel Anderson will say when he hears? Shanna Johnston is running around with a gang of men."

Shanna laughed too. "He will say he told them all along I was no good, and this proves he was right."

"Do you think he will be more upset you run around with a group of men or that you didn't invite him too?" Rose wondered.

Shanna shrugged. "I don't know why he would be upset at all. He's the one who broke the engagement, not me."

"True." Rose gazed at her friend. Shanna was still hurt by the betrayal.

"He is also the one who ran around spreading lies about me, not the other way around. So, I don't know what *he* has to be upset about."

"I think he tells those lies about you because he knows what a fine person you are, and he realizes he's been an idiot. Now Delphine Otis has his ring on her finger, Daniel is beginning to see the real girl. I think he realizes he made a mistake," Rose said.

"Now what kind of sense does that make? He had his chance. He not only broke the engagement, but he made sure no other man for miles around will get within three feet of me," Shanna protested.

"Exactly. He doesn't want any other man to have you, so he lies to keep them away. He wants you back, Shanna. He just hasn't figured out how to get rid of Delphine." Rose grinned. "Maybe we could help him out by tying her up and throwing her on a train to New York," Rose suggested.

Shanna chuckled. "I don't think we could pry the two apart long enough to tie Delphine up."

Rose nodded in agreement. "She does keep Daniel on a pretty tight string. Well, what about bumping her on the head after the women's society meeting tomorrow night? We could put her in the crate the fabric was shipped in and send her back as damaged goods or something."

Shanna rolled her eyes. She had no idea where Rose came up with her ideas. Rose was a kind person, and because she loved Shanna, she believed everyone else should too.

"In a couple of months, she would be in China, and our problem would be solved." Rose sounded thrilled with the idea.

"But then, if you are correct about Daniel, he would come after me again," Shanna said, playing along with Rose.

"You're right. Well, we could always get "your men" to kidnap him, take him for a little ride, and dump him in a ravine somewhere," Rose suggested

"What about the marshal? He keeps a pretty close eye on me," Shanna answered.

"Well, the only choice we have is for me to distract the marshal while you meet with your men and tell them what needs to be done." Rose wiggled her eyebrows. "I could *really* distract the marshal for some time."

"Rose! You and Shanna get in here! There's work to do!" Mrs. Tanner called from the door of the mercantile.

"We'll talk later," Shanna said softly. She gave her friend a quick hug. Rose was such a dear to worry about her feelings. Shanna glanced across the street. Her smile turned to a frown. "Come on, Rose, let's go before you-know-who comes back." Shanna pointed her chin in the direction of the telegraph office.

Rose looked. Daniel Anderson and Delphine were coming out of the building and walking in their direction. The girls hurried inside the mercantile. The screen door slammed shut behind them.

****

Reese was on his way back to the mercantile, when he caught the sound of Shanna's voice. He stopped and leaned casually against the side of the feed store, where he could hear the conversation but stay out of sight. He rolled a cigarette as he listened. He'd be looking into Daniel and Delphine as soon as he got a chance. Once the girls went inside, he stepped forward on the boardwalk and looked across the street. He had no way of knowing who "you-know-who" was, so he studied everyone in sight. There were a couple of wagons with farmers going by, a man leaning by the saloon, and a well-dressed couple coming out of the telegraph office. They were both tall and thin. The man had wavy brown hair, while the woman had vibrant red hair. Reese studied the pair closely. They walked across the street and entered the saloon. Was the woman Delphine? Why did Shanna want her gone? Was the man with her Daniel? Why would he come after Shanna? It was interesting the Tanner girl was in on whatever Shanna had planned. As for Shanna's denial about her men, she admitted they were nearby to the Tanner girl.

Reese put the cigarette into his mouth. He didn't light it. He wasn't much of a smoker at all. He only smoked when he was agitated about something and couldn't seem to calm down. In fact, he couldn't recall when he'd smoked a cigarette last, until this past week. He had several cigarettes since he met up with Shanna, and they hadn't helped him calm down at all. As soon as he believed he was getting it all figured, she threw a rock in his way. Sheriff Holden hadn't been much help, either. All the sheriff wanted to talk about was the

Turley Gang and their latest victim. When Reese questioned him about Shanna, the sheriff looked at him like he was crazy and said, "What do you want to talk about her for? She's got nothing to do with this," and then continued on about the Turleys.

One thing Reese knew for certain; *Shanna was Jenna* although she pretended otherwise. Reese lit the cigarette and inhaled deeply. She did one hell of a job pretending to be somebody else. He nearly fell for it, *nearly*. With Shanna's men close by, and her planning on making a move tomorrow night to get Delphine out of her way, he would stick to Shanna's side like butter on toast. Reese rolled the smoke around in his mouth. The Tanner girl figured she had what it took to distract him from following Shanna. Reese smiled, she was pretty, he did admit, but his taste ran more to capturing blonde vixens with claws and putting them behind bars.

Chapter 7

Shanna sat on the steps of the mercantile and looked up and down the empty street. It was well past dark. Uncle Joseph was supposed to be here by now. He told her to wait outside on the steps after work. Well, she'd been right here for some time. Shanna was tired and sitting here alone in front of the mercantile was making her drowsy. She wanted to get back to the claim and get her chores done, so she could go to bed.

Rose and Shanna had spent the better part of the afternoon and evening putting away the silk shipment which just arrived. Mrs. Tanner ordered the silk for Christmas last year. Now it was here, it was in time for this year's harvest dance. Rose squealed with delight over every bolt of silk as they pulled them from the shipping crates. They unrolled and measured every bolt, meticulously recording the exact yardage. Then, they rerolled every bolt carefully and stacked them in the supply room. The shipment cost a fortune. Mr. Tanner was anxious to get it sold and make his money back. He took a tiny sample of each bolt and pasted it on a blank paper for customers to view. The silk came in several different colors. Mr. Tanner wanted customers to see the variety he offered, without compromising the goods. The fabric was too costly and too fine to let every customer handle it. It was imperative to keep the waste cost down as much as possible.

"What color would you choose, Shanna?" Rose asked, dreamily touching the silk.

The question was ridiculous. Uncle Joseph would never allow Shanna to have something so fine, despite the money her mother sent him for Shanna's keep. He spent her money on cards and liquor.

"I think the purple one would look good on you," Shanna said, avoiding the question. She pictured Rose in the purple silk with her dark curly hair and sparkling brown eyes. The shade would complement her coloring. Mrs. Tanner was an excellent seamstress, and she would make the dress fit Rose's slender body as few could. Rose was a beautiful girl, and Shanna wondered for the hundredth time, why her friend remained single. Rose had a delightful sense of humor and a quick mind. She would make someone a wonderful wife. It was a shame none of the men in Rock Creek realized what a treasure Rose was.

"Thank you, but that's not what I asked you. Which color would you choose?" Rose insisted.

Shanna looked again at the neatly piled bolts. Her eyes were drawn to the pink one. It was silly, but if it made Rose happy, she could play along. "This one, I would choose this one." Shanna allowed her fingers one small touch, and then shoved her hands into the oversized pockets of Aunt Sara's faded orange calico dress.

Rose looked around and removed the bolt of pink silk from the stack. She hid it under a pile of gingham, making sure it could not be seen.

"What are you doing?" Shanna asked in alarm.

"I'm taking care of my best friend," Rose announced.

"How? I can't pay for the silk and your father will be upset when he realizes the pink silk is missing. I will lose my job. Uncle Joseph will be furious—"

"I'm not letting you go to the harvest dance in Aunt Sara's old rags. I have a plan. It's going to work out fine. You must trust me. Okay?"

Shanna didn't know what to say. She opened her mouth to protest but Rose stopped her.

"Trust me, Shanna. Please?" Rose pleaded.

Despite every cell in her body screaming at her to tell Rose to put the silk back, Shanna nodded her head. She couldn't tell Rose no about anything, not when she begged. Customers came and left. Shanna thought long and hard about the situation. She would have to talk some sense into Rose about the silk.

The doorbell jingled and Delphine sauntered in followed by Daniel.

"Where is the silk I've been hearing so much about?" Delphine asked. She stopped and looked Shanna up and down. Then she giggled. "Where did you get that ugly dress? I can't believe Mr. Tanner lets you work in his store. You're so shabby. Having you wandering around in here has got to be bad for business."

Rose shot out of the back room. "There's nothing wrong with Shanna, and Daddy likes having her here. She's a hard worker."

Delphine rolled her eyes and giggled again. "If you say so. I'm so glad I didn't eat lunch yet. I have a delicate stomach, and I don't think I'd be able to keep my food down after looking at Shanna, dressed as she is. What do you think Daniel? Isn't Shanna revolting?"

Daniel gazed at Shanna, then looked away. He

agreed Shanna sickened him too. His eyes wandered to her bosom and stayed there.

Rose stood with her hands on her hips and glared at Delphine. "Daddy doesn't like it when I tell customers to leave, but in your case, I'm going to make an exception."

"Let's find out what they want first," Shanna said. She turned to Delphine. "What can we help you with?"

"She doesn't deserve our help," Rose insisted. "Who cares what Delphine Otis wants?"

"Your daddy, especially if Delphine is spending her daddy's money," Shanna pointed out.

"Fine," Rose conceded. "What do you want, Delphine?"

Delphine looked from one to the other. "I want silk."

Shanna grabbed the card with the silk samples and set it on the counter in front of Delphine. "These are the colors we have."

Daniel's gaze remained glued to Shanna's chest.

Rose noticed too. She moved in front of Shanna and whispered, "Why don't you go sweep the back room?"

"Good idea," Shanna said and hurried to the back.

Delphine was still looking over the silk selection when Shanna returned.

"It's a shame there isn't any pink or purple silk. Those are my favorite colors," Delphine exclaimed. "You would think, with the variety of colors available, those two shades would be among them."

Shanna glanced at Rose.

Rose smiled sweetly. "We don't have silk in those colors."

Shanna helped Rose wrap the bolts of silk Delphine purchased in paper.

Delphine walked out with seven bolts of the beautiful silk. Daniel trailed along behind carrying the rather large parcel, his face a mask of irritation. Delphine took the prettiest colors. She didn't want anyone coming to the harvest dance looking as nice as she planned to look.

The day passed quickly. Soon, it was closing time. Everything was put away and locked up. The Tanners retired to their rooms above the store. Shanna sat down wearily on the front steps of the mercantile and waited for Uncle Joseph. *Where is he?* It was getting late, and she still had all her chores to do before she could go to bed. Shanna glanced toward the sheriff's office. Reese was framed in the window gazing at the mercantile. The man kept her in sight all afternoon, just like he promised. Shanna sighed. Rose thought it was romantic. Shanna thought it was annoying.

Shanna still smarted over Delphine's comment. She had no choice in dress. Uncle Joseph let her wear Aunt Sara's old dresses, and that was all. Shanna often wondered what it would be like to wear a dress made for her, a dress that fit. She knew the orange gingham she had on did nothing for her complexion or her hair. She wished with all her heart she had dresses of her own, a family of her own, and a life of her own. It wasn't the case. She did the best she could to survive.

A sound caught Shanna's attention. She stood up. It sounded like the side door of the mercantile by the loading area. The door had a squeak and then a groan as the hinges swung the door open. Shanna got to her feet and walked around the mercantile to investigate. *The side door was wide open!* Shanna shut and locked it before locking the front door. She glanced at the upper windows of the mercantile. The lights were out except in the Tanner's bedroom. Shanna frowned. *Was someone trying to rob the mercantile?* She moved closer to the door and stepped quietly inside. She knew the layout by heart, avoiding the items close to the door, and entered the main room of the mercantile. She looked around, giving her eyes a chance to adjust to the darkness.

The dark form of a man stood next to the gun counter. Moonlight streamed in the window and shone on his face. He had a pointy nose and a bushy beard. The man held a sack. He was busy filling it with guns and boxes of bullets.

Suddenly, the door to the mercantile opened. Mr. Tanner stood in the doorway holding a lantern high in his hand. "Who's there?" he shouted. Mrs. Tanner was right behind him. She took the lantern, while Mr. Tanner pulled out his rifle.

Shanna doubted the Tanners realized they made perfect targets. The light from the room behind them highlighted them in the darkness of the shop. The man at the gun counter dropped the sack and grabbed for his gun. Shanna looked around and plucked a hoe from a display beside her. The robber ran toward her, leveling his revolver in Mr. Tanner's direction. Shanna swung the hoe and caught the man on the side of his head. He let out a bellow of fury and charged at her. He plowed into her, knocking the breath out of her, and shoved her through the open door. He flung her away from him as hard as he could. Shanna went flying and hit into the feed store attached to the side of the mercantile. The man turned his gun to shoot at her. Shouting came from across the street. Footsteps were coming dangerously near. The man looked at the unconscious face of the woman at his feet. The shouting came closer. With a growl of anger, the man holstered his gun and disappeared into the shadows.

****

"Shanna, open your eyes." Reese shook her gently. He got no response. He knelt and pressed his head against her chest. Her heart still beat. Reese shook her again.

"Shanna, open your eyes. Look at me." He stared at her pale face. She took quite a hit. Mr. Tanner stood anxiously behind him, trying to keep a little distance between the marshal and the crowd of townspeople. The town was gathering fast, trying to see what was going on.

"Shanna!" Reese shook her again and this time she let out a groan. He sank back on his heels and waited.

Shanna groaned again. She opened her eyes and blinked up at him. Where was she? She hurt all over and someone kept shaking her. Everything was blurry. There were voices all around her. "Is she all right?" the voices asked over and over. "Who is it?" another voice asked. Shanna closed her eyes and prayed the world would quit spinning.

"She's fine. Give her some space," Reese said.

Shanna frowned. Marshal Reese was here, hovering over her. She should have guessed. If something went wrong, he was involved somehow. Like the train getting blown up. Hadn't she traveled to Omaha every year since she was ten, and everything proceeded just fine? This year, the marshal got on the train, and look what happened. Bad things naturally followed him wherever he went. Shanna levered her sore body into a sitting position. She leaned back against the wall behind her and looked around. She sat on the boardwalk between the mercantile and the feed store. Everyone was staring at her, including Reese.

"What happened, Shanna?" Reese peered at her. At least he wasn't standing over her, waving his gun in her face like last time.

"I don't know," Shanna answered.

Reese stared hard at her and waited. His lids dropped over his eyes, shielding his thoughts.

"She saved my life," Mr. Tanner said. "There was a robber in my store by the guns. Shanna hit him over the head when he tried to shoot me."

"How did Shanna know there was a robber in your store?" Reese asked. He turned back to Shanna. He observed her closely.

"I heard the side door open, and I went to see why." Shanna could see Reese didn't believe what she said.

"Maybe it wasn't closed tight," he suggested, studying her.

She rolled her eyes to let him know what she thought of his suggestion. Her chin lifted a notch. "I closed the door and locked it myself. It was shut tight."

"If Shanna says she locked it, she did," Mr. Tanner said quickly. "Are you okay, Shanna?" Mr. Tanner looked anxiously at her.

"I'm okay, Mr. Tanner." Shanna folded her trembling hands in her lap.

Sheriff Holden walked up and motioned for Reese to come and talk. Reese glared at her, warning her he would be back, and walked away. Mr. Tanner took her by the elbow and carefully helped her to her feet.

"I think the marshal is upset because you could have been killed coming into the mercantile after a robber like you did. It took courage, but it was foolhardy. What if he shot you? Rose would never forgive me or anyone else. She would skin me alive if anything happened to you. You must think about things before you act. I do appreciate you keeping the man from shooting at Mrs. Tanner and myself, but you need to be more careful."

Shanna nodded. Mr. Tanner didn't know she could take care of herself. Nobody did except White Eagle.

"We are going over to the sheriff's office, Shanna." It was a command. Reese stood in front of her, hands on his hips.

Shanna frowned at his domineering posture. "You go to the sheriff's office. I'm going home." Shanna turned away but nearly fell when she put weight on her right leg.

Reese didn't bother arguing with her. He scooped her up in his arms and strode toward Sheriff Holden's office, holding her tight against his chest.

"Put me down," Shanna said angrily.

Reese grinned. "I should have thrown you over my shoulder the first day. It would have been a lot easier and a lot faster."

"Put me down, now!" Shanna demanded.

Reese ignored her. He carried her inside, kicking the door shut behind them. He strode toward the back of the jail and deposited her on a bed in one of the cells.

Sheriff Holden hurried after the marshal, the frown on his face made his handlebar mustache droop even further than normal. He locked the outside door once they were all inside his office to keep the nosy townspeople out of the discussion.

"Get used to this look," Reese suggested to Shanna, pointing at the bars surrounding them. "You're going to be seeing it a lot in the near future."

Shanna didn't reply. She reeled from the pain in her backside and along the right side of her body. When Reese set her down, it hadn't been easy. Plopped would be a more accurate description. The pain made her eyes water. Reese leaned against the bars and folded his arms. Shanna curled over on her left side, away from his prying eyes, and wrapped her arms around her middle. She breathed through the pain and waited for Reese to go away.

Sheriff Holden entered the cell with two cups of coffee in his hands. He gave one to Reese and drew a chair up to the narrow cot. "The doctor should be here soon," Sheriff Holden said to no one in particular.

Shanna nodded to let him know she heard and rolled to her other side so she could see the sheriff.

Sheriff Holden took a sip of his coffee. "Tell me what happened, Shanna."

Reese pulled a chair up too and waited. Shanna ignored Reese and focused on Sheriff Holden. She told him everything she could remember.

"How did you know the sound you heard was the side door to the mercantile?" the sheriff asked.

"It makes a particular sound, and I recognized it," Shanna answered.

"Were you able to see the man?" Sheriff Holden asked.

"Only a little. He was wearing dark clothes and no

hat. He had dark hair, a pointy face, and a bushy beard."

"How did you manage to see so much in the dark?" Reese asked dryly.

"There was moonlight coming through the window. The man turned and I saw his face." Shanna shook her head. The marshal obviously thought she had something to do with this. When would he get it through his head, she was not evil? "Are you going to accuse me of robbing the mercantile? Or maybe hiring someone to do it for me? Or better yet throwing myself around so everyone would think somebody else did?" Shanna asked.

"No one is accusing you of anything," Sheriff Holden soothed. He glanced from the marshal to Shanna and back again. "We are asking because we think the robber was a member of the Turley Gang," Sheriff Holden explained. "If it was, we are going to be keeping a real close eye on you."

Shanna attempted to move her right arm and winced with pain. Reese frowned. He leaned forward to get a better look at her arm.

"Did the man see your face?" the sheriff asked.

"I don't know. It happened rather fast. He pulled his gun and was going to shoot Mr. Tanner, so I hit him on the head with a hoe. His gun hit the floor. The last thing I remember was the man knocking into me, and then I was flying. I hit into the side of the feed store and everything goes blank after that. I suppose he could have seen my face. I don't remember," Shanna said slowly.

Chapter 8

"What were you doing at the mercantile so late?" Reese asked.

"I was waiting for Uncle Joseph. Why do you think it was the Turley Gang who tried to rob the mercantile?" Shanna asked.

Sheriff Holden and Marshal Reese exchanged glances.

"We found a white bandanna tied with a square knot sitting on the gun counter," Sheriff Holden said.

A white bandana was the only evidence the Turley Gang left at their crime scenes. It was always left in a conspicuous spot so everyone would know who committed the crime. The Turleys moved their lair from place to place in the unorganized territory of the United States, completely outside the jurisdiction of the local sheriffs. They plundered everything and everybody, without consequence. The Turleys never left witnesses to identify them. So, nobody knew who they were, except by reputation and the white bandanna with the square knot left at the scene.

Terror crossed Shanna's face, and Reese frowned. Why would she be frightened of the Turleys? "Did you recognize the man, Shanna? Is he anybody you know or have seen before?" Reese asked. He stared at her intently. What did Jenna have to worry about? With her men close by, her well-being wouldn't be a concern.

"No," Shanna answered, and Reese believed her. He stared at her. His gut told him she was telling the truth. She didn't know who the man was. The bandana said the man was a Turley, but Jenna didn't know him? How was it possible? Maybe the Turleys weren't part of her plans after all. Which caused him to wonder, what was?

Somebody started pounding on the sheriff's door. Sheriff Holden got up to answer it. Reese tried again. "If the Turley Gang thinks you can identify the man, they're going to come looking for you," he stated.

"And in looking for me, they will be coming to—"

"Kill you," Reese answered.

Shanna dropped her head and rubbed her arm thoughtfully. Reese studied Shanna's face and wondered what she was thinking. She looked so young and alone, and so damn pitiful. He wanted to take her into his arms and kiss her. He wanted to hold her, and then take her back to his room, where he would make slow, sweet love to her. He wanted to tell her it was going to be okay. Only it wasn't. After everything there was between them, it would never be okay again. Her innocence was all a façade. It's all it had ever been.

"...not going to wait for some doctor. I want my niece right now so I can get for home. It's late enough as it is. Sara is going to have a fit." Joseph Johnston appeared around the corner followed by Sheriff Holden and Doctor Horace. Reese shook the sensual thoughts from his mind and got to his feet. He stepped away from the narrow cot, allowing the doctor space to examine the patient.

"She caint be hurt bad. She's sittin' up real purty. Now move aside." Joseph was trying to shove his way into the cell, but Sheriff Holden stood squarely in his path.

The sheriff nodded at Doctor Horace and moved so the doctor could enter the cell. "I'm afraid I can't do that Mr. Johnston. Doctor Horace needs to check Shanna over. She took quite a hit. I want to be sure she's okay before I send her home."

Joseph Johnston was not happy with the news. He was a thin man with graying hair and a long, crooked nose. His brown eyes were sunk into his head, and he smelled like liquor. Reese drew in a breath and almost choked. He took a wild guess on where Uncle Joseph had been all night.

"You cain't. I'm Shanna's legal guardian, and I say she comes now!" Uncle Joseph demanded.

Sheriff Holden crossed his arms and stared at the thin ugly man. "Speaking of being her legal guardian, maybe you care to tell me where you've been all evening? You left Shanna to sit alone on the mercantile steps. If you had come and got her, and taken her home, none of this would have happened. Maybe I should arrest you for endangerment."

"Now see here—" Uncle Joseph blustered.

Sheriff Holden reached for his handcuffs, and Uncle Joseph took a quick step back.

"All right. Let the doctor check her out. I'll wait," the man grumbled.

Doctor Horace was already seeing to the patient.

Reese stood against the far wall. His arms folded across his big chest. He observed everything the doctor did closely.

When he was finished, the doctor snapped his case shut and turned to the sheriff. "Nothing seems to be broken. Her right side took most of the blow. She will be sore for a few days, but she will be fine."

"Thank you, Doctor." Sheriff Holden shook hands with the doctor and moved aside so the doctor could leave.

Uncle Joseph immediately started to whine again. "See? I told ya the girl wasn't hurt. Come on, Shanna. Sara will pitch a fit if we're too much later."

Shanna moved to slide off the bed, and Reese was suddenly right there helping her. He took hold of her left arm and slid her forward onto her feet. He held her arm for a second until he was sure she could stand on her own.

"Who the hell are you? Get your hands off my niece!" Uncle Joseph bellowed.

Sheriff Holden stepped forward. "Joseph, this is U S Marshal Reese Calhan. He's the one who's come to catch the Turley Gang."

Uncle Joseph turned to Reese. His eyes widened as he looked all the way up to Reese's face. "Is that a fact?" Uncle Joseph said. "Well, you keep to huntin' criminals and leave yer hands off my niece."

Reese narrowed his gaze but didn't answer. He didn't like this squirrelly-eyed man, and he always trusted his gut. Reese's gaze followed Shanna as she limped toward the door. She was favoring her right side. She was going to hurt like hell come morning.

"Hurry it up, Shanna! We're late enough as it is," Uncle Joseph bellowed.

Shanna stood by the wagon, uncertainly. Reese spanned her waist, lifting her easily, and set her up on the seat. "Thank you," Shanna whispered.

"My pleasure," Reese drawled. He felt a little

guilty for the way he set her on the cot earlier. Whoever hurt her, didn't know who she was or what she was capable of. Which made Reese wonder where Shanna's men were. If they were nearby, why the hell did they let her take a hit? Something wasn't right. Reese frowned as he considered what happened. Shanna went in alone without a gun to face a robber. Then she hit the man on the head, rather than let Mr. Tanner get shot. The old Shanna wouldn't have cared one way or the other. She sure as hell wouldn't put her life at risk for some shopkeeper. Hadn't Shanna planned to get rid of someone named Delphine? Reese rolled a cigarette and walked back inside to talk to Sheriff Holden. He poured another cup of coffee and straddled a chair.

"So, what do you make of the situation?" Sheriff Holden asked. He took a sip of his coffee and waited for Reese to answer.

"The Turleys are definitely in the area. I think the one who came tonight might be a recruit."

"Why do you think?" Sheriff Holden asked.

"They like to send the new man alone into town to do small jobs. Then, if something goes wrong, it doesn't matter. They aren't losing anyone of value. It also lets the gang see how good a recruit is under pressure. If it had been an older member of the gang, he would have killed her," Reese said.

Sheriff Holden nodded his head. It made sense. "Do you think Shanna is in danger?"

"It's hard to say. If the man was a recruit, maybe, maybe not. It depends on what the man saw and how valuable he is to the gang."

Sheriff Holden took another sip of his coffee. "I don't like it. Shanna's a good girl, sweet as honey straight from the comb. She's got enough to deal with between Daniel Anderson, Delphine Otis, and her aunt and uncle. She doesn't need to be hunted by some cutthroat gang as well."

Reese had to ask. "How so?"

"Well, the Anderson fellow made a fool of himself over Shanna. Shanna's not a real pretty girl, as I'm sure you've noticed, but she's got character. She's as sweet as God makes 'em, Well, Anderson, he started courting Shanna. Shanna was happy as I ever seen her, over the moon in love, and couldn't believe a man like Daniel Anderson would be interested in someone like her. Then Nathaniel Otis and his uppity daughter moved to town. Next thing you know, Anderson is following the Otis girl around like she was Christmas candy and him with a sweet tooth. Anderson called Shanna a whore. He tore her down in front of the whole town. He told folks Shanna had the same disease the saloon girls have. He hurt the girl bad, and some of the folks like to poke fun at her. Rose Tanner stood by her and demanded proof. The rumors died down when Anderson proposed to the Otis girl. Some of the town folk had sense enough to see Anderson was lying to cover his own ass. He had to have an excuse for breaking his engagement to Shanna and then proposing to the Otis girl and her daddy's money so soon after. Shanna's a good girl. Just because she doesn't look like the other girls and wears those God-awful dresses of Sara Johnston's is no reason to treat her poorly. Shanna will make somebody a good wife someday."

Reese digested this for a minute or two then asked, "What about the aunt and uncle?"

"Here's the strange part. Joseph and his wife lived

in Deadwood years ago. Joseph got into trouble with a gunslinger there. He owed the man money from a poker game. The gunslinger threatened to kill Joseph and his family if he didn't pay up. Joseph disappeared, and two weeks later, he showed up with the money and paid the man off. Then he hitched the wagon and moved to Rock Creek. Sara had a brother with a claim here. Her brother died some time back, but they never even came to the funeral. The whole time her brother lived here, they never visited. Then one Sunday morning they rolled into town and took up the homestead like they lived here their whole life."

"Why is it strange?" Reese asked. It seemed a common enough thing.

"Because folks don't know the Johnstons or anything about them. They don't trust outsiders much. When they noticed how different Shanna was from the Johnstons, folks got to talking. They wanted to know why Shanna was different and why the Johnstons never visited Sara's brother. So, I did a little digging around. I wired the sheriff in Deadwood. Joseph Johnston likes to drink, and he likes to gamble. He got into trouble several times. He disappears and when he returns, he has cash to pay his debt. The strange thing is, one day he brought a blonde-haired little girl back with him from wherever he got the money. The Johnstons never had any children of their own, and suddenly they have a little girl who don't look at all like them. The whole situation was strange."

"So, what made Joseph move to Rock Creek?" Reese asked. He wanted to see if this story matched up with what he knew about Jenna.

"The sheriff of Deadwood said when Joseph got

into trouble with the gunslinger it was the last straw. The gunslinger shot up the saloon and killed several people. The owner of the saloon had enough of Joseph and his cheating. He told Joseph he'd kill him if he ever stepped foot in his establishment again. Now, Joseph likes his cards and his drink. So, he moved here where nobody knew anything about him. They brought Shanna with them."

"How old was Shanna when they brought her to Rock Creek?" Reese asked.

"Oh, I'd say about eighteen maybe nineteen. She was awfully shy. It's a damn shame neither Joseph nor Sara ever took to her. Poor Shanna has had a hard life." Sheriff Holden got up to get more coffee.

"It is a shame," Reese agreed, "but things like this happen all the time."

"Here's the thing," Sheriff Holden said, "they don't act like family. I suspect things aren't good at home for Shanna. She's come to town with bruises, hurt arms, and legs with no real reason on how she got them. I've been wondering for a while if the uncle strikes her, but I haven't been able to prove it."

"So, where was Shanna before they brought her to Deadwood?" Reese asked. He was close to getting answers. He could feel it. Reese leaned forward.

"Nobody knows," Sheriff Holden answered. "They showed up here with Shanna one Sunday morning, just like I told you."

Reese slumped back and shook his head. Dammit. The timeline fit in with what he knew about her. She was eighteen when they were together in Chicago. She must have come west shortly after. The question was, why? "As wrong as all this is, you can hardly claim it's strange. Many wives and daughters get beaten by their husbands and fathers when they're drunk and can't hold their liqueur. Often the men don't care where their women are either, unless they need them for something," Reese said.

"True, but then Shanna looks nothing like the aunt and uncle. They have dark hair and brown eyes. There's no way Shanna is their relative. She is completely opposite of everything they are. I've wondered many times if Shanna was kidnapped or something. Like I said, it's strange."

Reese nodded. He established two things in the course of the evening, Shanna didn't know the man in the mercantile, and she came west right after the explosion everyone believed killed her. It wasn't much, but hell, it was something. He never asked about Jenna's childhood, so he had nothing to dispute. He would take what little information he had.

"Well, Marshal Calhan, let's get some shut eye. Dawn's a coming and we want to find the robber's trail while it's fresh," Sheriff Holden said. He picked up the lantern and followed Reese out on to the street, locking the door behind them.

Chapter 9

Two riders covered in dust waited in the foyer of the two-story brick mansion on Jefferson Street, Chicago. They were waiting to see the boss. Frenchie was thin with a wispy mustache and dark, wavy hair. He had narrow gray eyes and was good with a knife. He spoke fluent French and had a passion for all women.

Iverson, on the other hand, was a large heavy-set man. He was a bit slow physically and mentally. He cared nothing about women except to gratify his needs. Explosives were his passion. He knew everything there was to know about explosives and the different chemicals used to create them. Nothing brightened Iverson's day like blowing something up, which is why he had been sent on this mission with Frenchie. The door opened, and a liveried butler escorted them into the room where the boss sat behind a large gleaming desk.

"Is it done?" the boss asked.

Frenchie and Iverson glanced at each other and then at the boss. "Well, sort of," Frenchie answered.

"Sort of? Do you have his body or not?" the boss demanded.

"We did what you said, boss. We placed the charges where they would do the most damage. We blew the train to pieces. Not one car stayed on the tracks. The Union Pacific is still picking up the pieces.

It was a beautiful explosion," Iverson said his expression dreamy. Frenchie nervously twisted his hat in his hands. Nobody liked to tell the boss the mission was a failure. Things got ugly when that happened.

"Where is Marshal Calhan's body?" the boss roared.

Iverson and Frenchie both inched toward the door. "We were wondering if your contact knew for a fact Marshal Calhan was on the train. Maybe your contact made a mistake." Frenchie hoped fervently this was the informant's failure and not his.

"My informant was sure. He watched Marshal Calhan board the train! Now where is his body?" The question was asked softly this time. It scared them worse than being yelled at.

"It wasn't there. We don't have his body. We searched the whole area and never found it," Iverson admitted. "We waited for a couple of hours after the blast and then went through the whole train."

"Everyone was dead, but Marshal Calhan wasn't there," Frenchie added.

The boss leaned back in the chair and took a puff of a cigar. *How like the marshal to cheat death.* The plan was well orchestrated. Reese couldn't have known something was going to happen. The informant at the train depot had done his job and brought the information as soon as Reese bought his ticket in Chicago. They were aware he would change trains in Omaha and ride into Pine Bluffs. It was the perfect plan. *How did the marshal escape? It should have worked! Dammit!* The boss looked over to the two men. They were sweating profusely as they waited to see what the boss' decision would be. The boss took another puff on the cigar. No one was as good with explosives as Iverson. They had another job coming up, and explosives were part of the plan. Frenchie would be needed, too. So, the men would live for the time being. Still, they needed a lesson for disappointing their boss.

The boss nodded slightly to the butler. Iverson and Frenchie were taken out. They would both be missing a finger before nightfall. It was a sad thing but necessary. Men must learn to obey.

****

Reese took the telegraph and wandered outside to read his message. Sergeant Baxter was his boss from the old Chicago days, the days before and after Jenna's betrayal, and the days following the explosion. He wanted to know if Sergeant Baxter had any new information on the Delaney Gang, or on Adam Delaney. He needed to make sense of what was going on with Jenna, why she went by Shanna, why the people of Rock Creek thought they knew her, how she was involved with the Turley Gang, and about a hundred other things which didn't make any sense. Sergeant Baxter sent a reply to Reese's inquiry.

Marshal Reese Calhan Rock Creek. Stop.
No new info on Delaney Gang. Stop.
Adam Delaney surfaced in Chicago. Stop.
Seen a week ago. Stop.
Nothing else new. Stop.
Sergeant Baxter Chicago

So, was it a coincidence Adam Delaney surfaced after so many years the same week Reese ran into Shanna on the train? Reese didn't believe in coincidences. There was some connection between Shanna showing up, and her uncle's sudden appearance after seven years as a recluse. Reese needed time to think about what the connection was. He intended to get some answers out of Shanna one way or another. He ran into a wall every time he thought he'd figured something out, and he was getting real sick of it.

They hadn't been able to track the robber more than a few miles out of town the morning after the robbery at the mercantile. Reese waited the next night outside the women's society meeting. Nothing happened. Shanna didn't even come, claiming her side was too sore. Which, Reese supposed it could be. Still, he felt like all kinds of a fool when the society let out, and all the women stared as they exited the schoolhouse. He did his best to appear at ease as he leaned against the schoolhouse and tipped his hat at twenty or so women. Sunday morning Reese decided he'd been patient long enough. Today he would get some answers. He had been in town a week and knew less than he did the day he arrived. There was only so far Shanna could go before he caught her and made her talk.

****

Shanna shook Reverend Wilson's hand on the way into church. She was getting the full use of her arm back, and it felt good. She followed Uncle Joseph and Aunt Sara into the little church and took a seat on the bench behind them. Aunt Sara always insisted there was not enough room on the church bench for the three of them. So, Shanna would take the seat right behind them. Somehow after Shanna was seated and reading her Bible, the church bench grew because Harry and Mable Clayton always managed to fit into the same space which was too little for Shanna to sit on. It must be a divine manifestation, Shanna supposed. Truthfully, she was getting used to being part of the background, or she was until the day she met Marshal Calhan He liked making her the center of attention, like the night of the burglary. Everyone saw her outside on the boardwalk. Everyone watched the marshal scoop her up and carry her into the sheriff's office too. Everyone noticed how long they were in there. Folks in town were having all sorts of fun imagining why. Shanna picked up her Bible and started to read. No sense in dwelling on that humiliation again.

As more people entered the church and took their places, the bench beside Shanna remained empty. Shanna bowed her head and kept reading, pretending she didn't care. Everyone stared at her and whispered. Rose caught Shanna's eyes and smiled her big smile. Shanna couldn't help smiling back. Rose was such a dear friend.

A commotion at the back of the church caused Shanna to look around. Daniel Anderson and Delphine Otis walked through the door. Delphine's high-pitched whine filled the little church. Marshal Calhan stood right inside the door talking quietly with Reverend Wilson.

Delphine gave a cry of delight when she spotted the marshal and held her hand out. "Marshal, it is so lovely to see you again. You simply must come to Daddy's for dinner sometime this week. You've been here for two whole weeks, and we've hardly seen you at all," Delphine cooed. She fluttered her eyes at him.

"I've been busy, ma'am," Reese replied. He shook her hand and dropped it.

Shanna smiled.

"Oh, I know, you've been looking for the man who tried to rob the mercantile. It's not as if a crime was committed or anything important was taken. Surely, you can afford to come socialize a little here and there," Delphine said, brushing away his comment. She ran her fingertips down Reese's arm as she spoke.

Shanna rolled her eyes. Good heavens, Delphine was slobbering all over Reese, and right in front of Daniel, too! Shanna looked sideways at Daniel to gauge his reaction but was disappointed. Daniel seemed every bit as excited to the see the marshal as Delphine was.

"Thank you for the invitation, but I must decline. It's business first," Reese said, stepping out of Delphine's reach.

"What a shame." Delphine pouted. Her eyes followed Reese hungrily.

"Daniel Anderson." Daniel extended his hand toward the marshal.

"U. S. Marshal Reese Calhan," Reese said and shook his hand.

Shanna didn't see what happened after because her view became blocked by all two hundred and fifty pounds of Mark Jacob. He ushered all five of his children onto the bench beside Shanna. Mr. Jacob sat down between his children and looked over at Shanna. He stared at her breasts. Shanna held her Bible high in front of her face so she couldn't see the disgusting man. He'd been married twice already. Both wives died in childbirth, and Mr. Jacob was looking for wife number three. Shanna had no idea why the filthy man looked in her direction, but he could look elsewhere. Shanna could barely see Rose over the top of her Bible. Rose pulled a face when Mr. Jacob sat down. Shanna dropped her eyes to keep from giggling. When she looked back up, Rose turned sideways in her seat and wiggled her eyebrows suggestively. Shanna dropped her Bible an inch and shook her head in response. She had no idea why the man chose to sit on her bench either. Maybe Mr. Jacob figured she was desperate because she was twenty-five years old and unmarried. What he didn't realize was Shanna would never fall to that level of desperation.

Mr. Jacob made a pretense of stretching, and suddenly the man's arm was along the bench behind her shoulders. She didn't dare look. She could smell him and knew he scooted closer. Shanna leaned forward; her Bible still high in front of her face while she thought about what to do. She wouldn't be able to listen to the sermon with Mr. Jacob sitting so close. His smell made her eyes water. She was disgusted by the brazen way he dropped his arm onto her. Shanna shook her shoulders, and the man moved his arm to the top of the bench. She pulled her kerchief from her oversize pocket and held it tightly against her nose, pretending she had a sneeze coming. How in God's name was she going to get out of this? She couldn't get up and leave, the town would go berserk wondering why.

"Is this seat taken?"

Shanna looked up in surprise and realized Reese stood beside her. Marshal Reese would have to do, at least he smelled better than Mr. Jacob. "No, it's not." Shanna smiled and scooted her knees clear to the left so the marshal could step around her.

He took his seat beside her and stretched his long legs out in front of him. Mr. Jacob mumbled something under his breath and moved to the other end of the bench, sandwiching his children in the middle.

Shanna glanced heavenward and whispered a fervent, "Thank you."

"You're welcome," Reese answered settling back in his seat with a smile.

Shanna glanced at the marshal. He obviously thought her gratitude was meant for him, not for divine intervention. Shanna leaned back also. Her breath caught. They touched shoulders, hips, and knees. The warmth from his body heated her to her core. Shanna shifted in her seat. Just when she got used to Reese's suspicious nature and accusations, he had to go do something nice, like rescue her from Mr. Jacob, or worse, he kissed her. Shanna remembered the way his hungry hands roamed her body so possessively, while his hot mouth reduced her to a quivering mass of sensitized nerves. She shivered with awareness. The man was too damn handsome for his own good. Shanna opened her Bible and pretended to read. She had a hard time making out the words on the page in front her. She couldn't think clearly with Reese pressed against her. Reese chuckled beside her. Then, his hand appeared and turned her Bible right side up. Shanna closed her eyes and prayed for a bolt of lightning. If only she could disappear without a trace. If God were merciful, he'd help her out.

Nothing happened. Shanna closed her Bible and set it in her lap. Her face was hot. She didn't want the marshal to see her hands shaking. She hoped to God he couldn't feel it, either.

Shoulder space was tight, and Reese eased his left arm out and laid it along the back of her seat like Mr. Jacob had. This time she didn't feel any disgust. In truth, her stomach hitched a little at the contact. The erotic smell of Reese Calhan surrounded her. He smelled like sandalwood, the outdoors, and coffee. She thought about his kiss again, and heat flooded through her. Her mind conjured up images and feelings which had her breathing fast. Shanna had no idea what Reverend Wilson talked about. She hoped to God fornication wasn't the topic of his sermon, or she would go to hell for sure. Because fornication with Marshal Reese Calhan was all Shanna thought about the whole two hours of the Sunday service.

****

Reese glanced down and noted Shanna's flushed face. He could feel her body trembling against him. Was she thinking about him the way he was thinking about her? Naked images of their sweat soaked bodies filled his mind. Her breathing increased. Reese smiled. Jenna remembered. He could tell by her reaction. Reese groaned inwardly. It was too damn easy to want this woman, especially when she smelled so damn good and looked so innocent. Her softness made him forget everything but how damn good she felt when he held her naked body to his and did all the things he wanted to. Reese was jerked back to reality when Sheriff Holden tapped him on the shoulder.

"We got us a little problem," Sheriff Holden said.

Reese nodded and got to his feet. He intended to get some answers from Shanna today, and all he had accomplished so far was indulging in fantasies about the woman that had him hard and aching.

Reese followed the sheriff outside. "What happened?" Reese asked.

"A cabin just got hit by the Turleys a couple miles

up the river," Sheriff Holden said as he climbed into the saddle and turned his horse east. Reese nodded. He mounted Pegasus and nudged him into a full gallop. He was right behind the sheriff.

Chapter 10

Little Alfred Turley was in big trouble. Scar Redding was the boss of the outfit holed up near Rock Creek. It was his job to strip the area and report back to Mack Turley, leader of the Turley gang. Scar recently returned from a trip to Chicago and was not one bit impressed with Little Alfred's bungled attempt at robbing the mercantile in Rock Creek. They were supposed to be in possession of all the ammunition the store had, but they weren't. Little Alfred, who wasn't little at all, merely thin with a bushy beard and dark hair, only managed to make it back to camp with two boxes of ammunition, *two boxes.* The only reason Little Alfred wasn't shot on the spot for his incompetence was, his older brother Mack wouldn't like it if Little Alfred was dead.

Scar Redding stared at Little Alfred. While Scar was in Chicago, he gave Mack the items the gang "collected" and reported everything was going according to plan. The gang had plans to rob the army payroll at Fort Buford. Mack sent Little Alfred along to learn how they did things. He wanted his brother to be in on the take when they collected the payroll. The problem was everything was not going according to plan. How could they take Little Alfred on a dangerous job like robbing Fort Buford if he couldn't even rob a little one-man mercantile in the middle of nowhere?

Scar scratched his head and looked at Little Alfred. He shouldn't have agreed to train Mack's brother. It was turning out to be a nightmare.

Alfred shifted nervously from one foot to the other. Scar was a big man, bald as an egg with a big scar across his face. He weighed all of two hundred and sixty pounds and was a son of a bitch, even on his good days. "I know I messed up, Scar, and I'm really sorry," Little Alfred said, "If the dang girl hadn't showed up outta nowhere, I would have the guns like you wanted."

"Did she see your face?" Scar asked.

"No, it was too dark," Little Alfred answered hastily.

Scar eyed him. He didn't think Alfred knew one way or the other. "Did you see her face? Would you recognize her if you saw her again?" Scar asked.

"Yeah, I think so," Alfred said.

"So, you saw her, but she didn't see you? It doesn't make any sense. If you saw her, then she saw you," Scar said. His hard look made Little Alfred squirm.

"I can fix this, boss. Give me another chance. I'll take care of the girl. Nobody will know a thing," Alfred assured him.

Scar stared at Little Alfred until his eye started to twitch. "See you do, or being Mack's brother won't save you," Scar growled.

****

Little Alfred spent the next few days lurking around town watching the girl and looking for his chance to make Mack proud. The burning cabin along the river was a ruse to get the two lawmen out of town. It worked well. Little Alfred peeked from his hiding spot behind a large tree as both men galloped past.

Sundays were good days to start fires. Everybody was in church, and nobody expected there to be an attack on Sunday. He smiled at his own cleverness and took the long way around to the cabin where the girl lived. He ditched his horse down by the creek so he could get away easy and headed to the old barn. He found his spot behind some barrels and hunkered down under an old tarp. Then, he waited.

It was late afternoon when the door to the cabin opened and closed. It was about damn time. His legs were cramped, and his butt was sore. Alfred left his hiding place and hurried to the cabin door. He rolled the water barrel standing outside until it blocked the cabin door. Then he lit the cabin on fire. Alfred doused the backside of the cabin with oil earlier, and now it lit up with one little match. Bright yellow and red flames licked up the side of the old wood cabin and spread to the roof. Smoke filled the sky. Alfred had to step back to get away from the heat. Soon, the whole cabin blazed with flames leaping sky high. Little Alfred waited for the screaming. The girl had to be getting hot and running out of air. Nothing happened. Little Alfred looked toward the door. From what he could see through the smoke, the barrel still blocked it shut. He crept slowly toward the cabin, unaware someone else was behind him. Something hit him in the back of the head, and it was the last thing Alfred knew for some time.

****

Shanna was hot and tired. The four-mile walk from town out to her uncle's claim had been long and dusty. Uncle Joseph and Aunt Sara took the wagon to the Claytons' for dinner, so Shanna walked home alone.

She hung her bonnet on the hook by the door, and went to the pantry to see what there was to eat when she heard something outside. She peered through the little window to see a man roll the water barrel in front of the cabin door!

Shanna walked quietly to the little partitioned off space she called her room. Uncle Joseph liked to lock her in when he was in one of his moods. Her room at the claim was little more than a closet. The good thing about it was it had an outside wall. The first time Uncle Joseph locked her in her room, she pulled and dug at the boards until several of them came loose, allowing her to slip outside and escape. Shanna kept her little cot shoved against the loose boards along the outside wall, so Uncle Joseph didn't know they were loose. She used them now to escape. Shanna rounded the house in time to see Little Alfred light the cabin on fire. She recognized him from the mercantile and stepped back out of sight. Shanna edged toward the barn as the cabin caught fire, and flames leapt toward the sky. Once inside the barn, Shanna kept her eye on the man while she thought about what to do.

Reese was right. The man must be part of the Turley Gang, and he wanted to kill her. The man paced and stared at the cabin, mumbling. He looked toward the door and frowned. He must know she wasn't in there, but how? Did it mean he would keep trying to kill her until he had her body? Suddenly, Shanna was mad. She wasn't going to wait around for this man or any other member of the Turley Gang to kill her. She would kill them first. White Eagle always said it was better to take your enemies by surprise than to wait for them to attack. Shanna picked up a shovel and headed toward the man.

****

Reese rode back into town, tired and sick to his stomach. He headed for the sheriff's office. What kind of man would trap a family inside their cabin and burn it to the ground with them in it? Only a sick, degenerate animal would do such a thing. No man would be able to live with himself afterward. According to Sheriff Holden, the owner of the cabin was a decent hardworking man, with a young wife, and two small children. So, why kill them? Why them of all the people who lived around these parts? The bastard hadn't killed them for money. They were poor farmers with nothing of value. Reese rubbed his head. It was a hard thing to sift through the hot ashes for the bodies. They found all four of them, charred beyond recognition. Sheriff Holden and Reese dug them out and laid them in a row for the undertaker to gather up. The undertaker would make coffins, and the funeral would be tomorrow. Reese was sick with disgust.

He ran his hand through his hair and poured a shot of whiskey. He downed it in one swallow. He needed something to chase the last few hours from his mind. The images of the charred bodies were burned into his mind, and he would never get the smell of burnt flesh out of his memory. Reese poured another shot of whiskey and downed it too. His second week in town and he was not only smoking but drinking as well.

Sheriff Holden stepped through the door and stopped. "We got more trouble, Reese. Someone burned the Johnston cabin while we were out."

Reese got to his feet.

"There's more. Shanna is missing. We don't know

if she was in the cabin when it burned."

Reese went cold all over, "What about the aunt and uncle?"

"They rode out to the Claytons' after the church service. Rose Tanner says Shanna walked home alone." Sheriff Holden's voice was grim.

A stone settled in Reese's stomach. They made Shanna walk four miles out to the claim, alone? He grabbed his hat off the desk and slammed it on his head. "Let's go!" Reese swung onto Pegasus and galloped away before the sheriff could respond.

It was dusk when Reese rode into the yard on Johnston's claim. Small flames still licked the last of what used to be a cabin. The air was thick with smoke. Reese took a minute before he climbed off his horse. He had to prepare himself to see Shanna in the same condition as the poor family earlier in the day. He stepped out of his saddle and walked toward the house. He stopped halfway between the cabin and the barn. He knelt and studied the earth. There were signs of a struggle, and two pairs of prints, one a man's and the other Shanna's. There was blood. A fist closed over his heart and squeezed it hard. Whose blood? It was impossible to tell. There were prints to and from the barn. Reese followed them. He saw Shanna's prints and found the makings of large fire. Looking up, he saw rope dangling from one of the rafters. Someone was strung up over a fire. Reese swallowed tightly. He squatted. Most of the prints were Shanna's. That meant she had the man dangling overhead. There were several splashes of blood around the fire. Shanna must have wounded the man. It was his blood, not hers. Reese got to his feet and looked around. There were knives lying on a wooden bench. His gut clenched. That would account for the blood. Jenna enjoyed torturing people who got in her way, especially men. She was up to her old tricks. Any doubts he had about her identity flew away the second he saw the knives. Did the man tell her what she wanted to know? There was a reason Jenna let the man live. What was it?

Reese followed both sets of prints out of the barn. He followed them toward the stream. There was more blood. The brush was trampled flat where a horse was tied for several hours. He studied the ground around him. Both sets of prints walked to where the horse was tethered, then disappeared. Shanna got on the same horse as the man who set the cabin on fire. *But why*? Reese whistled for Pegasus and stepped into the saddle.

Sheriff Holden rode up a minute later. He looked around and spotted Reese by the stream. "What do you make of it?" Sheriff Holden asked.

"It's the same man who set the fire earlier today, same prints, same horse." Reese pointed to the prints made by the horse's hooves. One hoof had a crack in it.

"Same prints we followed after the mercantile was robbed, too," Sheriff Holden agreed. It was the same man. "What about Shanna?"

"She's alive, and I'm going to follow her to the Turleys' hideout," Reese said.

Sheriff Holden looked surprised. "How do you figure?"

Reese pointed at the two sets of prints. "She walked down the path with the man who bungled the robbery at the mercantile and set both fires. She climbed on his horse. We know he is part of the Turley Gang because he left the white bandana. If we follow the horse, we find Shanna and the Turleys."

"Shanna might not be alive when you get there," Sheriff Holden commented.

Reese nodded his head. He already thought the same thing. "Well, either way, we need to find Shanna and bring her back," Reese said. He wheeled Pegasus around and started after the tracks.

"Reese! It's going to be dark soon. You won't be able to follow the sign. What do you plan on doing then?" Sheriff Holden asked.

"I plan on following the trail until I find who's at the end of it. I'm going to get those bastards. I'm not letting them get away again," Reese said as he rode away.

"I'll come after you as soon as the sun's up!" Sheriff Holden called. He didn't know if Reese heard him. He suspected it wouldn't make a difference to the man either way.

Chapter 11

Shanna sat with her back to the tree, her hands tied together in her lap. Alfred willingly bound her hands together once they neared camp. He wanted everyone to think he captured her on his own. They would shoot him if they knew the truth. His head was still bloody from the whack she'd given him. Shanna promised she'd say he ran into a tree if anybody asked. She could have killed Alfred after she knocked him unconscious with the shovel, but she didn't. The Turleys would only send somebody else to finish the job. Shanna figured Alfred already blabbed everything he knew about her to the whole gang. It was only a matter of time before somebody else tried to kill her. She wasn't going to wait. She would take all of them out before they had a chance to do more than send Alfred. It was the reason she was here, sitting beneath the tree.

Shanna watched Little Alfred approach the big man he called Scar. It hadn't been hard at all to convince Little Alfred to take her back to the gang's hideout with him, once he came around from the whack she'd given him. When he noticed he was tied and hanging upside down from the barn's rafters, he decided to be quite agreeable. In fact, when she gathered sticks for a roaring fire right beneath his head, he begged her to tell him what she wanted him to do. When Shanna laid out her uncle's hunting knives, saying her Indian family taught her how to scalp and gut people, Little Alfred started crying, begging her to let him take her back to his boss. It wasn't true. White Eagle's people only killed animals for food and never scalped a soul. They were kind and gentle, but Little Alfred didn't need to know. Once he agreed to take her to camp, she pulled her knife out, so he knew who was in control. After that, he was no trouble at all.

Shanna studied the camp. There were at least a dozen men wandering around. They all stared at her and took turns threatening her with all kinds of horrible things, but Shanna didn't listen. She was busy studying faces and the layout of the camp. It was a good hideout. The entrance was hidden by a shelter of trees and brush. They camped in a hollow near the river and used the river to wash away their tracks. It was quite a clever way to hide their sign, Shanna decided. They must be getting ready for some big job. Several men were unloading barrels of gunpowder, and crates of dynamite. The boss had a map spread out on a table in front of him. One man stood near Scar. He wore a patch over one eye and looked like he might be a half-breed. The boss man, Scar, was the only one who worried Shanna. He looked like a mean bastard. He kept turning to stare at Shanna in a way that caused her shiver. She didn't know what it was exactly. She felt like a piece of meat instead of a person, when he looked her way. She didn't doubt the man meant to kill her. It was late afternoon and Shanna was tired. She kept her gaze on Scar while he decided how to get rid of her body once she was dead.

****

"I can't believe you're dumb enough to lead the

bitch to our camp," Scar said through clenched teeth. "When I said take care of the situation, I meant kill the bitch, not escort her here to meet the whole crew."

"She knows Marshal Calhan. I thought you might want to get some information out of her before we kill her," Alfred said grinning like he contributed something important.

"Now why would you think such a thing? You're dumber than I figured. I think Mack sent you out here so he didn't have to put up with your stupidity. The girl means nothing, and I know more than I care to about the bastard Marshal Calhan. Why would I want to know more? Kill the bitch and ditch her body. We got other things to do."

Snake Eye, the half-breed with one patch over his eye, leaned toward Scar. "Do you know this woman?" he asked.

"What's there to know? She's seen our faces. She needs to die." Scar turned to the man on his right, but Snake Eye stopped him.

"This woman is the Delaney bitch. You kill her, and Adam Delaney will hunt you down and tear you apart." Snake Eye glanced in Shanna's direction. She stared back without blinking. Snake Eye glanced behind him toward the stream, then looked back at Scar.

"I don't know Adam Delaney. I don't care, neither. I say the woman dies." Scar nodded at a thin man with pistols tied low on his legs. Snake Eye turned around and headed for the stream as fast as he could go.

****

Shanna rubbed her wrist reassuringly against the revolver she carried in her large over size pocket. The dress was so baggy no one noticed the bulky lump in her pocket. She'd dropped it in there before she left the barn with Little Alfred. Shanna kept her eyes on the men as they talked. Little Alfred frowned, and Shanna figured the conversation wasn't going the way he thought it would. Then, the half-breed turned and hurried away, as the gunslinger headed in her direction. It was time to die.

While she waited beneath the tree, watching the camp, Shanna took her knife from its scabbard and worked on the ropes binding her hands. The ropes lie in pieces in her lap. She held the knife by the handle with both hands held together in her lap and waited. She didn't want anyone to notice she was no longer tied up.

The gunslinger stopped a few feet in front of her and palmed his gun. Shanna threw her knife. It lodged in his throat, ending his life. She jumped to her feet and ducked behind the tree. Then she headed for the stockpile of gunpowder. She moved so suddenly, it took the men several minutes to realize what happened. By then, it was too late. She raced toward the gunpowder and rolled behind the stockpile of explosives. It was all stacked together. Men were running everywhere, and Scar was yelling orders. Shanna ran as hard as she could for the clump of trees beyond the explosives, hiding behind the biggest one. She crouched low against the tree and taking aim, shot the barrels of gunpowder. The explosion nearly shook the teeth from her head. There were several more explosions as the barrels of gunpowder and the crates of dynamite caught fire. Shanna hoped every one of the bastards died. They didn't deserve to live after what they had done to people all over the country. The stories she heard about the Turleys while she worked in the mercantile were enough to make her sick. She stayed behind the tree for several minutes to give the gunpowder and explosives time to die down. There was a ringing in her ears which wouldn't quit. Shanna uncovered them and listened. There was no sound at all. She stood and cautiously looked around the big tree. Fire was everywhere. Nothing moved. The bodies of the Turley gang littered the ground. Shanna nodded her head in satisfaction. The devil was greeting his own. Shanna tiptoed over the bodies and debris to retrieve her knife. She brushed the dirt from her clothes and then started in the general direction of Rock Creek.

****

Reese followed the trail as long as he could. It got dark way too soon, and he stopped to make camp for the night. As the first rays of the sun appeared, Reese was ready to start again. He'd had all night to think. Why did Shanna go with the man? Why hadn't the man killed her? Why hadn't she killed him? Maybe the Turley Gang didn't realize who she was until the man attempted to burn her alive. Maybe once they realized Shanna was the leader of the Delaney Gang, they took her along to make plans. Reese figured they were after the army payroll. It was the only big thing happening in these parts. This kind of job would require gunpowder, dynamite, men, and lots of ammunition. Then again, where were Jenna's men? Surely Adam Delaney wouldn't leave Jenna alone out here without protection. Yet, Reese found no sign of her men. He stared at the hoof prints in the dirt. He didn't know of a time Jenna didn't have several gang members following her around. One thing was sure, whatever the reason Jenna rode with a Turley, he wouldn't find any answers until he found her.

Late in the afternoon, there was one hell of an explosion, and Reese looked in the distance. The explosion was followed by several more. They came from the general direction of the horse trail he followed. If Shanna was alive, she had something to do with the explosion. There was no way something like that coming from Shanna's suspected location would happen without her being involved in it. She had a thing with explosives and explosions. Reese nudged Pegasus in the side and hurried toward the smoke. He found Shanna all alone, walking about a mile from the blast. He trotted right up, slid from the saddle, and yelled in her face. She stopped and stared, confusion in her expression. He pointed in the direction of the blast and asked if it was where the Turley Gang camped. Shanna still stared at him. She didn't understand what he said. He stood stock-still. *She couldn't hear a damn thing!* Reese looked toward the blast. She had been way too close, and her eardrums were probably blown. He found a tree stump and motioned for Shanna to sit.

Sheriff Holden rode up a few minutes later. "You found her!" He climbed down from his saddle and walked toward Shanna.

"She can't hear you. She must have been too close to the blast," Reese said.

When Shanna looked up, she caught sight of Sheriff Holden and smiled.

"You headed toward the blast or back to town?" the sheriff wanted to know.

"I'm headed toward the blast. I want to know what the hell happened, and where the Turley Gang is." Reese nodded toward Shanna. "She isn't going to be a lot of help without her hearing."

Sheriff Holden nodded. "Let's go then. Shanna can ride with me."

"I'll take her." Reese scooped her up and put her on his saddle. He climbed on in front and she wrapped her arms around his waist. They rode back the way she came.

****

Shanna leaned against Reese and closed her eyes. She was so tired, she could hardly think. She hadn't slept much riding with Alfred Turley. The man was a weasel, and Shanna didn't trust him. Plus, she held her knife in his back all night while they rode as added incentive to take her where she wanted to go. Her mind buzzed from the explosion. She hoped the Turleys all rotted in hell for the things they did. She should be scared for taking them on alone, but she wasn't. White Eagle would be pleased with her decision to face the enemy instead of hiding from them. With the Turleys gone, she didn't need to worry about someone coming to kill her, and Marshal Reese could go back to Chicago, or wherever he was from. It would be heavenly to walk around without him following her. In a day or two, she would be rid of his unwelcome presence and his ugly accusations. She could get right back to being lonely. Shanna frowned. Why did the thought of him leaving make her sad? She was used to being alone and taking care of herself. With Reese, she was safe. He wouldn't let anything happen. He was too interested in arresting her to let her come to any harm. Shanna sighed. She would think about it all later after she rested her head for a minute. She laid it against the marshal's back. The heat of Reese's body and the rocking motion of the horse lulled Shanna into a deep dreamless sleep.

****

They had to approach the Turley camp from the steam. Everything else was still smoldering. Reese looked at the destruction with practiced eyes. He climbed off his horse, taking Shanna with him. He set her on her feet, and then he scouted for sign. Sheriff Holden climbed off his horse, and they poked through the ashes and debris until they figured out what happened. Shanna leaned against a tree, trying to stay awake.

"Think it was the Turley Gang?" Sheriff Holden asked.

"If it was, most of them are dead. Looks like one man got away in the stream, see?" Reese pointed at a set of prints entering the water.

"Looks to be about a dozen men, near as I can tell. All of them blown to bits, except the one who ran away. You figure on going after him?" Sheriff Holden asked.

"I do." Reese looked toward Shanna. The bodies here were unrecognizable. If this camp belonged to the Turley Gang, then where were Shanna's men? How had she escaped? And why would she take out the Turleys on her own? Reese kicked at a smoldering log. He was no closer to getting answers today, than he was yesterday, or the day before. He was getting tired of it. "We'll see you back in town," Reese made a move in Shanna's direction. He aimed to keep her close until he figured out who died here.

Sheriff Holden put a hand on his arm. "Shanna will be coming with me."

Reese frowned. Sheriff Holden didn't know who

Shanna really was.

"Son, you take Shanna alone with you on the trail, and folks in town will throw her out. After the things Anderson accused her of, no decent family will have anything to do with her."

Reese glanced toward Shanna as she leaned against the tree. He couldn't afford to let her out of his sight, not if he expected to get any answers.

Sheriff Holden misunderstood the marshal's silence. "I don't know how things are in Chicago, but Shanna's a good girl. She'll need a wedding ring on her finger before she spends any time on the trail alone with you, or folks in town will have a fit. They already give the girl a hard time. Best let me take her back with me."

Sheriff Holden was right about the town gossip, but Shanna wasn't a good girl. Reese needed to know what she did and where she went while he was gone.

"You'll keep a good eye on her for me?" Reese asked. He should tell Sheriff Holden what he knew about Shanna. Problem was he didn't know where to start. Reese was still trying to piece it all together. Then there was the fact the sheriff probably wouldn't believe Shanna was a lying, cheating, thief who would sell her own mother to the devil for a bag of gold. He figured he could talk the sheriff into keeping a close eye on her, though, while he chased after the man who escaped the explosion.

"I sure will, son, I sure will." Sheriff Holden grinned. Reese endured the wink and the clap on the back. Whatever convinced the sheriff to keep Shanna under his eye was worth the embarrassment. Reese stepped into his saddle and rode off after the man who escaped.

Chapter 12

Reese trailed the man to a cave hidden in the rocks by the river. Whatever the man was after, he took and left the rest. Reese found stolen guns, missing jewelry, and crates of dynamite with Union Pacific stamped into the wood. He also found several cases of liquor from a saloon which was robbed a few months back. All reported missing, following a raid from the Turley Gang. Reese could see where the barrels of gunpowder had been kept before their recent removal. He also found a box containing white bandannas. So, it *was* the Turleys who died in the explosion. Reese made a mental note on the cave's location and continued following the man's sign. The man headed east. Reese followed him until he reached Fort Buford. The fort was a busy place with men of all trades coming and going. Reese lost the man among the crowd. It was impossible to follow any kind of sign, and he never got a good look at the man to give an accurate description. There were too many strangers, too many people, and Reese had to admit defeat. He wouldn't find the man at the fort in any event. On a hunch, Reese decided to ride to Pine Bluffs. If the man worked for either gang, he'd be headed for Chicago. He would need to catch a train, and the closest depot was in Pine Bluffs. Reese headed out, hoping to catch the man before he got on a train. He wanted to see who he was trailing.

After several hard days in the saddle, Reese rode into Pine Bluffs. The train to Omaha left earlier in the day. Reese leaned on the counter at the train station and eyed the Union Pacific Railroad employee. He pointed at his badge. "I am U. S Marshal Calhan," he said. "I'm looking for a passenger I believe is headed for Chicago."

"Does this passenger have a name?" the ticket master asked. He squinted at the marshal, his old eyes taking the marshal's measure.

"I don't know a name. Who do you have who has bought a ticket to Chicago in the last two or three days?" Reese asked.

"Well, if you don't have a name, son, how do you plan on finding the passenger you're lookin' for?"

"He would be rough looking, with gold teeth, piercings, or tattoos. Anyone stand out in your memory as someone you wouldn't want to meet alone in the dark?" Reese asked.

The old man scratched his sparse white hair. "Well, there was one fella, real dark skin, looked like a half-breed. The man had a patch over one eye and was in a hurry. He kept lookin' over his shoulder. He bought a ticket to Chicago and left early this morning."

Snake Eye! Damn it to hell! It had to be Snake Eye! Reese remembered him from the old days in Chicago. He was Adam Delaney's assassin, *and he'd been with the Turleys!* Was it a coincidence? Reese doubted it. He slammed his fist on the counter. Double damn. Shanna was in Rock Creek, probably planning some big job with her men, while he chased all over the country for nothing!

Reese headed for the telegraph office. He sent a

telegraph to Sergeant Baxter updating him on the recent events involving Jenna and the Turley Gang. He wanted Sergeant Baxter on the lookout. Adam Delaney's sudden appearance in public after seven years and Snake Eye's presence in the Turley Gang had to mean something big was going down. If Adam Delaney moved west, Reese would need all the help he could get. Once he sent his telegram, Reese jumped on a tired Pegasus and hurried back to Rock Creek.

****

Adam Delaney motioned for him to enter and leaned back in his chair. Snake Eye walked toward the desk where Adam Delaney sat. He hoped the man still paid good money for information on Reese Calhan. He was a couple of days later than he planned to be, thanks to Marshal Calhan. The marshal was a hard man to shake and nearly had him before they reached Fort Buford. From there, Snake Eye disappeared, catching a ride into Pine Bluffs and a train into Chicago.

Adam Delaney watched Snake Eye approach. He looked like a pirate with the patch over one eye. No one would guess this half-breed was a professional marksman, an assassin Adam used in the past.

"I'm told you have information for me," Adam began.

"If you are interested in information on Reese Calhan, I do," Snake Eye answered.

Adam inclined his head and waited.

"The usual price?" Snake Eye inquired.

Adam nodded.

"Marshal Calhan is in Rock Springs. The local sheriff requested him personally to capture the Turley Gang, who recently moved to the area."

"Who is this Turley Gang? I do not know them," Adam said.

Snake Eye studied Adam's face. "It's been a long time since we talked, Mr. Delaney."

Adam nodded his head again and waited.

Snake Eye danced his way around what he wanted to say. "I heard tell your niece died in the sting operation seven years ago, what with the explosion and all."

"No, she's alive," Adam laced his fingers together.

"She's running your operation then?" Snake Eye wondered.

Adam studied the man in front of him. "Yes, she does."

"It seems your niece knows the Turleys. She blew about a dozen or so of their men to hell a few days ago."

Adam wasn't surprised, "She does those kinds of things sometimes."

"So, you know the Turleys? Or at least your niece does?" Snake Eye persisted.

Adam's eyebrow rose. "What's your point?"

"Mack Turley's little brother was blown to hell with them, and Mack will be looking for blood."

Adam Delaney shrugged. If he hadn't heard of the Turleys, they weren't a threat. He took out a cigar and lit it.

"The other thing is, if you're looking to start operations out west, I want in."

"I'll keep it in mind," Adam said blowing out a puff of smoke.

"Is Jenna planning on taking over the Turley job? If she does, I want in on it, too," Snake Eye added.

"I'll mention it," Adam answered. Snake Eye nodded. He wasn't sure now if Adam was even interested in his information. Mr. Delaney looked downright bored with the whole conversation. Adam tossed a small bag in Snake Eye's direction and waved him from the room. Snake Eye waited until he was outside before he opened the bag. *Not bad.* Adam Delaney still paid well for information. It was hard to tell what Adam Delaney thought. If he liked what you said, you lived. If he didn't, you died.

Snake Eye was a shrewd man. He wanted to make sure he was on everybody's friend list and stayed off any hit list. He headed for Mack Turley's. It would be best if Mack heard about Little Alfred's death from him, rather than somebody else. Since he was the lone survivor of Scar's crew, he didn't want anyone accusing *him* of setting off the blast. Mack Turley took the news like Snake Eye figured he would, once he quit punching holes in the wall and kicking anything and anybody in range.

Mack turned to Snake Eye. "Who did it? Who is responsible for blowing up my men and killing my brother?" Mack was a large Irishman, with fists the size of hams. He had dark brown hair and the disposition of a bear. He looked furry and soft until he was riled, then he turned mean and deadly. Right now, he was riled.

"Jenna Delaney," Snake Eye said. He stayed well out of Mack's immediate vicinity.

"Don't know her." Mack paced back and forth as he talked.

"She runs the Delaney Gang for her uncle, Adam Delaney." He got Mack's full attention. Everyone knew who Adam Delaney was. Adam ran the biggest gang in

Chicago. He was the kingpin and had been for many years. Adam Delaney was rich, he was power, and he was king of the streets.

"Why would Delaney kill my men or my brother? I got no fight with him!" Mack roared. He punched another hole in the wall.

"Don't know." Snake Eye shrugged.

"Tell me what you do know," Mack suggested.

"The Delaney woman rode into camp with your brother Alfred. He had her tied up and thought Scar would want to question her. The Delaney woman was there when Alfred bungled his recruit job. Scar told him to kill her. Alfred brought her back to camp. She caught Slim in the throat with her blade. Then she blew the gunpowder and the men to bits when she escaped," Snake Eye said.

"How did you get out?" Mack wondered.

"I told Scar she was bad news. He wouldn't listen. I kept my eye on her and when she made her move, I ran for cover." Snake Eye waited while Mack digested the information.

"What about my brother?" Mack asked,

"He was standing next to Scar when the gun powder caught fire."

Mack stared at the floor. "Where's the girl now?"

"Last I knew she was in Rock Creek," Snake Eye answered.

"I'll give you ten thousand in gold to kill the girl before she gets back to Chicago," Mack said quietly. "This stays between you and me. You tell anyone, I'll deny it and kill you myself. The less people know about this, the better."

"You have a deal." Snake Eye left the building.

Chapter 13

Reese returned to Rock Spring several days later. First thing he did was head for the sheriff's office. He needed an update on any new developments in his absence. He also wanted to find out what Shanna had been up to while he was gone. The sheriff assured him all was quiet. Quiet meant trouble in Reese's experience. The sheriff hadn't had to deal with gangs the way Reese had. Reese decided to have a look.

The first thing he noticed was Shanna. Her appearance was drastically different. Either her hearing was back, or she knew how to read Rose's lips. Shanna stood on the porch of the mercantile talking with an animated Rose while she swept the weathered steps. Rose's arms were going every which way while she talked, and Shanna was laughing. Shanna wore a rose-colored calico dress. She was curved in all the right places. Her dress clung to her luscious figure leaving little to his imagination. It fit her like a glove. The bodice molded her generous breasts pushing them up where they strained against the fabric and lace, threatening to spill out. Reese's mouth grew dry. He shifted on to his other leg and continued to stare. His gaze lowered to her narrow waist, then on to the gentle flare of her hips. They swayed as she swept. Reese's blood heated up. He couldn't take his eyes off her. Memories of Chicago flooded his mind, memories of

Jenna, memories of being with Jenna, and memories of loving Jenna. He remembered those heated sweat-soaked nights even if she didn't. The thought rankled a little. She should remember something, shouldn't she? She should remember him. Reese stared. Why the hell was she wearing revealing clothing again? Was she looking for a man? His gut twisted up, and he didn't like it. He was gone for a few days and suddenly everything changed. Shanna had no business walking around like that. She was too damn sexy for her own good.

Reese glanced around. The other development he noticed was how busy Rock Creek was. The streets were swarming with dust covered, saddle-sore cowboys, and every one of them was staring at the two young women in front of the mercantile. It was too bad he couldn't unload both his pistols into the lot of them. "It seems the population of Rock Creek increased considerably while I was gone," Reese commented.

"Cattlemen. Most of them are cowboys driving their herds to market. There are several outfits that arrived in town at the same time." Sheriff Holden looked up and down the busy street. "You best get some rest. Most of these boys are headed to the saloon. They'll be looking for women and drinking. About midnight the fighting is going to start. It's going to be a long night."

"Seems to me they're already looking for women," Reese said. He nodded toward Shanna and Rose.

Sheriff Holden looked around. Most the men on the street were eying the girls all right.

"Shanna's asking for trouble dressed the way she is," Reese commented.

Sheriff Holden's eyebrow rose as he considered Reese's statement. "She ain't dressed any different than any other girl in town."

"The hell she isn't! Look at her!" Reese said. He was angry again. If Shanna wanted to dress like a prostitute, it was her business.

"I am looking son. Maybe you need to go see Doc and get your eyes checked. I admit Shanna looks a might different wearing Rose Tanner's dress instead of them old rags Sara Johnston gave her, but it's nothing different than any other girl is wearing." Sheriff Holden grinned. "You're upset because you don't like other fellers looking at your girl."

"She's not my girl," Reese said dryly.

"Then you're a damn fool," the sheriff commented and walked away to find his deputy.

Reese went on the prowl. He wanted to know what else was different in town. If any of Shanna's men rode in while he was away, he'd find them.

****

It was well after dark when Shanna left the mercantile. Uncle Joseph insisted she walk out to the Claytons' claim rather than stay with the Tanners until they rebuilt the little cabin. The Tanners invited Shanna to stay with them, but Uncle Joseph wouldn't let her. He said he needed to keep an eye on her. Customers kept them busy well after closing time, and it took a while to get the store straightened and clean so Shanna could go home. Uncle Joseph got upset if she stayed late. She was too tired to argue with him tonight. Shanna walked down the main street heading west. It was a couple of miles out to the Claytons' claim, and Shanna trudged forward. Light from the saloon spilled out onto the street and piano music filled the air as Shanna hurried past. She wasn't fast enough. Several drunken cowboys stood around the entrance. One of them blocked her path. The fumes from his breath made Shanna want to gag.

"Hey, pretty lady, what you doin' all by yourself?" He made a grab for her, but Shanna sidestepped him.

Another cowboy caught her by the arm. "Give us a kiss," he said.

"Let go of me," Shanna commanded, jerking her arm free.

"Not until you give us a kiss." The other men gathered around. The saloon girls were all busy with other customers, and they hadn't had a turn yet.

"I won't ask again. Let me go," Shanna said. She took a step back. The cowboy laughed and pulled her toward him, intent on taking a kiss. Shanna punched him in the nose and stepped around him. Someone caught her arm and several other men grabbed her dress and anything else they could get hold of. Shanna caught the hem of her skirt and pulled it up to get to her knife. Rose's dress didn't have pockets. A shot sounded over her head.

"Let the girl go," Reese said. He sat on Pegasus; his pistol aimed at the men surrounding her. Did he think she needed his help? She didn't. He should know. She'd proved it often enough. The men stepped away from Shanna grumbling about the injustice of the marshal's interference. Reese nudged Pegasus forward and held his arm down to help her up. Shanna sighed. It beat walking for two miles in the dark all the way out to the Clayton's claim.

Once Shanna was settled on his lap, Reese nudged

Pegasus forward. "What in the hell are you doing walking down main street this time of night?" he demanded.

"What difference does it make?" Shanna asked. She was too tired to listen to a bunch of threats from Reese.

"The difference is those men were drunk. You were out on the street alone and they thought you were fair game. They had you dead to rights," Reese growled. "I figure they have the right to be dead for making you a game. They don't know what you're capable of."

Shanna didn't care who got dead or what kind of game they played. She wanted to go home and get some sleep. What business was it of his where she went and what she did? She was irritated. She was tired of Reese poking his nose in her business, too. "So?" Shanna tossed her head. She didn't need Reese following her around pretending like he cared one way or another. His only interest in her was arresting her for someone else's crime.

"So, if it's a man you want, all you had to do was ask. I'm more than willing to scratch your itch," he whispered in her ear.

Shanna shivered as the heat of his words spread over her like wildfire. He wanted her. It explained why he was so angry. Shanna leaned against him, the fight going out of her. She wanted to soak in the heat of him. Uncle Joseph would no doubt beat her again for being so late. Maybe if she let Reese hold her and touch her, she could forget for a minute what a burden she was. Uncle Joseph and Aunt Sara blamed her for the loss of the cabin. Uncle Joseph took every opportunity to beat her, so she knew how upset he was that she let the cabin burn. Neither her aunt nor her uncle mentioned the fact she nearly died in the fire. Reese may be confused on her identity. He may threaten to arrest her every minute, but he was handsome as hell. His kisses made her forget. His touch made her feel wanted.

"I'm going out to the Claytons'," Shanna confessed. Reese should know which direction she was headed if he planned on giving her a ride.

Reese sucked in a breath. "What is it you see in the Claytons? Are you setting your cap for one of their boys? If you are, you're making a big mistake. Those boys can't give you what you need. What you need is a man. You need me," Reese said against her neck. His arm was wrapped tightly around her rib cage, his breath warm against her skin.

Reese's arousal pressed against her backside, and she shifted in her seat. Heat flooded her secret place, and a strange throbbing pulsed through her. Her breathing quickened. Shanna shifted against him again. She gasped at the contact. What was it about him that made her feel so damn good? The harder he became, the wetter she got.

"Say you want me," Reese licked the side of her neck and kissed the line of her jaw. Shanna leaned in. She wanted Reese to kiss her like he did before and groaned at the memory. What did he say about a man? Shanna decided she didn't care. She was warm all over, and Reese was doing the most incredible things. The movement of the horse caused constant friction between her backside and the hard length of Reese's arousal. Shanna squirmed again when Reese's hand covered her breast, his fingers rubbed against her nipple through the fabric of her dress. She moaned out loud and shifted against him, her breathing coming fast.

****

He could smell sunshine and roses in her hair. He could feel the softness of her breasts. She shifted her rounded backside against his aching arousal, and Reese gritted his teeth. It had been too damn long since he'd lost himself in her beautiful body. Seeing Shanna earlier in the day reminded Reese of how damn sexy she was. The long-ago memory of their lovemaking had him rock hard and throbbing. He wanted her. He wanted her hard and fast, until he couldn't think about anything but her tight, wet sheath and how damn good she felt. She panted through soft, parted lips. She stared at his mouth, her eyes a liquid blue setting his blood on fire. She rubbed against him again and closed her eyes at the contact. Reese nearly dropped his reins. He knew the look. Shanna wanted him all right. Reese nudged Pegasus into a gallop. He remembered a little spot further up the road where the grass was thick and soft. The shrubs would hide them from view, and he could take his time undressing her and tasting every inch of her beautiful body. "Don't worry, sweetheart, I'll take care of you." Reese pulled Pegasus to a stop and slid to the ground holding Shanna against him.

****

"What if I don't need you to take care of me?" Shanna asked. Her arms were around his neck, her warm breath whispering across his face. Reese tilted her face up to his. His hot mouth settled on hers, his tongue swept inside to mate with hers. He stroked her tongue. White-hot heat spread through her. Shanna held on for dear life. Reese's hands caught her by the buttocks and pulled her hard against him. Shanna gasped and pressed closer. She trembled against him. Reese growled low in his throat.

"You need me, Shanna, admit it," Reese said. He thrust a knee between her legs, and Shanna buckled at the sensation shooting through her. She wrapped her arms around his waist to keep from falling. Reese reached for one of her full breasts, squeezing it through the taught fabric of her bodice. Shanna whimpered with pleasure. The space between her legs was on fire, she squirmed against him, gasping at the friction the movement caused. With his rock-hard thigh between her legs and his arousal pressing into her belly, Shanna nearly swooned with desire. Reese lowered her slowly to the grass and lay on top of her. He spread her legs with his knees and settled between her thighs. His mouth was on hers, his tongue thrusting and stroking. His shaking hands were everywhere. Shanna was lost in a heated sea of ecstasy. Shanna had no idea Reese undid her bodice and pushed her chemise down, until the cool night breeze blew across her naked breasts. She looked at Reese in surprise. His eyes were dark with passion as he looked at her.

"God, you're so beautiful." Reese growled. His head lowered, and his hot mouth closed over one pink nipple. Shanna arced off the ground as he suckled. A sharp cry escaped her. She whimpered, her head thrashing side to side. Somehow his suckling was connected to the warmth between her legs. She needed him to touch her there. She shifted restlessly against him, wanting, and needing. Her hands gripped his shoulders, and Reese rocked against her pelvis, imitating the mating act. Pleasure shot through her, but it wasn't enough. Her hands were frantically running over his shoulders and back. She needed to touch his skin. Reese leaned back on his knees. He undid his shirt and threw it to the ground, and then he settled between her legs once more. Shanna sighed with satisfaction as her hands learned every contour of his back and shoulders. His skin was like melted caramel, smooth, warm, and salty. Her mouth found his neck and she sucked and licked until he growled his urgency. His mouth found her other nipple, and Shanna fell apart. She gripped him tightly around the neck as his suckling shot heat through her stomach into the junction between her thighs.

****

Reese put his hand under her skirt and slid it slowly up her thigh. She had to be wet for him. She was too damn responsive to not be. His hand encountered her knife in its scabbard before he got a chance to find out. Cold, hard reality crashed over him like a dunking in the Missouri River right after winter thaw.

"Dammit to hell!" Reese sat up. He shoved her skirts up to her hips and looked long and hard at her knife. He pulled it from the scabbard and held it up in the moonlight. He needed this reminder of who Shanna was before he made the biggest mistake of his life. "I've got to be the dumbest ass around to let you get to me twice. Why did you kiss me back, Jenna? You made it clear how you felt about me seven years ago. Why play me for a fool? Were you going to stab me in the back as soon as my guard was down to get me out of the way?" Reese asked softly as he turned the blade in the light of the moon.

Shanna sat up and attempted to grab the blade from

his hands. Reese pushed her back. Passion and longing vanished. Shanna shivered in the cool evening breeze. "You're the one who kissed me. Not the other way around." Her eyes sparked fire at him.

Reese got to his feet and threw her dress over her near-naked body. He threw the knife on the ground. "It was a mistake I won't make again." He stomped into the darkness without looking back.

Chapter 14

One week, three days, eleven hours, and twenty-six minutes. That's how long it had been since Reese dropped Shanna off at the Clayton claim the night he'd held her naked in his arms by the river. It wasn't like he was counting the days or noticing the hours. He had more important things to do, like wonder where in the hell Shanna's men were, and why he'd fallen for her once again. He was a damn fool to let Shanna's beauty and sensual nature get under his skin. He'd done it before. He should be a smarter man, a whole hell of a lot smarter. He'd also spent his time trying to get information out of her. She hadn't so much as looked his way since she'd slipped from Pegasus outside the Clayton's front door. Reese couldn't stop thinking about her and the passionate way she'd responded. Then, he would think about the damn knife strapped to her thigh reminding him of who she was, and he'd get mad all over again.

Shanna limped into the mercantile the morning after he dropped her off. Her face was bruised on one side, and her eye was swollen shut. Reese demanded answers, and Shanna simply turned away. She had nothing to say. Reese was stumped. He understood why she didn't want to see him or talk to him. If he were honest, he'd admit he didn't want to talk about what happened either. Shanna got under his skin like no woman he ever met, and it wasn't something he was proud of. If he were smart, he'd get as far away from her as he could get. Only, he wasn't smart, and his desire for vengeance far outweighed his sense of self-preservation. He could head back to Chicago anytime he wanted now the Turleys were all dead. He wasn't going anywhere, though, not until he found out why Shanna was in Rock Creek and what Adam's interest was here. He assumed Shanna had some connection to the Turleys. Only she'd killed them all and was in no hurry to leave town. There must be something else keeping her here. Reese started to question everything he knew about her.

In Chicago, Jenna never went anywhere without several of Adam's men acting as bodyguards. He assumed they would be in Rock Creek or somewhere close by. He kept her under surveillance constantly, and he hadn't been able to find out where they were or how she communicated with them. Adam Delaney was not a fool. If Shanna was here, he wanted something, and he would exact revenge for the bruising on Shanna's face. Whoever hit her, was a dead man. Reese wanted the man's name so he could catch Adam's men in the act. The real question bothering him was why did Shanna live with Joseph and Sara Johnston? What connection was there between the two and Adam Delaney? Was Adam the one who loaned Joseph the money to pay off his gambling debt? If so, why? What did Adam get out of the deal? And why send Shanna halfway across the country to live with the Johnstons? What was the connection between them and Mary Johnston of Omaha? Reese decided to send another telegram to Sergeant Baxter. Maybe he could dig something up on

Joseph Johnston and Adam Delaney.

****

Shanna looked out the window of the mercantile toward the sheriff's office. Reese stood in the doorway watching just like he'd done every day since that night. His eyes followed her everywhere. She couldn't sleep. She had shadows under her eyes. She noticed them this morning when she brushed her hair. Every night she lay on her bed reliving the scene in the grass over and over until the sun peeped over the horizon. Then, she would rise and woodenly begin her day. She couldn't eat a darn thing either. Everything she put in her mouth got stuck in her throat and made her gag. Her mind refused to function. Her entire life was blurry, and it was all Reese's fault. She handed her broom to Rose. "Will you sweep the steps for me?" she asked. Shanna turned from the window to straighten a shelf.

"Of course," Rose answered as she took the broom. "Why don't you go talk to him? He stares at you so hard I swear he's going to break something," Rose joked.

Shanna turned sad eyes in Rose's direction, "He thinks I'm Jenna."

Rose frowned, "So? He's always thought you were Jenna. Why does it bother you now?"

Because she'd nearly given herself to him, that's why. Then, he called her Jenna and accused her of wanting to stab him. Truthfully, stabbing him wasn't what she wanted to do until he called her Jenna. Then, she wanted to carve out his heart, scalp him, and chop him in little pieces.

"I'm just tired of him thinking I'm somebody else." Shanna turned away and continued her task. Rose went outside to sweep.

The bell over the door jingled. Delphine Otis strolled in pulling her fur coat closer around her. Her coat was mink and cost a fortune. Daniel bought it for her in Chicago last week. The weather was still warm, but Delphine wore it everywhere so everyone could see it.

Shanna pasted her brightest smile on her face. "Good afternoon. What can I help you with?"

Delphine stroked her hands up and down the soft fur. Her eyes stared right through Shanna. "I want someone else to help me."

Shanna rolled her eyes. "Rose is outside. The Tanners are at the fort. I'm the only one there is."

A sly smile stole over Delphine's face, "Is that so?" She strolled over to the dry goods counter. Most of the silk was gone. One bolt of brown silk remained on the counter.

"It's such a shame you won't be coming to the harvest dance. Everybody is going, and I'm going to be the most beautiful woman there." Delphine looked at her from under her lashes. Shanna waited. Delphine had more to say.

"I'm going to dance with the handsome marshal. I'm going to let him hold me in his arms and dance in front of the whole town." Delphine smiled and giggled. "You may as well know I have my eye on him. I want him." She leaned against the counter, her eyes on Shanna's face.

"What about Daniel?" Shanna wondered. She didn't care one way or the other.

"You can have him if you want him. I've decided I want Marshal Calhan. He's such a handsome man and so muscular. He makes Daniel look like a boy. Once the marshal realizes it's him I want, it shouldn't be any trouble to take him away from you. I took Daniel easy enough." If Delphine had a tail, it would be twitching like a cat's right before it pounced.

"I don't want Daniel," Shanna said, "and you can have Marshal Calhan. I don't know why you think I care one way or the other." Shanna shrugged. "Is there something at this counter I can help you with?"

Delphine narrowed her gaze on Shanna's face. "Of course, you care. I see the way you stare at the marshal when no one is watching. I've decided he's mine, so stay away from him." Delphine smiled smugly. "You know I always get what I want, and I want the marshal. So, be warned."

Shanna shrugged again. Reese wasn't as easily swayed as Daniel. It might be interesting to watch someone tell Delphine no for the first time. Then again, Reese might decide he liked Delphine. She might be the kind of woman he enjoyed. Shanna wondered why there was a sharp tug on her heart at the thought.

"Why won't Shanna be at the harvest dance?" Rose asked from behind Delphine. Both women jumped at the sound of Rose's voice.

Delphine recovered quickly. "Because she has nothing to wear." Delphine turned to Shanna, malice gleaming in her dark eyes. "You could wear one of Rose's old dresses, but then *everybody* would know. It must be so humiliating to know everybody who looks at you knows you're wearing somebody else's dress loaned out of charity. It's too bad you have nothing of your own to wear and no one to care. Perhaps if you had a family or a man who wanted you, it would be different. I swear, I don't know how you get up in the morning. It must be so depressing to realize you're never going to be good enough to be part of anything. Nobody wants you, and nobody ever will." Delphine turned to leave. She smiled at both girls. The bell over the door jingled as it shut behind her.

"Don't listen, Shanna. You do have somebody to care! You have me!" Rose fumed.

"I know," Shanna said softly. She didn't know what she would do without Rose.

"You do have something of your own to wear, or at least, you will." Rose slid the bolt of pink silk from its hiding place. Rose's purple silk was being sewn. The pink silk had yet to be paid for. All the extra hours Shanna put in had only contributed a small amount toward the purchase of the pink silk. Uncle Joseph's bill at the mercantile grew daily, and there hadn't been much to put aside for the silk.

Shanna shook her head at Rose. "Delphine is right about the dance. I won't be going."

"Why not?" Rose demanded. "I can talk to Papa, I'm sure we can figure something out." She sounded more convinced than she was. Mr. Tanner wanted to know why the books weren't balancing out on the silk shipment.

"It's all right, Rose. I don't want to go anyway." The last thing she wanted to do was look at Reese Calhan. Looking made her remember what a fool she was and what nearly happened in the dark. Reese was such an intelligent man, it still astonished her he got her name mixed up with another woman. Why couldn't someone want her for her?

Rose gave Shanna a quick hug. "Damn the

marshal."

Shanna looked at Rose in surprise. "Why are you damning him?" Rose never swore.

"Oh, I don't know. I just think he has something to do with you being so sad. It makes me feel better to think cuss words. I know he hurt you," Rose said.

Shanna shook her head. "It only hurts if I let it."

"What will you do while everybody is at the dance?" Rose asked. Shanna read the concern in her friend's eyes. Rose would worry about her the whole time unless she came up with a good excuse.

"I think I'll rob the fort, then run away to Chicago," Shanna said.

Rose giggled, "Won't you need help? The fort is an awfully big place."

Shanna batted her eyes imitating Delphine when she flirted. "Of course not. Who would suspect a sweet, little girl like me? Why I bet I could walk right into the fort and get those handsome soldiers to load my wagon up with all their gold without noticing a thing!" Shanna adjusted the bodice of her dress, so her breasts nearly fell out of the top. With an exaggerated swing of her hips, she mimicked the way Delphine walked and talked.

Rose went into a fit of giggles. "What if the soldiers get suspicious?" Rose asked wiping tears from her eyes.

"Then I will give them a little kiss or two. They'll be so busy looking down my bodice and trying to get my attention, it won't even cross their minds they've been robbed until well after I'm gone," Shanna said.

Rose sobered. "You aren't coming to the dance, are you?"

Shanna hugged her friend. "No, but it is okay. There won't be anybody at the dance I want to see or dance with, and I'll be so busy it won't matter." Shanna turned away to hide her anguish.

****

Rose nodded, still not convinced. She must get Shanna the silk, but how? "Sounds like Papa and Mama are back. You go help them unload, while I put this silk away."

Shanna nodded and went out the side door. Rose picked up the pink silk and stroked it softly. If she had the money, she'd buy it for Shanna. It was plain old meanness for Delphine to say those things. Delphine had it in for Shanna, always had. Rose was so busy with her thoughts, she didn't realize Reese stood at the counter in front of her.

"How much would it cost to make a dress?" Reese asked.

Rose jumped. She glared when she noticed who the customer was. "How much of what?"

Reese pointed to the pink silk. "How much of this."

"Well, it depends on the size of the dress. Who is it for?" Rose inquired. If he said Delphine, she swore to God, she'd grab one of Papa's guns and shoot him. She wasn't going to let him hurt Shanna again.

"Shanna. She's not going to the dance because she needs a dress, right? And this is the stuff she wants a dress out of?" Reese eyed the silk.

"You want the whole price including paying a seamstress or just the price of the fabric? Because the way Uncle Joseph runs Shanna around, she won't have time to sew it." Rose was proud of herself for thinking of it. Joseph Johnston wouldn't let Shanna go to the dance if he knew she had fabric and wanted to go.

"I want the whole price. How much?" Reese asked.

Rose told him an amount she figured would get Shanna some new stockings and a hat, too. Reese needed to pay one way or another for hurting Shanna.

Reese didn't say a word. He counted the money out and then some extra. "Can you see the dress is ready in time for the dance?" he asked.

Rose tried not to let her mouth fall open. "Sure," was all she managed to say. Maybe the marshal wasn't such a bad man after all. Rose teetered toward thinking Reese was sweet and practically a god one more time.

****

Reese nodded and left the mercantile. He'd heard the whole conversation, and it would be easier to keep an eye on Shanna at the dance. He had no way of knowing if she intended on robbing the fort, or if it was a distraction like the night of the women's society meeting. Either way, he wanted her where he could monitor her. It sounded like Rose was intent on her going to the dance. The only hold up was Shanna didn't have a dress, if he understood the conversation correctly. At the dance, he'd have help keeping an eye on her. He figured Sheriff Holden would be easy to rope into helping him watch her. Sooner or later, Shanna would have to show her hand. When she did, he would be ready.

Chapter 15

"Come in here, Shanna, there's something I want you to see." Rose anxiously tugged on Shanna's arm as she led her up the stairs. Shanna's dress had just been delivered. Rose dragged Shanna down the hall to her bedroom. She kept it a secret until now because Shanna would only come up with some excuse or another not to go to the dance. If she didn't know about the new dress until the day of the dance, it gave Shanna less time to protest. The silk dress was laid out on Rose's bed. She put her hands over Shanna's eye before opening the door. Shanna stopped short when she saw what lay on Rose's bed.

"How? Where?" She looked at Rose. She didn't know what to say.

Rose grinned. "It was the marshal. He gave me the money, and Mrs. Adams sewed it. I had her use my pattern and add a little in the bodice." Rose picked up the dress and held it up to Shanna.

"Try it on! I've been dying to see it on you since Mrs. Adams dropped it off."

"Why would Reese buy me a new dress?" Shanna asked.

"Maybe he feels bad about whatever happened and wants to make it up to you," Rose suggested.

Shanna frowned. Could it be true? Was he trying to apologize for calling her Jenna?

"I don't know if I dare touch it," Shanna confessed. Her hands were worn and calloused. What if she snagged the fabric by mistake?

"I'll help you," Rose offered.

Together they got it on Shanna and buttoned up. Rose sighed with happiness. The dress fit Shanna just the way Rose imagined it would. She was stunning.

"Oh Shanna, you're beautiful. Marshal Reese won't be able to keep his eyes off you!" Rose danced around Shanna in excitement.

"I'm not sure I dare wear it, it's so fine. I'm doubly sure I don't want the marshal staring at me," Shanna confessed.

Rose brushed her comments aside. "I'll be right by your side, and everything will be fine. Besides, I think it was generous of the marshal to pay for all of this. Now, come on. Let's get our baths and get ready for the dance."

Shanna had no idea what to say. Butterflies filled her belly. She was going to the dance in a new silk dress! What's more, Reese paid for it all. Did it mean he wanted her for her and not as Jenna? Shanna wasn't sure if she was allowed so much hope.

****

Reese stood with his back to the wall watching the townspeople gather as the dance got under way. The schoolhouse was decorated with leaves and acorns. Pumpkins, squashes, and all things apple burst from every corner symbolizing fall and the harvest. Against the far wall, a refreshment table was set up with jugs of hot apple cider and baked goods of every description. Men walked in stamping their wet feet on the floor and hanging their heavy woolen coats on the pegs nailed next to the door. The women followed behind carrying more baked goods and dragging their children with them. They greeted each other happily and got their donations and offspring settled. Daniel Anderson appeared with Delphine on his arm, her mink coat covering her to her knees, and a lofty smile lighting her face. She singled Reese out with one sweeping glance over the crowd. Reese felt her staring from across the room. The woman had a predatory look in her eye. He glanced her way wondering what her game was. The second he did, Delphine looked away pretending disinterest. Reese narrowed his gaze. He met more than a few man-hungry dames in Chicago. They all played the same game of cat and mouse. Reese turned his attention back to the door. He wasn't interested.

Sheriff Holden walked over to stand beside him. "Looks like a pretty good turnout," he commented.

Reese nodded his agreement. He faced the door so he would know the minute Shanna arrived. When he did see her, he wasn't sure it was her. The Tanners entered laughing and stamping their feet. A pretty girl in a heavy woolen cape followed Rose. The Tanners hung up their coats still chuckling amongst them. The girl took off her woolen cape revealing a pink silk gown clinging lovingly to the girl's luscious figure. Reese drew in a tight breath. Whoever she was, she was mighty easy on the eyes. The beautiful girl in the pink dress turned, and Reese got a good look at her face.

"Will you look over there?" Sheriff Holden whistled. His eyes stared at the same vision holding Reese speechless. Shanna had the most perfect body Reese had ever seen. The pink of the dress set off the faint blush in her cheeks and the blonde of her hair. She looked like a princess, and it hurt to breathe. Reese glanced about the room to see what reaction the townspeople had to Shanna's transformation. He caught sight of Daniel Anderson and Delphine Otis. Daniel's mouth was open like a wide-mouth bass. Delphine was snarling like a cougar ready to make a kill.

Rose must have noticed them too, because she grabbed Shanna by the elbow and dragged her across the room to a group of young people. The young men turned red, and either stared at the floor, or gaped. Shanna looked round the room nervously. The old Jenna would revel in the attention. This Jenna didn't. Reese growled. He could feel her embarrassment from where he stood. He needed a cigarette and a stiff shot of whiskey. Reese headed toward Shanna, dodging handshakes and townspeople. He was intent on rescuing her when Delphine blocked his path.

"Good evening, Marshal, care to dance?" Delphine smiled shyly. Her slim hands reached toward him.

"No." Reese stepped around the woman, but Delphine caught his arm.

"Please, Marshal?" She pouted and peeked up at him from beneath her lashes.

Reese carefully removed the woman's claws from his arm. "I'm sorry, Miss Otis. Perhaps your fiancé would care to take a turn with you." Reese sidestepped in time to see Daniel Anderson grab Shanna by the arm and shake her.

"What seems to be the problem?" Reese stood beside the two. He glared at Anderson to let him know what he thought of the situation.

Shanna pulled her arm from Daniel's grip. "Mr. Anderson refuses to take no for an answer."

"It must be catching," Reese murmured.

"My, my, somehow Shanna found the only bolt of pink silk Tanner Mercantile had." Delphine walked up and stood beside Daniel. Her eyes looked Shanna up and down. She narrowed her gaze. "I asked if the silk came in pink and you told me it didn't." Delphine looked from Daniel to Reese and back at Daniel. Her expression turned calculating. "Does Mr. Tanner know? I'm certain you didn't pay for it. How did you manage to get it out without anyone knowing? Did you steal it, Shanna?"

Shanna's face heated. She looked back at Delphine. "I did not steal it. It was bought and paid for."

Reese watched Shanna with interest. Normally, she would have chewed up and spit out anybody bold enough to accuse her. This Shanna blushed and fumbled for an answer.

"Perhaps we should ask Mr. Tanner," Delphine insisted. "We all know what kind of woman you are, Shanna. Someone of easy virtue wouldn't have a problem taking something that didn't belong to them." Her gaze rested on Reese. "Why don't you arrest her, Marshal? We all know Shanna didn't pay for it. You can see how guilty she looks."

Reese opened his mouth to tell the woman to mind her business when Rose cut him off.

"The silk was paid for, and it belongs to Shanna. We told you there wasn't any pink or purple the day you came in, because we bought them both." Rose stepped in between Reese and Shanna and pulled Shanna's arm through hers. "You're welcome to ask Daddy if you like. He will tell you the silk is all accounted for." Rose squared off with Delphine. She returned glare for glare.

With Rose by her side, Shanna gained confidence. "Why don't you mind your own business, Delphine?" Shanna asked.

Daniel's eyes narrowed. Delphine took a step back. She stared at Shanna and Rose arm in arm for a minute. Then she tossed her head. "Come on, Daniel." She grabbed Daniel's arm and dragged him over into the corner where the two of them held a violent, whispered conversation.

Rose turned and stared at Reese. "Shanna wants to dance. Why don't you ask her?"

"Rose!" Shanna's face got red.

"Miss Johnston? Would you care to dance?" Reese held his arm out, and Shanna slid her arm into his. They danced around the floor in a waltz. Both were quiet were several minutes.

Shanna gazed up. "Thank you for the dress." Her voice was sincere.

Reese glanced at her face. In all the time he'd known her, he'd never heard her thank anyone unless it was calculated to advance her ambitions. "You're welcome."

Tonight, he watched her fumble for something to say, blush in embarrassment, and say "thank you." What was happening here? Something was wrong. Reese focused on the crowd as they danced. He stared at every individual. He wanted to make damn sure her men weren't hidden among them. He saw nothing and frowned as he considered what he might be missing.

****

Shanna saw Reese's frown and the tiny bud of hope sprouting in her bosom dissolved in ashes. Why had he paid for her dress? It wasn't to appease her for calling her Jenna, obviously, so why then? The dance ended, and Reese led her to the Tanners. He stepped back to his corner where he could watch the whole room.

Shanna stood stiffly beside Rose. It was a mistake to let Rose talk her into coming. She trembled from the confrontation with Daniel and Delphine. She didn't know why it embarrassed her when Delphine accused her of having easy virtue. It was the same thing Daniel said about her. Shanna didn't know what Reese thought, but Shanna proved what they said about her was true the night beside the river. She stared at the floor. She was mad at Rose for suggesting Reese ask her to dance. Being in his arms was a painful reminder of what almost happened. Rose wanted her to be happy. Somehow, she got the idea Shanna's happiness involved Reese. Shanna liked the dress, and she loved Rose for thinking of her, but she hated being here. She hated herself for believing Reese cared. Whatever the reason he paid for her dress, it had nothing to do with her or an apology. She gazed at him beneath her lashes. He had his back against the far wall; his muscular arms folded over his broad chest. He could view the entire room from where he stood. Who was he looking for? Why was he still in Rock Creek? He should be on the train headed back to Chicago, not here making her miserable. One young man claimed Shanna for a dance, and she circled the floor completely indifferent to the young man and his attempts to charm her. She watched the marshal instead. Reese studied them through half closed eyes. She couldn't make out what he was thinking. Why didn't he just go away and leave her alone? He had the chance to talk when they danced, and he stayed silent. What was it he was waiting for?

****

Reese leaned back as the pair circled the floor. Shanna's partner looked about fourteen. He held her way too tight, and his hand could move up an inch or two. His gaze circled to Daniel Anderson and Delphine Otis staring intently from the other side of the room. Daniel looked lustful. Delphine looked furious. For the next hour and a half, Shanna danced with one young man after another, while Reese watched from his corner. Nothing happened, and nobody new entered the building.

At ten o' clock, the Tanners made ready to leave and donned their coats. Daniel Anderson left the building out the back door, and Delphine headed toward Reese for the third time that night. Reese exited through the back door too and made his way around front. Daniel Anderson stood in the shadows watching as the Tanners and Shanna got into their buggy and started back into town. Reese waited. Once the Tanners were gone, Mr. Anderson passed him in the dark, headed back to the dance muttering furiously under his breath. He didn't trust the man. The way Anderson stared at Shanna told Reese he was up to no good. Reese followed the Tanners home and waited outside the mercantile until the sun rose. He passed a quiet night and an even quieter morning. Nothing happened. He scouted the ground for any sign he may have missed, when he came up with nothing, he headed to his motel room, and his bed. He needed some rest, and then he would go through it all again and again until he figured out what he was missing. He was confused by the dance and Shanna's inconsistencies. Where the hell where her men, and what was she up to?

****

Two days later, Rose Tanner threw open the door to the sheriff's office and stumbled inside. She had a wild, crazed look in her eyes. "They've taken Shanna!" she cried hugging her stomach and breathing deeply.

"Who? Who's taken Shanna?" Reese asked. Sheriff Holden's boots came off his desk and hit the floor.

Rose leaned against the doorjamb to catch her breath. "I don't know. Shanna stayed at the Claytons' last night and she hasn't come into work yet."

Sheriff Holden scratched his head. "Well, now, Miss Rose, that's not reason enough to believe Shanna's been taken."

"But she's *never* this late, and I know something's happened!" Rose said.

"What makes you think it did?" Reese wondered.

Rose steadied her breathing as she explained her fears. "There's been somebody watching us, somebody watching her. Shanna and I found boot prints under my window. She found the same boot prints around the Claytons' house right outside the room she stays in. There are hoof prints in the dirt under the tree out back at the Claytons'. Strange horse prints."

"Now, you're both just a couple of girls. I'm sure the prints are ones your father made and probably Mr. Clayton. I don't see any reason to believe they're strange. Shanna probably wandered off the path or something," Sheriff Holden soothed. "What do two girls know about reading sign?" Sheriff Holden chuckled. "I'm sure it's nothing."

Reese frowned. It might be a good idea to check it

out. "Show me where you found the boot prints," Reese said ushering a flustered Rose out the door in front of him. He nodded at the sheriff. "I'll take care of this."

Reese followed Rose Tanner to the side of the mercantile, right beneath Rose's window. *I'll be damned. There are boot prints in the dirt.* They were too big to be Mr. Tanner's. These prints belonged to a man at least six foot tall. Mr. Tanner was five and a half, tops.

"See," Rose said. She waited.

"I see," Reese answered. "When did you first notice these prints?"

"About a week before the dance. Shanna found them and showed them to me. We've been watching, and every night there's more," Rose said.

"Ever see any horse prints here? Or only at the Claytons'?" Reese asked.

"Well, we didn't at first, but then Shanna found these yesterday." Rose walked around behind the house and sure enough, there were horse prints, a lot of horse prints. Reese knelt beside a fresh one. Something kicked him in the gut. Whether it was anxiety or satisfaction, he didn't know. This horse belonged to Snake Eye. If he was here, he had Shanna. Whether she went willingly or against her will, was the question. Either way, they had only a little time to determine which it was.

Chapter 16

Snake Eye stopped his horse two miles out of town. He figured this was as good a place as any to kill the girl and dump the body. Funny how he'd been able to take her without much of a fuss. Where were the Delaney men? Where were her bodyguards? He'd snatched the girl as she walked alone along the dirt road into town with no one around at all. She was a hellcat. He had the scratches on his arm and face to prove it. She pulled a knife on him, too. If it weren't for the time he spent as a member of the Delaney Gang, with their dirty fighting, she would have ended him. Snake Eye spit on the ground and dismounted. He pulled Shanna from the saddle and dumped her bound body on the ground beside his horse.

At first, he'd been going to shoot the bitch, but every time he got close, the damn marshal showed up. He didn't want Marshal Calhan anywhere near when he killed her. If the marshal knew he was in the area, he wouldn't get away. Snake Eye didn't plan on dying anytime soon. Plus, he planned on spending the ten grand Mack Turley promised him for killing the girl in style. He'd decided to head to Mexico for a spell. Ten thousand would get him by for some time. Snake Eye grabbed Shanna by the hair and set her back against a tree. He'd found this spot a couple of days ago when he decided shooting the Delaney bitch in town would get him dead. This spot was away from the main road and surrounded by brush. Several trees grew together in a little cluster. With all the shrubs, he'd be able to do the job and ditch the body without being spotted from any direction. Snake Eye spit again as he stared at the bitch. She was a pretty little thing. He could see why Delaney would be upset if his niece got dead. She was also talented, and Delaney would not only be out a niece, but a valuable member of his gang. Snake Eye got down on his haunches and looked into Shanna's eyes. There was no fear and no emotion. The girl stared right back without blinking. Snake Eye pulled the gag from her mouth. This would be so much more satisfying if the bitch would at least scream or beg for mercy. She did neither.

Snake Eye pulled her knife from his boot, where he'd stuffed it after she tried to stab him. He held the blade up in the sunlight. It was a good knife. His eyes narrowed on the eagle cut into the handle of the blade. He knew the symbol.

Snake Eye turned to Shanna. "This knife bears the mark of an eagle."

"Yes." She stared at him without blinking.

Snake Eye leaned in close. "Tell me where you got this knife."

"From White Eagle," Shanna said.

"Who is White Eagle to you?" he asked in Cheyenne.

"My friend, and the father I never had," Shanna answered him in kind. She knew the language.

Snake Eye stood up. He had to consider carefully. *Who was this girl?* "What name are you known by?"

"Shanna Johnston. White Eagle called me beautiful

flower," Shanna answered in Cheyenne.

"Beautiful flower," Snake Eye murmured.

How could this niece of Adam Delaney know Cheyenne? Or his father? This was the last thing he expected when he set out to find and kill Jenna Delaney. Snake Eye studied her while he considered what his next action would be. The tension eased out of him. He was curious now. "How do you know White Eagle?" he asked.

Shanna drew her knees up and leaned back against the tree. The bindings on her wrists and ankles burned where they restricted the blood flow to her extremities.

"I got lost in the woods when I was ten years old. I was cold and hungry. White Eagle found me and took me to his village. His people were kind and cared for me. I often went back and visited White Eagle. For several years, White Eagle was my only friend. He taught me many things and gave me the knife as a gift. White Eagle was a father to me and took me in as his own. I owe him my life."

Snake Eye nodded. He couldn't kill this girl. His father, White Eagle, would curse him forever if he harmed one who meant so much. Snake Eye stood up and paced. Mack would never know if he killed the girl or not. He could go to Chicago, tell Mack the girl was dead, collect his reward, and head to Mexico. Once Mack realized the girl lived, Snake Eye would be too far away for Mack to find.

Snake Eye sat down on his haunches once more. "No one must know you are alive. I let you live because of White Eagle. He was my father. If he took you in as his own, it will grieve his spirit if I harm you. I will not dishonor him. Mack Turley wants you dead. He hired me to kill you. If he knows you live, he will send others, so beware." Snake Eye cut the ties binding her and helped her to her feet. "Stay away from Chicago. Stay away from the Turleys. Say nothing. Let no one know what happened here."

Shanna nodded her head. Snake Eye handed her the knife. He thought about the Delaneys and a smile crossed his face. Snake Eye was good at covering his own tracks.

"Tell your uncle Mack Turley sent a man to kill you." If Adam Delaney knew Mack had a hit out on his niece, maybe he would gun down Mack Turley and relieve Snake Eye of the problem.

Shanna looked startled. "Tell my uncle?" she asked. She put her knife back in its scabbard and straightened to face the half-breed.

"Your uncle ought to know Mack Turley is gunning for you."

Snake Eye swung into the saddle and turned his horse to leave. He came face to face with Marshal Calhan.

The marshal had his gun aimed at Snake Eye's chest. "Get down off your horse." He had Snake Eye dead to rights.

Snake Eye decided to spur his mount to knock Reese to the ground. He got a bullet in his chest for the trouble. He went down with a thud.

****

Reese covered the fallen man with his gun while he slid off his horse. He kicked the body to determine if Snake Eye was dead or alive. He was dead. Reese turned to look at Shanna. He'd heard the last of the conversation. The Turleys were gunning for her, and

Snake Eye wanted her to tell her uncle. Well, he had one gang member down and the possibility of getting Adam Delaney was improving. If he kept an eye on Shanna, she would lead him to her uncle. Reese was encouraged for the first time since he got on the train in Chicago. He didn't want Shanna to know he'd heard what they said.

"You okay?" he asked. She didn't appear to be concerned about anything much. Her eyes were trained on Snake Eye.

"Can we bury him?" she asked quietly.

Reese looked from her to the body. "You got a shovel?"

Shanna shook her head.

"Then he goes back to town, and the sheriff will see he gets buried." Reese said. He took Snake Eye and slung him over his own saddle. He tied the half-breed so he wouldn't fall off and then remounted Pegasus. He looped the reins of the other horse to his pommel while he helped Shanna up. He held his arm out. "Come on, Shanna. Let's get you back before Rose Tanner decides to come look for you herself."

****

Shanna grabbed his arm and let him pull her onto his lap. She was glad to be alive. She wanted to bury the half-breed. She owed him that much. White Eagle would expect her to mourn the loss of his son. Once she got back to town, she'd pester the sheriff until he buried White Eagle's son properly. "I hate riding like this," she commented. She was too damn close to the man, and it irritated her.

"Why?" Reese's breath blew hot across her neck. Shanna shivered. *He* was the reason she didn't like it.

Reese settled Shanna, and holding the reins to the other horse, they headed toward town.

"It's uncomfortable," Shanna said at last. She hated herself for wanting a man who cared so little. He should at least call her by the right name.

"Next time you sneak off to visit one of your men, try to give Rose Tanner some kind of excuse. She was hysterical this morning when she came tearing into the sheriff's office to report you missing," Reese whispered in her ear.

Shanna stiffened in surprise. *He thinks I planned this? I damn near fainted hanging upside down over the saddle. My stomach will never be the same. I was scared as hell!* "I didn't sneak off. The man ran out of the bushes and knocked me over with his horse. Then he tied me, gagged me, and took me to the cluster of trees to kill me."

Reese chuckled. "So why didn't he kill you?"

He didn't believe her story. Shanna was mad as a wounded bear. Reese was amused over her abduction and near death? What kind of a marshal was he anyway? "He would have except he noticed the eagle on my knife and changed his mind," Shanna answered.

Reese chuckled again. "You two seemed mighty cozy when I rode up. Not what I'd expect from a supposed abduction and near murder. You looked to me like two members of a gang plotting together."

Shanna wanted to punch him in the teeth. Honest to God this man tried her patience. "So, *this* looks cozy does it?" She held up her wrists where the skin was raw from being bound. Damn the man! Why did he always have to think the worst about her?

Reese looked at her wrists and frowned. His

amusement vanished. Shanna swung her leg over the saddle and slid to the ground before Reese realized what she intended. She was tired of the questions and tired of Reese thinking she was an evil woman. He stopped Pegasus and held his arm down. Shanna kept walking, ignoring him, and his arm.

"Get back on the horse, Shanna," Reese commanded.

"Go to hell," Shanna answered.

Reese ground his teeth together. "You plan on walking all the way back into town?" he inquired.

"Damn straight I do," she said. Maybe a brisk walk was what she needed to keep her from killing the marshal and earning a place in jail.

Reese wheeled Pegasus directly in her path causing her to stop. "Maybe if you started telling the truth, *Jenna*, I would believe you," Reese said.

If she had a gun, she would have shot him on the spot. "I am telling the truth. I have told the truth. My name is *Shanna*. I was abducted. The half-breed did not kill me because of the eagle on my knife. He knew White Eagle and let me go." Shanna stepped around Pegasus and kept walking. Why couldn't God answer her prayers and strike Reese down with a bolt of lightning? Just once, if God could answer this *one* prayer, she'd do anything. She'd join a monastery, go on a month long fast, care for the sick and needy, anything. If Reese dissolved into a pile of ashes, it would solve *all* her problems, and she wouldn't have to go to jail for murder.

"Okay, *Shanna*, who the hell is White Eagle, and why would Snake Eye care?" Reese asked.

"White Eagle is a Cheyenne chief who rescued me

as a child. He became my rescuer, my friend, and the only family I had other than Mama. I don't know why Snake Eye, as you call him, would care, but he did. He cut the ropes binding me and let me go as soon as he knew I was a friend of White Eagle. He said White Eagle was his father."

Reese laughed. "How did you manage to convince him you knew White Eagle?"

Shanna said something in Cheyenne.

Reese frowned. "Did you call me a slobbering calf?"

She smiled. "Only if you know the language."

****

Shanna knew Cheyenne. Reese twisted the information around in his mind. It followed what Sheriff Holden already told him but confused the hell out of him. The old Shanna wouldn't have cared enough to learn Cheyenne. She had a lofty view of the world and considered anything other than French and English a trash language. So why would she learn Cheyenne? Maybe all she knew was one or two sentences and used them as back up for special occasions. As for her story about being abducted, he'd check into it. She had been bound, so part of her story was true. He would do some scouting around as soon as he dropped the body off with the sheriff and returned Shanna to the mercantile. Rose Tanner was probably driving Sheriff Holden to drink about now.

Chapter 17

Rose Tanner wrapped her arms around Shanna and led her across the street. Reese watched them go and then went to backtrack Snake Eye's trail. Reese found the sign right at the bend in the road. There were signs of a struggle. Snake Eye ran her down with his horse, exactly like Shanna said. Reese didn't know what to think. He sat for a while on his horse and studied the sign before him. What was he missing? Snake Eye *knew* Shanna was Adam Delaney's niece. Why would he be so stupid as to abduct her and try to murder her? Was Snake Eye covering his tracks? Maybe Snake Eye joined the Turleys, and when Shanna blew the gang up, Snake Eye ran to tell Mack Turley. Thing was, his life wouldn't be worth spit if Adam Delaney found out. Snake Eye wasn't a stupid man, though. Is that why he let Shanna go and told her to tell her uncle about the hit Mack Turley put on her? Adam would wipe out the Turleys for the principle of it and to make an example of them. That must be it.

Reese headed back to town. Shanna would be staying at the Tanners' tonight. Sheriff Holden made sure Joseph Johnston knew, and there would be no argument about it. Reese found Sheriff Holden and updated him on the where and how of Shanna's abduction. Then, he headed to the telegraph office to update Sergeant Baxter.

****

Shanna and Rose spent the rest of the afternoon quietly. Mr. and Mrs. Tanner were gone to the fort, and there weren't many customers. So, it left plenty of time to talk.

"Weren't you scared?" Rose asked as they straightened the dry goods counter.

"Of course, I was, silly, but you can't let on you are. It gives your captor a sense of power when you act scared. You never want to give anyone power, Rose." Shanna was matter of fact.

Rose was incredulous. "How do you know so much?"

"White Eagle taught me, plus I see it in Uncle Joseph's face. When I cried and begged him to not hit me when I was younger, it made him happy. Then, he'd hit me more just to see me cry. I quit letting him see my fear a long time ago. He still hits me plenty, but I don't let him enjoy it," Shanna answered.

Rose nodded slowly. She was horrified. She already guessed Uncle Joseph hit Shanna sometimes but hearing her talk about it so matter-of-factly was something else. Rose wanted to take a whip to the man for hurting her friend. "Why do you let him hit you? I would hit him back or go tell the sheriff," Rose said.

Shanna looked at her friend. "I could, I guess, but Mama made me promise to not give Uncle Joseph any problems. Mama is terrified of something, and I don't know what it is. She told me my life is in danger, so I must live with Uncle Joseph and Aunt Sara. If I made Uncle Joseph mad enough to send me back, I don't know what Mama would do."

Rose put her hand on Shanna's arm. "I think your

mama needs to know he hits you. You should tell her next time you go see her."

Shanna sighed and shook her head at Rose.

"I wish you could live with your mama. It would be sad for me because you are my best friend and I would never see you, but it would be better for you. No one would hit you or make you walk miles by yourself in the sun and the snow. You would probably get new clothes and make new friends, and you would have your mama. You would be so happy!" Rose's smile fell. "And I would be alone." Tears gathered in Rose's eyes as she thought about how lonely she would be without Shanna.

****

Shanna gave Rose a quick hug. "I'm not going anywhere, Rose, so you don't need to worry." Shanna folded a pair of jeans and replaced them on the shelf. "Mama said she sent me out here to protect me. She told me there were people who would kill me if they knew I was alive and where I live." Shanna said it slowly as the events of the last few days crashed in around her. The Turleys hadn't been around when she was ten. Mama had been talking about someone else. But who? Did Reese know? Did it have something to do with Jenna or the Delaneys? A lot of people knew more about her and her life than she did. Was there a connection? She would ask Mama who wanted her dead next time she went to Omaha. Only now, there were more people trying to kill her. The half-breed told her Mack Turley wanted her dead. He also told her to tell her uncle. Somehow, she didn't think Uncle Joseph would care.

Shanna was exhausted from her ordeal and fell

asleep the second she laid her head down on Rose's feather pillow. It was morning way too soon. Mrs. Tanner hurried them through breakfast and cleanup before the mercantile opened for the day. Shanna grabbed the broom from its place in the corner and went out to sweep the boardwalk in front of the mercantile and the stairs. She felt someone staring at her and turned to find Daniel Anderson a foot away, leaning against a post watching her intently. "What do you want?" Shanna asked rudely. She hadn't forgotten his tenacity at the dance. She wanted him to go away.

"I want you." Daniel straightened from the post and took a step closer. She had on a light blue calico dress of Rose's today. It was a little snug in the bodice. She was completely covered but with Daniel gawking, she felt naked. Daniel's gaze dropped to her chest. He stared for a full minute, looking her up and down.

Shanna shuddered. She wished she could stab him with her knife. "Where's Delphine? You know, your fiancée?" Shanna asked dryly. "The woman you can't live without. The woman so pure and innocent she could outshine the angels of heaven?" Shanna deliberately threw his own words back in his face. The words he used on her the day he broke off their engagement to court Delphine. "Why don't you go find her? After all, I'm so used and diseased you might catch the pox talking to me."

Daniel stared at her mouth. "Delphine is none of your concern. There's no need to be jealous. I've decided I want you." Daniel lunged suddenly, grabbing her by the arm and pulling her against his body. His breath blew hot across her face.

Shanna wanted to gag. He smelled like whiskey

and cigar smoke. When he leaned in closer, her knee came up hard. Daniel fell to the boardwalk groaning with pain. She smiled in satisfaction and then spit in his face. Shanna bent down getting nose to nose with the howling man. "What *you* want is not my concern. I *don't* want you. Touch me again, and I'll cut your throat," she said. Shanna kicked him in the groin to emphasize her point. She stomped into the mercantile. Daniel Anderson was becoming a pain in the ass. She was not interested in him at all. She hadn't been since the day he verbally abused her in front of the whole town. He was loathsome, greasy, and utterly disgusting. Shanna shivered with revulsion. Daniel could go back under whatever floorboard he crawled out of. She glanced out the mercantile window a few minutes later and saw Daniel limp away.

The day passed quickly, and Shanna put Daniel Anderson out of her mind. It was only as she walked along the lonely dirt road in the dark to the Claytons' claim, she became uneasy. Someone was watching her. Usually, it was Reese. This was different. Come to think of it, she hadn't seen much of Reese all day at all. Usually, he was underfoot, and every time she turned around, she tripped over him. The quietness of the night pressed down on her. Shanna quickened her step.

It happened when she reached the back door of the Claytons' cabin. One minute she was fine, the next she was unconscious.

****

Daniel Anderson looked in satisfaction at the crumpled form of Shanna on the ground at his feet. He set his club down and picked her up. He threw her limp body over the saddle of his horse and headed to the empty trapper's cabin down by the river. She was such a bitch. Who did she think she was? Shanna was nobody, a penniless, lowdown nobody. She should be begging for his attention, not crippling him on the steps of the mercantile. He had no idea how many of the town's folk witnessed his humiliation. She would pay dearly for what she'd done. He thought about her comments. What did Delphine have to do with his wanting Shanna? Delphine didn't need to know what he did with Shanna. It was none of her business. Shanna was nothing but a piece of skirt to roll around in the hay with. Once he plugged Shanna a few times, he'd be done with her and go back to Delphine. He was doing the bitch a favor to show her he wanted her, and she was too stupid to know it. It had taken him some time to walk upright again. He would punish her for the pain she caused him. He'd bend her over a chair and ride her until he couldn't stand. Then, he'd lay her on the bed and pump into her until she was so sore, she couldn't walk for days.

Daniel was so busy envisioning the things he wanted to do to Shanna, he almost fell from his saddle when his horse suddenly stopped. He looked up.

Marshal Reese Calhan sat on his big stallion blocking his path. The marshal's pistol gleamed in the moonlight. It was aimed directly at him! "Good evening, Mr. Anderson. I'll be taking Shanna." Reese cocked the hammer of his gun. The sound echoed in the stillness of the night.

"This isn't what it looks like—" Daniel attempted to bluff his way through.

Reese stopped him. "It's exactly what it looks like," Reese countered. "Climb off your horse slowly.

Keep your hands where I can see them."

Daniel slowly slid from his horse. Reese dismounted, keeping his gun trained on Daniel all the while.

"I found Shanna unconscious. I was taking her back to town so the doctor could have a look. I didn't do anything wrong," Daniel insisted.

Reese snorted. He took the cuffs from his belt and cuffed Daniel's hands together.

"I've been following you for some time. I know you took Shanna from the Claytons'." Reese led Daniel to a tree and tied him to it.

"I was taking her back to town to see the doctor," Daniel persisted.

Reese stopped. He swiveled toward Daniel Anderson "Town is over there." Reese pointed in the opposite direction. "The way I figure it, you wanted to teach Shanna a lesson for refusing your attentions earlier today."

The marshal must have seen everything. Daniel stared into the marshal's eyes and decided to beg. Delphine would kill him if she found out. "Don't tell Delphine, please? Whatever you do, let's keep this man to man, between you and me."

Reese chuckled. "A man wouldn't go after another girl behind his fiancée's back. Nor would he abduct a girl for telling him no. Nothing you've done so far makes you worthy of being called a man."

Lightning lit up the sky. Daniel got a glimpse of Reese leading his horse away into the darkness. Shanna was still slung over his saddle. "Wait! You can't leave me out here! You can't leave me alone in the dark tied to a tree! Bring my horse back! Wait!" Daniel called.

The marshal didn't even look back. They disappeared into the darkness. Daniel stared after them. *Now what?*

****

The storm began in earnest. Sheets of cold rain sliced through the air drenching the countryside. Within minutes everything was soaked. Reese looked back at Shanna draped across Anderson's saddle. They wouldn't make it back to town, not like this, not in the dark. Soon everything would be muddy and slippery as hell. He couldn't risk one of the horses tripping. Reese turned his horse in the opposite direction. He'd scouted the area around here looking for Shanna's men. He knew there was a deserted cabin up ahead. He looked back to make sure Shanna was okay before continuing.

Reese had been talking with Sheriff Holden earlier in the day when he noticed the scene in front of the mercantile. He hadn't even made it halfway across the street to help Shanna before she had Anderson on the ground howling like a cub. Anderson was a coward and wouldn't take Shanna's rejection well, so Reese followed him. Once he realized Anderson was headed out to the Claytons', he went back into town to tell Sheriff Holden what was happening. Reese suspected Anderson was going after Shanna. Sure enough, Anderson abducted her out back of the Claytons' cabin. He read the sign and followed as quickly as he could while the light held out. Once he knew what direction Anderson traveled, he remembered the old cabin. He didn't doubt it was where the bastard intended to take Shanna.

The old cabin would come in handy, now. They would be out of the rain. With any luck he would be able to make a fire. They would hole up there until

161

morning. The night would be cold and damp, because of the storm. The cabin would provide shelter and hopefully a little warmth.

Anderson would be dry enough under the tree. Good thing he'd told Sheriff Holden where he was going. Reese made a habit of letting the sheriff know where he was headed. If there was any trouble, help would be on the way. When he didn't return, the sheriff should start looking and no doubt find Anderson. If Anderson was as big of a coward as Reese suspected, once the rain started, he would be making enough noise to lead a deaf posse right to him. Reese glanced back at Shanna again. She needed to get warm and dry before she got sick. Reese spotted the roof of the cabin along the bank and nudged Pegasus to walk a little faster.

Chapter 18

Reese kicked the log in the fireplace of the old cabin, causing the fire to flare up. Bright orange and yellow flames licked against the back of the fireplace. He threw another log in the fire and looked over at Shanna for the tenth time since he laid her down. She hadn't moved. He stepped over to the old cot standing in the corner of the cabin and felt for a pulse. Anderson must have hit her hard. She should have woken up by now. The steady beat of her heart against his fingers reassured him, and he let out a breath of relief. He looked at her chest and noted the rhythmic rise and fall. He nodded in satisfaction. There was an egg size bump on the back of her head, and other than the fact she hadn't come to yet, she appeared to be fine.

Reese studied Shanna's pale features and noticed her shiver slightly. He frowned. He'd hoped she would wake up so she could undress herself. She wouldn't get warm until she was out of her wet clothing and a dry blanket covered her. She looked so young and innocent when she slept. Her dark lashes fanned against her pale cheeks. A sudden urge to protect her filled him. He shook the feeling off. Seeing her like this reminded him of the way it used to be between them. Back when he thought she was innocent, and he still believed in love.

Reese rolled Shanna to her side and unbuttoned her dress. He pulled the sodden fabric from her limp body and then tugged her shift over her head. He removed her shoes and stockings and set them by the fire to dry. He returned to the bed. Her full pink-tipped breasts gleamed white in the flickering fire light. He found her knife strapped to her thigh and grimaced. He removed the leather sheath and set it beside her clothes. Reese reached down and pulled her knickers off her long legs. He stood for a minute looking at the delicate beauty lying naked before him. She was perfect in every way. Reese did a thorough investigation of her body. He was merely looking for injuries he told himself, although the little voice inside his head mocked him. He desperately wanted to touch her again. Once he felt along every limb and pressed against her ribs, he was satisfied nothing was broken. Then, he allowed his eyes to look their fill. He took in the fall of blonde, silken hair, the generously round, pink-tipped breasts, the tiny waist, the curve of her hips, and then the long, slim legs, and delicate feet. His gaze was drawn to a mole on her right hip. Had it been there before? It *had* been a little more than seven years since he'd last seen her naked in bed. She had it before. He simply forgot.

Shanna stirred, a low moan coming from the back of her throat. She turned to her side, her hands coming to rest beneath her cheek, and she was still once more. Reese gathered his blanket from where he set it beside his saddle on the floor and covered Shanna. He spread the rest of her clothing out where they would dry and then removed his own. Once he had all the clothing spread in front of the fire, he looked around the sparsely filled cabin. There was one chair, the cot, and a kettle. Other than the wood he'd carried inside for the fire, there was nothing else inside the cabin other than

Shanna and himself. Reese looked from the chair to the cot where Shanna slept. Making his decision quickly, he climbed into bed beside her and pulled his blanket over them both. He'd be damned if he was going to sleep naked in a chair all night while she slept soundly on the bed with his blanket. They'd shared a bed once before. They could do it again. It would be just for tonight. Reese turned on his side and pulled Shanna against him. He was asleep a few minutes later.

****

Shanna was having the most incredible dream. She dreamed she was in bed with Reese, and he was doing the most shocking things to her body. The last thing she remembered was walking alone in the dark and someone hitting her over the head. Somehow, she had gone from a cold, dark, scary, place to this hot, sensual pleasure, and she wanted it to continue. His warm, hard body pressed against her, and she shivered as his hot mouth kissed, licked, and sucked its way from her neck down to her breasts. Shanna leaned back to soak up his heat. God, he felt so good. Her dreams had never been this vivid before. Her body quivered with desire. Reese rolled Shanna on to her back, covering her with his heat. Shanna could feel the long, hard length of his arousal pressed against her. She didn't want to open her eyes in case she woke up. Reese was different when she was awake, cold, aloof, and accusing. She liked this warm sensual place and she wanted Reese to keep holding her, licking her, and sucking her.

White-hot heat grew in her stomach as his lips and hands explored her body. It pooled in her secret spot between her legs. Shanna cautiously opened her eyes and met the slumberous blue gaze of Marshal Calhan. It was real. He was here, and he was touching her. She sighed with pleasure, wrapping her arms around Reese's neck, and pulling him close against her. Reese parted her legs with his knee and settled between her thighs. His mouth covered hers, his tongue sweeping inside to mate with her tongue. His hands found her breast. He squeezed and measured them with his palms. Then his fingers found her nipples. Shanna arched her back to meet his warm teasing touch.

Reese drank from her mouth like a starving man. A large warm hand found its way between her legs, and Shanna moaned with pleasure. He stroked her heat with his long fingers. He rubbed his hand against her. She thrashed side-to-side, frantic for more. A large finger probed the soft folds of her femininity. She lifted her hips to meet his invasion and moaned again when he began to stroke her gently. Shanna spread her legs allowing his hand access. Reese leaned down pulling a nipple into his mouth and suckled. Shanna fell apart in his arms. Crying out and arcing against him as he lavished his attention on one nipple and then the other. He stroked her molten core until she was wet with desire. He groaned and penetrated her with his finger. Shanna cried out again, her hips rising to meet him, her breath coming past between her parted lips. Reese moved his finger in and out, imitating the mating act. Beads of perspiration broke out on Shanna's forehead. Her hands clawed at his back as she arced against him.

****

Reese felt his control slipping. He was rock hard and aching. It had been such a long time since he'd been inside this woman. He wanted to take it slow, to make it last, but Shanna's reaction made him lose his self-restraint. She was such a sensual wanton whenever he was with her. The memory of the earth shattering climaxes they shared before made him groan aloud. He needed to be inside her now. Reese moved his hand and centered his manhood at her entrance. Shanna was beyond thinking, beyond reason, beyond caution. She was lost on a sea of the most incredible rapture she had ever known. Reese pressed inside her. Shanna clutched at his shoulders, lifting her hips to meet him. Reese pulled back then surged forward a little more, tormenting her with desire. Shanna's head thrashed wildly. She panted against him, as she clutched at him, trying to draw him closer. Reese pressed forward in one big surge. He felt the barrier of her virginity tear. He stopped cold.

Searing pain sliced through Shanna. She cried out at the shock of his complete invasion. She couldn't double over with him on top of her, so she hit him to get his attention.

"Get off me!" she shouted as she pummeled him with her fists. Tears filled her eyes. She blinked them back angrily.

"What the hell?" Reese turned to stone as the shock of her virginity penetrated his mind. Reese stared down into Shanna's face. All traces of sexual pleasure vanished with the tearing of Shanna's membrane.

"Who *are* you?" Reese asked, his mind frantically trying to make sense of what happened. How the hell could she still be a virgin?

****

"Don't you *dare* ask me that again, *not here, not now, not ever!*" Shanna shouted. She had enough. The man was inside her, tearing her to pieces, and he wanted to know what her name was? "If you call me Jenna one more time, I swear before God and all the holy apostles, I will cut your heart out."

Reese moved uneasily at the mention of Jenna's name. "No, you're not Jenna, are you?" Reese said and shifted again. He stared at her as if he'd never seen her before.

Shanna gritted her teeth. The pain was slowly leaving, but Reese hadn't made any move to get off. Shanna shoved at his shoulder to get his attention. "Get off of me," she said wiping her tears away angrily.

"Hold still," Reese whispered against her neck. He caught her fists with one hand and leaning down took her mouth with his one more time. She bucked against him, but Reese held her still as he nibbled and sucked her mouth.

Slowly he teased his way inside and stroked her tongue with his. "Shanna, you taste so good." Reese whispered against her mouth.

Shanna stiffened when he said her name. He soon had her moaning against him. His hands wandered her body once more, exploring every inch of her satin skin. He teased, nipped, and suckled her sensitive nipples until she nearly went insane.

"Please Reese, please." she begged. She didn't know what she wanted for sure. Pressure built inside her, and it centered on him. She lifted her hips against him. The length of his arousal pressed deep. She shuddered against him. She began to writhe, her breath coming in short gasps. He pushed deeper. The liquid heat of her pooled around him as he moved slowly in and out. She gasped against his shoulder.

"Let me make this good for you. Let me love you,"

he whispered into her ear. Shanna heard the words, but she was beyond reason. Reese held her close, his mouth on hers as he plunged into her time and again. Shanna locked her legs around his hips gasping and panting as the full, hard length of him drove her over the edge. He rocked against her until she exploded in a million brilliant pieces. Waves of the most intense pleasure washed over her. She clawed at Reese's back screaming his name as he plunged into her faster. Reese drove hard. She screamed his name once more and shuddered against him. He shouted as his own release washed over him, shattering him to the core of his being.

He fell against her, completely sated, soaked with sweat, and breathing deeply. Reese wrapped his arms around her still trembling form, holding her close as he fought to regain control. Shanna still shook with the intensity of her release. She had no idea it could be so intense between a man and a woman. Minutes later, she looked up at Reese, a smile tugged at her still trembling lips.

****

Reese looked down at her as all the implications of their joining flooded his mind. He saw the tears in her eyes, and his gut tightened. He read the pain on her face, and he realized he'd hurt this girl deeply, in more ways than one. Her name was Shanna, and until a few minutes ago, she'd been an innocent girl. She'd been telling him the truth the whole time, and he hadn't believed her. He'd been rude and unkind, accusing her of terrible things. Yet she still lay here, smiling up at him. To round out the full count of his offences, he'd taken her virginity. He'd taken the one thing of value she possessed. He had to make this right somehow. He had to make it up to her. He couldn't hurt her and then leave her. Once he made this right, this thing between them now, then he would go about making all the other mistakes he'd made right. He would never hurt a woman on purpose. The knowledge he hurt this girl, both physically and emotionally made him wince. "Shanna, we need to talk."

Chapter 19

The train ride from Pine Bluffs to Omaha took forever. Shanna sat next to the window; her bonnet tied firmly beneath her chin where Rose tied it before sending her off to the fort with Mr. Tanner. The mail coach took an eternity to reach Pine Bluffs. There was only one other passenger, so it hadn't seemed as bad as her last trip home. Shanna shifted in her seat, bumping her case at her feet. She wasn't taking any chances with it being in the baggage car this time. No sir, her case was staying with her. Shanna looked at the Bible on her lap. It was the only book she had to read on the long train ride. She figured she was going to hell for sure for allowing Reese to bed her. All the Bible reading in the world wouldn't save her now. So, she left it in her lap.

Shanna stared blindly out the window. She thought about the night in the wood, reliving every minute. Reese was quiet and withdrawn after the haze of their lovemaking wore off. Shanna kept looking at him, while she cleaned and dressed. She tried to gauge what he was thinking, but his face was expressionless. Once they were completely clothed, Reese turned, his voice grim.

"This never should have happened," he'd said. Shanna didn't know how to take his statement. Did he mean it shouldn't have happened because she was Shanna and not Jenna? Or it shouldn't have happened because she'd been a virgin, and he hadn't enjoyed their coming together? Shanna waited to see what else he had to say.

Reese put his hands behind his back and paced as he talked, much like a commander preparing his troops for battle. "I admit I am to blame for what occurred between us, but what's done is done. There's no going back now. We must make the best of the situation." Shanna didn't like the sound of that. What did he mean by make the best of the situation? Shanna folded her arms over her chest in case he hurt her again.

"The only reason I touched you is because I thought you were Jenna—"

With a cry of outrage, Shanna bound from the cot and punched him dead in the face. She threw the door of the cabin open and ran.

****

Reese stumbled back in surprise. Why in the hell did she hit him and run? He was trying to talk about what happened, and she went all crazy on him. Reese hurried after her and stopped short when he came face to face with Sheriff Holden.

The sheriff looked from one to the other. "Is something happening here between you two?" he asked.

"No," Shanna said quickly. "I heard your horse and wanted to see if it was you or not."

Good excuse. Reese thought.

Shanna threw her arms around the sheriff in a quick hug, talking fast. "Oh, I'm so glad you're here. It's been such a long night, so dark, and cold, and rainy. How did you find us so fast? I was worried it would be hours before anyone found us. I'm starving. Do you have any food in your saddlebag?"

Sheriff Holden studied Shanna with one eyebrow up. "Marshal Calhan's horse, as well as Daniel Anderson's, are right there in the stable. You could have left at any time."

Shanna looked at him, blankly.

"I didn't want to risk it with Shanna in the dark and the rain. If one of the horses slipped, she could have been hurt," Reese said. He saddled Pegasus as he talked, and then turned to saddle Anderson's horse for Shanna.

"You made a good choice. The river's swollen, and there's a lot of mud between here and town. It would have been too dangerous in the dark. I'm glad you waited." Sheriff Holden still looked from one to the other, suspiciously. "Anything happen here, you want to tell me about, Shanna?"

Shanna looked right at Reese. "No, nothing happened. This was the most boring, uneventful, unimportant night of my life."

What the hell was that supposed to mean? Reese glared at Shanna. Something damn important happened. He'd taken her innocence and had the most mind-blowing sex of his life in the process. She could well be caring his child, even now. A child sure as hell was important! He intended to marry her; see to it she was properly taken care of. He'd take care of the baby and be the best daddy a boy could ask for. Marriage was also important, especially when it involved Shanna. Her acceptance of the situation sailed away with her innocence. He owed her for taking her virginity, and he was going to do right by her. Hell, it was all his fault! Shanna had been telling the truth. She wasn't Jenna. The fact she wasn't Jenna was also real important. It still didn't explain why she looked so damn much like her. Reese frowned. Another thought entered his mind. Mack Turley was gunning for *Shanna*, and Adam Delaney wouldn't give a damn because she wasn't his niece. Now he thought about it, this information was important, because now she needed *his* protection, which was important also. He intended to give her all the protection he could muster up. In the end, all of it was important *and* eventful. Reese gave Shanna a good glare.

Shanna climbed on Anderson's horse and with a glare of her own, set off for town. Reese would have gone after her, but Sheriff Holden stopped him.

"Let her go. I don't know what's eating at her, but it'll be better in town if folk don't see you two ride in together. Especially, if anybody finds out Shanna wasn't home last night." Sheriff Holden turned his horse toward the Claytons'. "Why don't you show me where Shanna was attacked instead? Give Shanna time to make it into town. If we come from a different direction, it'll be better for everyone."

Reese nodded. It made sense. The last thing he wanted was to give Shanna more trouble than he already gave her. She needed time to calm down. He had no idea what upset her. He wanted her calm when they talked, so he could explain how she was going to be marrying him, without getting punched again. The girl had a strong arm and threw a good punch, a real good one.

****

Shanna ran the horse all the way to town. Tears fell freely from her swollen eyes. The bastard! *He wouldn't have touched her except he thought she was Jenna!* The words cut through her, slicing into her heart. First. Daniel Anderson tore her heart to shreds and humiliated her in front of the whole town. Then, right when she no longer cared, and her heart was all wrapped up in indifference, Marshal Reese Calhan showed up and shattered her indifference. What was she going to do? She gave herself to him, every part of her heart and soul. In response, the only thing he had to say was he thought she was Jenna? How was she ever going to face Reese again after the things they did together? Why couldn't she fall in love with someone who wanted her? And not because she looked like someone else or reminded him of someone else? But because she was her and her alone?

Shanna stopped on the outskirts of town and wiped her face with her sleeve. She patted her hair and pasted a serene expression on her face. Then she walked the horse toward Tanner's mercantile.

Rose waved at her the second she stepped onto Main Street. She stood on the mercantile step and pulled Shanna off the horse in a fierce hug before Shanna got the horse stopped all the way. "Where have you been? I was so worried when you didn't come into work yesterday morning." Rose pulled back; studying Shanna's tear streaked face and frowned ferociously. Rose grabbed the reins, tied them to the post, and dragged Shanna through the mercantile and up the stairs to her bedroom. She pushed Shanna on to her bed and stood with her arms folded over her chest, much like her mother did when she scolded Rose for something, "Now, talk. What's wrong?" Rose said.

Shanna dropped her head. She didn't know where to begin.

"What happened last night? And don't you dare tell me nothing. I saw Sheriff Holden bring Daniel Anderson in this morning cuffed to his horse. I also saw Delphine charge into the sheriff's office, and I heard her screaming at Sheriff Holden to let Daniel go. So, talk."

"How should I know?" Shanna asked hoping her friend would drop the questions. A lot of things happened last night she didn't want to talk about.

"No. I'm not letting you deny anything. I saw Daniel yesterday after you left him on the sidewalk. He was one angry man. I *know* something happened. Then there's the fact you were riding Daniel Anderson's horse. You're not leaving here until I hear the whole story, now talk."

Shanna didn't know where to begin. She said as much to Rose.

"Okay. Then start when you walked home from work. What happened next?"

Shanna told Rose everything. Right up until she woke up, and then she lied. She couldn't tell Rose what happened between her and Reese. Couldn't tell her how she'd given herself to him, how she'd drowned in his touch, how she'd responded to him, how she'd ridden a wave of pleasure so high it erased her, and she became a part of him. She sat staring at the tied rug on Rose's floor. She also couldn't tell Rose how deep his words cut into her heart when he'd told her he only touched her because he thought she was *Jenna*. Tears filled her eyes and slid down her cheeks. She couldn't face him again, couldn't bear to see him, and she couldn't bear to hear more of his words. They hurt too much.

****

176

Rose wrapped her arms around Shanna's shoulders. She was a highly intelligent girl. As she studied the emotions chasing themselves over Shanna's face, she had a pretty good idea what happened. Rose squeezed Shanna's shoulders. "I understand, Shanna. Tell me what happened after," she said softly.

"He told me he would not have, you know, except he thought I was Jenna," Shanna choked out.

Rose was properly and completely indignant. "The beast!" she said. "What are we going to do? You can't let him hurt you the way Daniel did."

"It's too late," Shanna whispered, "much too late."

Rose was silent as she analyzed the situation. "What do you want to do now?" It shook her up to see Shanna hurting.

"I wish I could talk to Mama," Shanna said. "She would know what to do." Tears streamed from her eyes.

"Why can't you?" Rose asked thinking fast. "How much is a train ticket to Omaha?"

"Mama sends me twenty dollars every year to come. The train costs ten dollars. The rest is for the mail coach and to pay the people who let me ride in their wagon from here to Fort Buford."

"So, a one-way ticket from Pine Bluffs to Omaha should be about five dollars." Rose ran to her chest. She took out eight dollars. "There was money left over from your dress. I've been saving it in my chest to give to you." Rose placed the money in Shanna's lap. One way or another, she would get Shanna to her mama. Shanna never cried, not even when her uncle beat her. The fact Shanna cried now told Rose all she needed to know. She would go get one of Papa's guns and go find the marshal as soon as she got Shanna safely away.

****

Shanna looked at the money. A lonely, hopeful feeling fluttered in her breast. She could go see Mama! Shanna hugged Rose with shining eyes. "You are the dearest friend! I think this is exactly what I need, and I love you for thinking of it!"

"Where's the marshal, now?" Rose asked. "We need to get you out of town before he knows what's happening. With the way he watches you lately, we're going to have to be quite sneaky."

"He stayed with the sheriff. They were talking when I rode off," Shanna replied.

"Good, then we have time," Rose said.

"What about my things at the Claytons'? We will need to go out and get them without Uncle Joseph finding out, or he will stop me," Shanna decided.

"No. We don't have time. You will take several of my dresses, so nobody is the wiser," Rose answered.

"Rose—" Shanna began.

Rose cut her off. "Can't you see it's the only way? If we wait around, either Uncle Joseph, the marshal, or both will find out, and stop you from going. We can't risk it. You are taking my things. I won't hear any more about it."

Rose dragged her traveling case from under her bed and began filling it with clothing. She added a hairbrush, comb, and soap. Then, she snapped the case shut. "Come on, Shanna. Let's get you on a wagon for Fort Buford."

Chapter 20

Reese headed for the mercantile once he got back to town. He intended on having a talk with Shanna. There would be one or two things straightened out between them before this thing went any further. He had no idea why she'd been so mad. Hell, he'd only been trying to apologize and explain why things had gone as far as they did, and she up and punched him in the mouth. She threw a damn solid punch for such a little girl. Reese touched his swollen lip. It took him less than five minutes to discover Shanna was gone, headed to the fort with Mr. Tanner.

He spent the first few minutes explaining to Rose Tanner what his intentions were concerning Shanna. Rose was tight lipped as a youngster being given tonic until he mentioned the fact he loved Shanna and wanted to marry her. Then he couldn't get Rose to be quiet long enough to ask any more questions. Once he understood Shanna was going to see her mama in Omaha to get her broken heart fixed, and Shanna hoped Reese fell into the Mississippi, and she never had to see him again, he patted Rose awkwardly on the shoulder and got back on Pegasus. He'd make better time if he headed to Pine Bluffs cross-country than if he followed along behind and attempted to snag the same mail coach as Shanna. From what Rose Tanner said, Shanna wouldn't be happy to see him. The way Reese figured, the only one who could explain why Shanna looked so much like Jenna, would be Shanna's mama. He intended to follow Shanna and hopefully get some of his own questions answered. If Shanna was as upset as Rose thought she was, it would be better if Reese followed her from a safe distance until he knew where her mama was.

Reese made it to Pine Bluffs a full four hours before the mail coach arrived. He followed Shanna to the train station and leaned against the outer wall of the depot, staying out of sight while Shanna bought a one-way ticket to Omaha. After she walked off, he bought his own ticket and faded into the background to wait for the train. Reese took a seat in the back-passenger car where he could see the tip of Shanna's hat through the windows of the cars. He got one glimpse of her face and realized she was crying. Something akin to anguish squeezed his chest. Her face was all swollen, and her eyes were red and puffy. Reese shifted uncomfortably. He'd never seen Shanna cry, not during the robbery of the mail coach, not following the incident with Little Alfred Turley, not even with Snake Eye. She hadn't even cried when Daniel Anderson embarrassed her. She was crying now, and it ate at his heart to know he was the reason behind her sadness. Reese settled back in his seat. He wanted to go to her, but somehow, he knew if she caught sight of him, he would never see her mama, nor would he ever see Shanna again. He needed answers, a lot of answers. The only one who might know those answers would be Shanna's mama. So, he was content to keep Shanna safe from a distance and see where she led him.

****

"Boss, we got a telegram from Pine Bluffs.

Marshal Calhan is on his way to Omaha. He will be there tomorrow afternoon." The man they called Whiskey John brought the news and waited for the boss's answer.

"Is he coming to Chicago?" The boss didn't look up but continued reading the newspaper on her desk.

"The telegram didn't say. It only says: *Marshal Calhan en route to Omaha. Be there tomorrow afternoon.* No mention was made at all of any additional ticket into Chicago." Whiskey John stared at the telegram. He thought she would be pleased with the news.

"Then he's staying in Omaha for some reason. Tell the ticket master he will get his usual pay for the information. Tell the boys to meet me at the office." She swung around in her chair and reached for the hat atop the rack on the left.

Whiskey John nodded and walked out. He hoped to God this time they caught the marshal. The boss was losing all sense of humor and at times was downright cranky. Only yesterday, Slick got a bullet in his shoulder for cracking a joke about a disfigured woman. The joke was funny, but she hadn't taken kindly to it. Whiskey John wanted to go looting and shooting like in the good old days. Anymore Marshal Reese Calhan was the only subject she was interested in hearing about.

Whiskey John sent the required telegram to the ticket master and thanked him for the information. The boss had a hand in every level of government and business. Nothing happened but what she knew about it, one way or the other. The ticket master would have his pay by the end of the week. Whiskey John found the boys and gave them the boss's message. Then he headed for the office.

The office was an abandoned warehouse by the train tracks. The door was chained shut to maintain appearances, but everybody knew it was the Delaney Gang's gathering place. Nobody dared enter but the Delaney Gang. They had an identical one along the tracks in Omaha. Adam Delaney liked to keep things simple. It avoided confusion with the less intelligent members of the gang.

Their boss stood in the center of the building; a riding crop held tightly in her hand. Whiskey John wasn't sure what the riding crop was for, but he wasn't about to ask questions. She waited until everybody was present and then laid out the plans. They were going to Omaha to capture Marshal Calhan, but not before they discovered what he was doing there. She wanted the marshal taken to the local office in Omaha. He was to be hanging from the meat hooks in the Omaha office within two days, alive. She had one or two things to discuss with the marshal. This caused the men to laugh. They knew what she wanted from the marshal. She blamed him for her years in exile and wanted him to suffer before they killed him.

****

All the way to Omaha, Shanna played and replayed everything she did or said to Reese. She thought her heart was protected and under control. She was wrong. The pain she endured from Daniel's betrayal and public rejection was nothing like listening to Reese tell her he only touched her because he thought she was Jenna. The words played over and over in her mind until she thought she would go mad. They kept time with the clack of the train wheels as they rumbled along the miles and miles of steel track. *"I thought you were Jenna, I thought you were Jenna, I thought you were Jenna."*

Shanna put her fingers in her ears, but the words only played louder. In desperation she opened her Bible and started to read. The words leapt off the page, mocking her. She'd opened her Bible to Genesis with all the begets. Shanna slammed her Bible shut and wrapped her arms around her middle. She could be involved in a begat right this minute.

She thought about a baby. A baby she and Reese made together. A tiny soul with Reese's blond hair and blue eyes. Her heart melted. A tiny innocent life who depended on her for survival. Shanna sighed. She wanted children, always had. The thought there might be one right now inside her, made her ferocious. She would have a family of her own. Her and the baby would be their own family. She wouldn't let Reese near her. If they'd made a baby, she'd move to Omaha, or somewhere far away, and raise the baby alone. Reese need never know he fathered a child. She'd keep her safe, care for her, and love her enough for both of them. It would be hers and hers alone. She wouldn't share with the man who fathered her. Not when he admitted he'd made a mistake and thought she was someone else.

Shanna spent the rest of the journey envisioning a beautiful, blonde-haired daughter with blue eyes. She thought about how she would teach her, how she would care for her, all the things she wanted to show her, and do with her. It was hours before she realized the reason she hurt so much, and the reason she could love a blonde-haired, blue-eyed child who didn't exist with such intensity, was one and the same reason. *She'd fallen in love with Reese.* Shanna nearly fainted when the realization hit her. She paled and held her Bible tightly to her chest.

"Are you all right, miss?" The elderly gentleman seated across from her leaned forward in concern.

Shanna dabbed at her clammy face with her handkerchief. "Yes, yes. I'm fine. Thank you for asking." She smiled at the old man to reassure him. "There is nothing to worry about. I simply had a little dizzy spell, sir. I'm fine now." She nodded to let him know she meant what she said and turned toward the window once more.

The train pulled into the station a few hours later. Shanna picked up her case and climbed off the train. She still had a shilling to hire a hackney carriage to take her to Mama's house. She whistled shrilly between her teeth and was soon on her way. Reese exited his car right before Shanna and turned away quickly before she recognized him. She whistled for a hackney, and he followed suit.

Two well-dressed men sitting on a bench at the station put down their newspapers and followed Reese. They signaled for a hackney carriage also and followed the marshal, who followed the girl.

****

Shanna knocked timidly on her mother's front door. She only visited once a year. She wasn't certain her mother was home. She had no idea what her mother did all year without her.

"Shanna?" Mary Johnston stepped through the doorway and wrapped Shanna in a hug. She looked up and down the street and then pulled Shanna into the warm inviting house. "My, it is so good to see you. I've missed you. Why have you come? Is something wrong? Come in, darling, and tell me why you are visiting for the second time."

Mary had Shanna seated in a chair, with a cup of herbal tea and a freshly made sandwich by her side, before Shanna could blink.

"Eat, darling, and tell me why you've come." Mary sat opposite Shanna in a soft cushioned chair and waited. Shanna took a sip of her tea. She glanced at the sandwich. She wasn't hungry. "I've made a terrible mistake, Mama," Shanna whispered.

****

Fear clutched Mary's heart. Panic raced through her system. Her first instinct was to run and get the gun she kept by her bed, but she didn't. She didn't know why Shanna was here. It would be best to let the girl explain. Mary willed her hands to relax and let go the fists they instinctively created. She took a deep calming breath while she waited for Shanna to continue.

"What mistake could you have made?" Mary was proud of her ability to keep her voice calm.

"I've fallen in love," Shanna whispered. Her head dropped and tears rolled silently down her cheeks.

Mary got to her feet. She went to Shanna's side and pulled Shanna against her. "Tell Mama all about him," she said as she stroked the silken, blonde head.

"He's a marshal, Mama, a U S Marshal, and a good one. He came to Rock Creek to catch the Turley Gang and while he was there, I fell in love," Shanna said.

Mary smiled. "It doesn't sound much like a mistake. Is he kind? Is he a good man?"

"He would be if he didn't believe I was somebody else," Shanna answered.

"Who does he think you are?" Mary wondered. Something inside Mary alerted her as soon as she asked the question. She knew what Shanna would say before she said the name. Mary said it with her. "Jenna."

Chapter 21

Shanna looked up at Mary in surprise. "Do you know her?" Shanna asked, bewildered.

A loud knock on the door made both the women jump.

Fear clutched at Mary's heart again. "Stay here, dear. If you hear me call out, run out the back and don't look back," Mary said.

"But why?" Shanna began but Mary hushed her.

"I will explain it all in a minute or two. Let me see who's at the door." Mary picked up the poker by the fireplace and carried it to the door with her. Cautiously, she peeked behind the door and met the blue-eyed gaze of Marshal Calhan. Mary saw the badge pinned to his vest and opened the door a little wider. "Can I help you?" She read the badge and guessed this man was the one her daughter spoke of. He was a handsome devil, tall, and muscular. She could see why her daughter liked him, but why would he know Jenna?

"My name is U S Marshal Reese Calhan, Ma'am. I'm looking for Shanna Johnston. I know she's here. I followed her to your house, and I'd like to speak to her. I also have a few questions I'd like to ask you as well, ma'am," Reese said.

Mary looked into the marshal's eyes, and her fear left her. This man was a good man. She would stake her life on it. She was never wrong in her intuitions of people. He had kind eyes. They searched the area behind her looking for someone. He had a worn, weary look about him. Mary guessed her daughter was the cause. "Come in, Marshal." Mary stepped back and allowed the marshal to enter the house. Mary bolted the front door behind him and led him into the parlor where Shanna was sipping her tea.

Shanna was startled when she saw Reese in the door and jumped to her feet angrily. "Why are you here? Did you follow me? I have nothing to say to you, so please go!" Shanna cried.

Mary put a hand on Shanna arm. "Sit down, darling. I think the marshal is looking for answers the same as you."

"I am," Reese said. He rotated his hat in his hands, his eyes searching Shanna's face with an intense, watchful look.

"Come, Marshal, you may sit here by me." Mary patted the settee next to her. Once Reese was seated, she started to talk. "I understand you have my daughter confused with a woman named Jenna," Mary began.

Reese nodded. He was strangely quiet as he waited for the woman to begin. His gaze lingered on Shanna.

"I always knew this day would come, but I hoped it wouldn't come so soon." Mary bowed her head. She gathered her strength. She would need it. What she had to say would be a shock. She hoped Shanna would understand what she'd had to do. "My name is Abigail Smythe," Mary began. Shanna drew in a breath and waited.

"I worked for the Delaney family in Chicago. I was hired by Robert Delaney as a companion for his wife, Alice. She was expecting their first child, and her confinement was difficult. The doctors recommended someone be with Alice constantly for her safety and the safety of her unborn child. Robert Delaney was head of Delany Steel and spent a great deal of time away from home on business. As Alice's pregnancy progressed, Robert started to send his younger brother Adam on company business so he could be with Alice. During this time, a particular gentleman approached Robert with a new metal far stronger than any metal we have known."

"Tungsten steel," Reese said.

"Correct," Mary agreed.

"Wasn't Adam Delaney running a gang?" Reese asked.

"He was. It was hard for Robert to send Adam on company business when he had a reputation as leader of the fiercest gang in Chicago. Alice questioned him, and Robert explained he thought if Adam had more responsibility he would stay out of trouble," Mary explained.

Reese nodded.

"Robert was pretty impressed with the test results on this new metal and made a deal with the man. I believe his name was Mushet. Alice suffered a setback soon after and was confined to her bed. Doctors feared the child would die if Alice gave birth too soon. Robert left Adam in charge of business and hurried to his wife's side. He voiced his misgivings to Alice on several occasions. About a week later, Robert received word Mr. Mushet was dead, and his plans on how to alloy the tungsten with steel were missing. Robert confronted Adam. Adam admitted to killing Mr. Mushet and presenting the plans as his own. Adam applied for the patent, and Delaney Steel would begin production. Robert was furious. Adam laughed at Robert's rebuke. Robert threatened to go to the police, and Adam threatened his life as well as the lives of his family. They had a tremendous row. Robert arrived in the middle of the night, frantic to get Alice away from the city. He had a carriage waiting. It was a dark, rainy night. I will never forget the horror as long as I live."

Mary took a sip of tea and began again. "The bumping of the carriage proved to be too much for Alice. Her contractions started in earnest. We were forced to stop at a little tavern and get Alice onto a bed. Robert hurried out to hide the carriage as best he could. I had no training on delivering a baby, but I was all there was. Alice gave birth to a beautiful daughter about midnight. I wrapped the child up in a blanket. Robert went out to check on the carriage and the horses. As soon as Alice was able, we needed to move her. Robert was convinced his brother was coming to kill them. After Robert left, Alice cried out. To our surprise, another daughter was born. Alice lay weak upon the bed, holding her first daughter. She decided to name the babes, Jenna and Shanna. I took the second babe into the other room to bathe and wrap her." Mary dabbed at her eyes. She didn't like to dwell on what happened next.

"So, I am a twin?" Shanna asked slowly. She looked at Reese. He was watching her intently.

Mary reached over and squeezed her hand. "Yes."

"What happened?" Reese asked. His eyes never left Shanna's face.

"It was when I was cleaning the second daughter, I heard the door crash open. I grabbed the baby and climbed into the wardrobe in the other room. I listened to Robert begging someone to let his wife and child go. Then I heard gunshots. Adam Delaney asked Alice what the baby's name was. She told him Jenna. He said he liked the name and shot Alice. I kept my babe tight against my chest and rocked her in my arms. She never made a sound. Adam Delaney told someone not to kill the baby because he wanted her. I never knew why. They looked in the room where I hid but never opened the wardrobe. The men left soon after. I waited for a spell and then checked on Alice. Both she and Robert were dead." Mary's voice rose in pitch as her emotions climbed higher. She looked at her hands. They trembled at the memories. She clutched them tightly together in her lap.

"How did Shanna end up in Rock Creek?" Reese asked.

"I worried Adam would search for me, because I was always with Alice. I was afraid someone would remember seeing me get into the carriage with her. If he knew of my presence, he would come looking for me and find Shanna. So, I changed my name to the name my brother used to escape the men he owed money to. We moved from place to place. We lived like gypsies, never staying in one spot for more than a few months. I couldn't let anyone know about Shanna. I lived in constant fear of Adam. When Shanna was ten, we came to Omaha to see my best friend. She was ill and needed help. She found this house for me and convinced me to stay. Living on the run, in constant fear of our lives, was wearing us both down," Mary said. Her gaze rested on Shanna. She searched her daughter's face for understanding.

"Uncle Joseph is a Smythe, too?" Shanna asked.

Mary nodded her head. "There's more. One day about a month after we settled here, I went to the bank. On my way out, I almost walked into Adam Delaney. He didn't recognize me. I kept my head down so he couldn't see my face. He was busy arguing with a little girl who looked exactly like you. I hurried past and ran all the way home."

"Jenna," Shanna said.

"Yes. I didn't know the two of you were identical twins until then. I realized if Adam Delaney got a glimpse of you, he would know exactly who you were. I don't know what stopped him from killing Jenna, and I couldn't be sure the same thing would keep him from killing you if he found out. I worried constantly about what to do. I didn't dare go out, and I kept you indoors with the drapes pulled shut."

"I remember being angry you wouldn't let me outside," Shanna murmured.

"I couldn't leave. My friend was still ill, and I was the only help she had. I couldn't sleep. I couldn't eat. The fear of Adam finding you drove me crazy. One day, my brother knocked on my door. He begged me to loan him some money, saying a gambler was going to kill him and Sara if he didn't pay up. I put him off. I was still busy worrying over my own problem, until the answer came to me. Deadwood was far away, and Adam Delaney would never find you there," Mary said. Her gaze rested on Shanna once more. All of this must be quite a surprise.

"Why would Uncle Joseph ask you for money?" Shanna asked.

"Because while I worked for the Delaneys, I had

everything I needed. I tucked my wages away in a savings account for the future. I made the mistake of loaning Joseph some once or twice. He got to thinking he could borrow money from me anytime he got into trouble."

"So, what did you do?" Shanna asked.

"I knew Joseph would never agree to take you to Deadwood. So, I made it a condition of borrowing the money from me. Joseph could have the money if he took you home with him. He was supposed to care for you, to keep you alive, and out of trouble. Sara promised to love you and make sure you were happy. I agreed to pay one thousand dollars a year to them for your care." Mary squeezed Shanna's hands again. "It was the hardest thing I've ever done, to bundle you up and send you away. I tried to explain it to you, but you were so young, and I didn't want to frighten you. I made Joseph and Sara promise to send you back once a year so I could see you. I didn't dare let you visit more often. I was afraid the more you were here, the more chance there was of someone seeing you and telling Adam," Mary said. "Forever after, it was my greatest fear Adam Delaney would get a glimpse of you."

****

Shanna didn't know what to think. She was dumfounded. She had a sister! A twin who looked exactly like she did! She glanced at Reese. He'd been telling her the truth the whole time. There truly was a woman named Jenna who looked exactly like her. She could see now, why he was so confused about her identity. Shanna gazed at him from beneath her lashes. The night in the old cabin, who did he want? Her? Or Jenna? She never got a chance to ask.

Men burst into the house from every angle. She was knocked to the floor and tied up before she had a chance to think. Mama's head was inches from hers. Reese was down too. A hood was thrown over Shanna's face. The last thing she saw before everything went dark was the fear on Mama's face and the fury on Reese's.

Chapter 22

They were dragged out of the house and thrown in the bottom of a carriage. Mama landed on top of her. Shanna tried to shield her from their captors' feet as they climbed into the carriage with them. Shanna had no idea where they took Reese. Fear caught her heart. He couldn't die! Not before she had a chance to question him about what he'd said the night by the river. "I'm here, Mama." Shanna whispered. She leaned closer to Mary, but someone shoved her back.

"Keep quiet," the man growled.

If they thought they were hurting her mother, they could think again. She wiggled her hands against the ropes binding them. She'd forgotten what White Eagle told her, and now the ropes cut into her skin. Her fingers were getting numb. Shanna inched her way toward Mary. Once her mother was next to her, she held still. Mama must be close to hysteria by now. They bumped along for a while, and then the carriage stopped. The men got out of the carriage, and more men's voices joined them. There was an argument going on. Shanna took the opportunity to talk to Mary. "Are you okay, Mama?" she whispered.

"Yes," Mary whispered back.

"Do you know who the men are?" Shanna asked.

"I recognized one of them. He works for Adam Delaney," Mary said. Her whole body shook violently.

Shanna was furious. "Can you reach my side?" she asked. "There's a knife under my skirt."

"I think so. Why do you have a knife, Shanna?" Mary asked.

"We'll talk later, Mama. Get the knife out, and put it in my hands.

Mary felt along Shanna's side until she found the knife. Shanna felt her pull it from the scabbard. Then Mary placed the handle into her bound hand. Shanna found the rope binding her mother. Cautiously she worked the sharp blade back and forth until Mary's hands broke free. Mary pulled the hood from her head and reached for Shanna.

"We don't have time, Mama. It sounds like someone is giving orders. They will be back in a minute. Do you have someplace safe to go?" Shanna asked.

"I can go to my friend," Mary answered. "She will help me."

"Good. As soon as they open the door, I'm going to make a distraction. You run away, and don't look back. I will find you."

"Shanna, I can't—" Mary began.

"Yes, you can. I can take care of myself. It will be easier for me if I know you are safe. Once I am free, I will leave a message at your house on where to find me," Shanna said.

"But Shanna—" Mary began again.

"Mama. It's going to be all right. I will come and find you. You have to trust me," Shanna said with more conviction than she actually felt.

"Give me the knife, Shanna," Mary insisted. Quickly she worked on Shanna's ropes until her hands were free.

Shanna sheathed her blade. The men's voices got closer to the carriage. Shanna pulled the hood from her head and climbed onto the seat by the door. Lucky thing they tied her hands in front of her instead of behind. Otherwise, she wouldn't have been able to get Mama free. "Here they come, Mama. Remember what I said, and run as fast as you can." Shanna braced herself as the carriage door swung open. With a cry she jumped at the men standing there and knocked them to the ground. Mary was right behind her. Before the men could react, she was out of the carriage and running down the street.

One man pulled out a gun and took aim. Shanna knocked him over and kneed him in the groin. The other man swung her around intent on backhanding her across the face and stopped. He froze in terror as he looked at Shanna.

"Boss?" the man asked. It was barely a whisper.

Shanna's mind worked quickly. They didn't know she wasn't Jenna. Shanna narrowed her eyes on the man. He nearly pissed himself.

"I didn't know it was you, I swear. No one told us you would be sitting in the house with the marshal. Otherwise, we wouldn't have tied you up and such. Sorry, Boss. We got the marshal, though. We sure did."

"Where is he now?" Shanna asked hoping she sounded like Jenna too.

The man looked at her curiously. "He's on the way to the office, like you told us. Whiskey John's got him tied up in the baggage car." He indicated a train behind them. "We were going to shoot you, I mean, the lady with the marshal. Sorry again, we didn't realize it was you. You probably want to ride up front on the train. We will get you a seat, Boss. Wait here. We won't be a minute." The two men scurried off, and Shanna breathed a sigh of relief.

Reese was still alive. They were going by train to the office, wherever that was. Chicago, probably. Shanna glanced around quickly. They were in a train yard. She headed toward the last car on the train Delaney's men indicated. She wasn't sure how she would get Reese free but being mistaken for the boss would make it easier. More men emerged from the baggage car and locked the door behind them. They gave her startled glances.

One big man walked toward her, a scowl on his face. "Is something wrong, Boss?" he growled.

"No, why would it be?" she asked.

"It seems you don't trust us to do the job, so you tagged along. I don't like you riding herd on me," he said. He stood directly in front of Shanna glaring at her.

"Nobody's riding herd. I was going to check on the prisoner." She thought she sounded convincing, until the big man took a step toward her. He wasn't acting scared like the other men were.

"When Adam heard you were setting up this party, he sent me along to see to it Calhan made it back in one piece. It seems your uncle wants to have a little talk with him, too." The big man chuckled. "Adam told me to keep an eye on the marshal. He said no one was to see him or talk to him along the way." The man meant what he said.

Shanna stood her ground. She sneered at the man. "Are you telling me no?" she asked.

The man paled a little. "I work for Adam, not you,"

the big man said.

Shanna turned away, "Then you won't mind me sending a telegram to my uncle telling him you were disobeying my order, will you?" She started to walk away. The big man stopped her.

"All right, you can check on the prisoner. Your uncle won't like you interfering. You know he won't."

Shanna nodded and waited while he unchained the door and slid it open. She stumbled into the baggage coach. It was dark inside, and it took her eyes a minute to adjust to the darkness. It smelled like leather, stale hay, and sweat. She looked around the stacks of baggage. Reese was chained to the far wall, the hood still over his head. Shanna hurried over and pulled the hood off.

****

"What the hell are you doing here?" he asked furiously. Once the men learned she wasn't Jenna; they would shoot her.

"I'm here to rescue you," Shanna said.

Reese took a deep breath to calm his pounding heart. "Shanna, sweetheart, I need you to listen to me." His eyes bored into hers. "They think you are Jenna," he said urgently.

"I know. How do you think I got in here? Now turn around so I can untie you." Shanna reached around behind him.

"Shanna, please sweetheart, you *have* to listen to me! Once they realize you're not Jenna, they will kill you! And I won't be able to do a damn thing about it. So, go! Run while you have the chance! Don't worry about me! Leave! You don't know what they'll do to you." Reese leaned toward her, his eyes burning.

"If I can get you lose, we'll go together," Shanna answered.

Reese didn't move. Suddenly, the door to the baggage car slid open. The big man stood in the door. He had several men with him and a length of rope in his hands. Reese growled low in his throat. He pulled against his ropes violently.

"Grab the girl," the big man said.

Shanna got quickly to her feet. "Lay one hand on me, and you'll wish you hadn't. Wait until my uncle hears about this!" she sneered.

"He already has. He says his niece Jenna is sitting right there with him, and he has no idea who you are, lady. He wants us to bring you along with the marshal so he can get a good look at you. He didn't believe me when I told him you looked exactly like Jenna." The big man stood in the doorway blocking her escape. The other men stood uncertainly behind him. They didn't want to be the one responsible for tying up the boss. Reese growled and then glared at Whiskey John. Shanna stared too waiting for an opportunity to attack. Reese recognized the look on her face and shook his head at her.

Whiskey John looked around at his men. "Grab the girl. She's not the boss, and Adam wants her tied and delivered!" he bellowed.

They still stood, staring. It wasn't until Whiskey John pulled out his pistol and threatened to shoot them all, they did as he asked.

"Shanna—" Reese began, but it was too late. She knocked the first three men down and had the fourth in a chokehold before he could say a thing. They backhanded her, splitting her lip. Shanna spit blood onto the floor of the baggage car.

Reese pulled frantically against his ropes, murder in his eyes. "Leave her alone you bastards. I swear I'm going to tear every one of you apart!"

The men took a step backward. Reese took a step forward. His ropes held him fast, but they all knew they were dead men if he escaped. His look of contempt promised retribution.

"She sure does fight better than the boss," one man said as he wiped blood from his mouth. Whiskey John grabbed Shanna by the hair and slammed her against the wall. The men tied her with the rope and threw her onto the ground beside Reese.

****

She'd barely had time to remember to pull her wrists apart the way White Eagle taught her. She wiggled her arms against the ropes. She had slack. With a little bit of time and a lot of luck, she should be able to get them both out of here.

"Best get what comfort you can from the bitch before we get to the office. The way I figure it, Jenna will take one look at your girl here and cut her up in little pieces. She won't like somebody else lookin' like her." Whiskey John laughed and they all walked out of the car, sliding the door shut behind them. They could hear the chain being drawn through the door handle.

Shanna leaned back against the wall, breathing hard. If Reese said, "I told you so," she'd kick him.

****

Reese was quiet for a time, his heart pounding furiously in his chest. "Whiskey John is right. Jenna wouldn't like you looking like her. Adam won't like it either," Reese said. He frowned. "Where's your mama?"

Shanna shrugged. "I helped her get away. She says she has a friend she can stay with where she will be safe," Shanna said.

He didn't even want to know how she did it. It was one less person to worry about. He wasn't sure how the hell he was going to get them out of this. It was every nightmare he had played out in real life. Now he knew there were two of them, and they were identical twins, so much made sense. They were as different as two people could be. Jenna was evil, and Shanna was good—plain and simple. He couldn't let Jenna or Adam hurt Shanna. He couldn't lose her now it was all starting to make sense.

Chapter 23

The train began to move, and soon they were rumbling down the track. "Why did you run away from me?" Reese asked.

"I didn't run away. I came to Omaha to see my mother," Shanna answered.

"You only come once a year. You already had your visit for this year a few months back, when you and I were on the same damn train together. This visit to Omaha is about something else. So, why did you run from me?" Reese asked again.

Shanna blew her hair out of her eyes and looked sideways at Reese. His head rested against the train wall. His gaze centered on the wall opposite. He wasn't even looking at her. Suddenly she was mad, mad she was tied up, mad he'd followed her to Omaha and was tied up beside her, mad her mama had been taken and nearly killed, mad she'd given herself to Reese, mad he'd taken her thinking she was Jenna, mad she'd fallen in love with him, and mad he loved Jenna and not her. "You knew about Jenna the whole time," she accused him.

"No," Reese said. "I knew Jenna and thought you were her. You look exactly alike."

"Alike enough you took me to bed thinking I was her!" Shanna spit on the ground. She was so upset she could hardly think straight.

Reese looked startled. "Shanna, let me explain," he said softly.

Shanna turned her head away, blinking rapidly. If he told her one more time, he only touched her because he thought she was Jenna, she would tear his heart out. She wasn't sure how she'd do it with her hands bound together, but she'd figure it out.

"I met Jenna while I was a detective with the Chicago police seven years ago. I oversaw the security of valuables. Things like shipments of gold, payroll for the railroad, bank transfers, and important people. We met at a social event where I'd been hired to protect the mayor. Jenna entered on the arm of her uncle. I was blinded by her beauty. She took my breath away. She was the prettiest girl I'd ever seen. I thought she was perfect, the perfect woman. I asked her out, and she accepted. We became friends and then lovers. She was so sweet and giving, completely unselfish, and so loving. I fell deeply in love with her."

Shanna sniffed. She didn't want to hear this at all. "I thought her uncle was head of the gang. Why was he invited to this social event?" she asked, despite her pretended disinterest.

"He was, is. He has never been caught. Everyone knows who he is and what he does, but nobody has any proof. Adam Delaney makes sure his hands are clean. Without proof, we can't arrest or prosecute him. He's also one of the richest men in Chicago. So, although nobody likes him, he's invited to all the big events because of his wealth."

Shanna snorted. "It doesn't seem right.'

Reese agreed. "Jenna was often at my house, and sometimes she stayed the night," Reese said softly. He waited for Shanna to say something. There was silence. "Not long after Jenna started coming over, robberies began to occur. The Delaney Gang hit several transports, one right after another. It was as if the robbers knew where, when, and by what road different shipments would come or go. I was completely baffled on how this gang knew so much about my work. Sergeant Baxter was my boss. He thought there must be a leak in the department somewhere. I agreed, and together we tried to figure out who it was. We came up empty handed. Then, we came up with a plan. We would send out different routes and time information with different detectives to see where the leak was," Reese paused.

"Where was Jenna?" Shanna asked.

"I'm getting to it. I had a made-up time and delivery route as well. Sergeant Baxter was convinced Jenna was the leak. I wouldn't listen. In my arrogance, I assumed I knew her. I was dead wrong. We set up a train car with explosives and had it come in at a certain time. It was supposed to contain a shipment of gold for the fort. I told Jenna I was going to the police station to do some paperwork and left the house."

"She stayed at your house a lot." Shanna's voice was emotionless.

"Yes," Reese said. He gazed at her face. It was a mask of indifference. He sighed wearily running his hands through his hair. "Hell, I need a cigarette and a bottle of whiskey." He closed his eyes to calm the rapid beating of his heart.

Shanna glanced at him warily. "Why?"

"To get me through the rest of the story." Reese was quiet for another minute then continued. "I went to the train station early. Sergeant Baxter and I hid, waiting and watching. Right as the car with the explosives arrived and was detached from the rest of the train, Jenna showed up on horseback. I was so surprised to see her. I didn't notice her men coming in from all angles. I jumped from my hiding place, to Baxter's dismay, and hurried over to Jenna. I tried to warn her away. Jenna called me a damn fool and told me to get lost. She said she wouldn't need me anymore with what she planned on collecting from the train. She told me she was done with me for good. She told me thank you for leading her and the gang to so many shipments. She laughed at how easy it was to get the information from me. I stood there shocked. I couldn't believe Jenna was part of the Delaney Gang. Then I realized she wasn't only part of the gang; she *ran* the gang. Right then, I started to see her for the first time. She stood there in a pair of men's jeans waving a gun in my face and laughing, telling me what a stupid fool I was. I thought she loved me. I grabbed her arm to stop her. She signaled at somebody behind me. I never saw her men coming. They surrounded me and beat me nearly to death. There wasn't a thing Sergeant Baxter could do to help. He shot at them and nailed a couple of the men. I got a couple too, before I went down. Once they heard the gunshots, they scattered. Jenna and two of her men headed to the train car. I yelled at her to stop, but she wouldn't listen. The explosion shook the ground. I was covered in debris. Sergeant Baxter made a dive for me and dragged me away before the explosion, or I would have died."

Shanna stared at Reese. Now things were starting to make sense to her too. No wonder he'd been looking in the bushes for Jenna's men all this time. "You said you wouldn't have touched me, but you thought I was her." Shanna's voice was barely audible. Reese looked at her. She stared back while she waited to hear his answer. Her heart beat furiously in her ears.

"It took me awhile to realize you are the embodiment of everything I thought she was." His gaze wandered over her beautiful face.

Shanna stiffened. "Meaning what?"

"It means I fell in love with a girl, the image of a girl. I believed the girl was Jenna, but she turned out to be something entirely different. It was all an act she put on to get information from me. Information she used to steal and murder. I could never forgive her for what she used me to do. I hated her with all my heart. I thought she died in the train explosion. I watched her run toward the train, watched as the door opened, and then the explosion blocked my sight." Reese shook his head. "I thought it was over. I thought she was dead. I was in the hospital for weeks. While I was laid up, Sergeant Baxter attended a memorial service for Jenna." Reese looked over at Shanna. "And then I carried you from a train seven years later."

Reese stared at the wall. "I had one hell of a time keeping it straight. You had me so confused. One minute you did just what Jenna would do. You carry a knife like she does. It's sheathed to your thigh on the same side. You throw it the same. You look the same, talk the same, and walk the same. I wanted to arrest you every time I looked at you. Then you would do something so out of character, like tend my wound and search for yarrow. You're also shy and quiet. Something Jenna is not. I figured it was all an act, that you were casing a job. You are everything I thought she was. It's like you are separate sides of the same coin. One side is good, the other is evil."

Shanna let his words settle around her. She dropped her head on her knees. He was as confused as she was. Shanna lifted her head and whispered. "That night by the river...who did you want...Jenna...or me?"

He never got the chance to answer. The chains rattled against the door, and then it slid open. They had not gone far. The office must be somewhere on the other side of the city. Whiskey John strolled into the car. He had his pistol out and several men followed him. "We are coming into the station." Whiskey John pointed the gun at them. He nodded to the men surrounding him.

"Get them up and get the hoods on them." Shanna was pulled roughly to her feet. A black hood was pulled over her head. It took four men to carry her off the train car. She put up quite a fuss, but eventually they got her to stand still. It was the pistol pressed against her head that convinced her to be quiet.

"Get walking!" Whiskey John commanded. The pistol nudged her between her shoulder blades. Shanna started to walk. She could feel Reese walking alongside her. It comforted her to have him there, even if she was still mad at him. Once they figured this mess out, they had a lot of talking to do. At least he did, Shanna decided.

Shanna stumbled and someone jerked her arm. "If you'd take the hood off, I wouldn't stumble," she said caustically.

The man beside her knocked her down. She'd had

about enough of these men. The man began to laugh, and she came up fighting. She rushed toward the laughter, catching the man in the chest, and knocking him on his backside. He hit the ground hard, spitting swear words.

"For God's sake." Someone pulled the hood from Shanna's head.

Whiskey John had his gun pointed at her. He held a hand out to the grungy bald man sitting on the ground. The man pulled out a pistol, and Whiskey John glowered at him. "Put it away. Boss wants to do the talking and the killing." The man let Whiskey John pull him to his feet.

He spit in Shanna's face. "Keep out of my way if you know what's good for you," he threatened.

"You knocked me down. I simply returned the favor," she said.

"Enough!" Whiskey John said, "Christ, it's like tending a bunch of brats." He nudged Shanna in the back with his pistol to get her to start walking. Shanna looked around. They were outside a huge warehouse. Three men walked ahead shoving Reese into a door at the back of the building. Whiskey John nudged Shanna again. They entered the building through the same door.

****

The building was large and mostly empty. There were barrels and stacks of wooden crates here and there. A musty odor permeated the air. Sunlight gleamed through a row of glass windows along the top of the walls. A large table stood in the middle of the room. Chairs were strewn about. Reese was tied to a wooden chair facing the table. Whiskey John nudged Shanna toward him. One of the men turned a chair around setting its back against the back of the chair Reese occupied. Whiskey John pushed Shanna into it and tied her to the chair. They pulled the hood from Reese's head. He got a good look around for the first time. He glanced at the meat hooks suspended from the ceiling behind the table and saw the bloodstains beneath them. This must be Adam's Omaha office. He liked abandoned buildings along the train tracks. It made gang-related comings and goings easier.

Whiskey John spoke quietly with the men off to the side. Reese studied the inside of the building, making note of the exits. It was too dark to see what lay beyond the table, other than the meat hooks. He suspected there was another door behind there somewhere. He had a door to his left and the door behind him where he'd come in. Reese studied the distance to the door on his left. It looked to be a couple hundred feet. The door behind him was sixty paces. He'd counted.

****

Shanna looked around, too, assessing the distance to the two doors. She didn't see the meat hooks because she had her back to the long table, facing the back door.

The big man stood talking with the other men off to her right. She had to think quickly. One way or another, they were getting out of this. Then, she and Reese were having a long talk.

"John!" A woman's voice rang out shrilly. Shanna felt Reese tense. Her stomach formed a knot. She knew who it was. Jenna. *She was about to meet her twin sister for the first time.*

Chapter 24

Whiskey John jumped at the sound of his name and hurried forward. Jenna had a mean temper, and he didn't want to rile it. He was too late. She was already riled. Jenna screamed his name again before he got to her. She held a skinny little man by the neck. Frenchie and Iverson followed dragging a short stocky man with them. Both the men were bound and gagged.

Jenna had blood on her arm and was swearing like a gutter rat. "Where the hell were you?" Jenna screamed. She dropped the man at Whiskey John's feet and put her hands on her hips.

"I was keeping watch on the prisoners. Who's this?" Whiskey John asked.

The man started to get to his feet, but Jenna gave him a swift kick in the gut. "They're dead, that's what they are. Four men jumped me outside the gate. One got a shot off and grazed my shoulder. Frenchie killed one, and one got away."

Whiskey John looked the men over. Something about the stocky one rang a bell. "This man is Mack Turley." He indicated the stocky man with his chin.

Jenna turned to the man. She drew a knife from the sheath on her thigh and cut the gag from his mouth. "Is the name supposed to mean something?" she asked.

Mack Turley spit in her face. "You blew up my brother, you bitch."

Jenna wiped her face. She smiled at Mack still holding her blade. Whiskey John swallowed. He'd seen the look before.

"It sounds like something I'd do. What was your brother's name?" Jenna asked.

Mack narrowed his eyes. "As if you didn't know. Why'd you blow Alfred and my men up? What threat were we to you?"

Jenna gave a little laugh. "You are no threat at all." She stared at Mack as if trying to make up her mind about something.

"I thought I was your explosive man." Iverson cut in. He pouted like a child when Mack talked about an explosion he wasn't part of.

"You are," Jenna answered and turned to Mack. "I didn't blow up your brother or your men, but I am going to kill you." Jenna lifted her knife and sliced the side of Mack's face.

Mack didn't make a sound.

Jenna smiled. "This one is going to be a lot of fun. Hang them on the hooks."

Whiskey John dragged Mack over and hung him and his man on the hooks.

Iverson was still upset. "Did you use somebody else because the explosion we set on the train didn't get the marshal?" he asked.

Jenna swung to Iverson. "No, but I am still mad at you over the failed train explosion. Good thing Whiskey John knows how to follow orders. I was going to kill both of you for failing, but I told John to get me the marshal, and there he is."

****

Reese leaned back. He should have known. He

thought Jenna was dead. He'd been a sitting target on the train with not one thought of Jenna or his health.

Whiskey John whispered in Jenna's ear and nudged his chin in their direction.

Jenna strolled toward Reese, an evil, seductive smile twisting her mouth. "Did you miss me, darling?" She leaned down and kissed him, a hard, ruthless kiss, then bit his lip. The bite drew blood. She laughed as she wiped his blood from her mouth.

"Adam had a memorial service for you. I thought you were dead. Everybody did," Reese said. He wanted to know how she escaped.

Jenna laughed shrilly. "I know, darling. That's what you were supposed to think." Jenna drew the tip of her blade down Reese's cheek. "I heard you call me as I went toward the train car. I stepped behind Baby John when Talcum opened the door. I am forever grateful I did. Baby John fell on top of me, protecting me from the blast. It didn't do much for him. They had a closed casket at his funeral." Jenna pulled a face. "Such a mess. It was cruel of you to put dynamite in the train car instead of gold." Jenna's blade drew blood. She wiped it away with the tip of her finger and smiled. "The explosion outside of Pine Bluffs was my way of letting you know I am still alive. It should have blown you to pieces. I'm mad at Iverson for failing me." Jenna's bottom lip stuck out. She pouted for as minute. Then slipped her finger into her mouth and licked Reese's blood away.

"Where were you all those years?" Reese asked. "I know you weren't in Chicago, or I would have heard about it. "

Jenna's eyes narrowed. "Adam sent me to Europe.

He was upset with me for getting in a relationship with you." She drew the tip of her blade over Reese's lips. "He said I bungled the whole thing. He was mad at me for confessing I was behind all the robberies. Adam can be such a spoilsport sometimes. I wanted you to know it was me. I wanted you to know how much I enjoyed using you." Jenna laughed. "You were supposed to die that day. I wanted to watch your face when you did. I wanted to watch you when you realized I outsmarted you, and I had the power to keep you alive or let you die." Jenna pouted again. "Only I didn't get the chance. The Chicago police showed up too fast. When you yelled and told me not to open the train car door, I realized it was trap. Damn you for that! I will never forgive you for lying to me. I want you to suffer as much as I suffered. That's why you're here, darling. You see, for punishment, Adam sent me away. For five years, I lived in Spain and then France. I couldn't come home, couldn't talk to my friends, and I couldn't ride with the gang. I hated you. Every day I thought of ways I wanted to torture you." Jenna's blade slid to his throat. She sliced a thin line across the front. "Oh well, you're here now. We have several surprises for you. You're going to beg me to let you die before I'm done with you." Jenna's eyes gleamed with malice.

Reese studied her through half-closed eyes. How had he thought this cruel, evil woman looked like Shanna? They were nothing alike. Shanna's eyes glowed with life, while Jenna's were dull and flat. Shanna's smile lit the room with sunshine and gaiety, while Jenna's was cruel and twisted. Even their bodies were different. Shanna was slim and lithe, whereas Jenna looked like she'd put on weight, especially around her hips. He wondered what happened to Whiskey John's brother. Now he knew. Baby John was barely eighteen when he died. He was a good kid.

Jenna stared at Reese for a long minute. Reese had no expression. Jenna's gaze wandered to the back of Shanna's head.

"What do we have here? Whiskey John tells me there's a woman here pretending to be me," Jenna drawled.

Reese tensed as Jenna walked around to get a good look at Shanna.

A little cry escaped her. She stared at Shanna. Her eyes wide in disbelief. "Who are you?" Jenna demanded.

****

Shanna felt Reese stiffen. She worked her trembling hands free of the ropes binding them while Jenna and Reese talked. She barely got her knife out and her skirt back down before Jenna appeared in front of her. Shanna held her knife against Reese's bindings. She worked the blade back and forth while Jenna studied her. Jenna struck her across the face and asked the question again.

"My name is Shanna," Shanna replied. The rope started to fray. Shanna had never been so frightened. Her sister hated her and wanted to cut her. She read it in her eyes.

"Why do you look like me?" Jenna demanded. Her eyes narrowed.

"We look alike because we are sisters," Shanna said swallowing. Her mouth was so dry it was a wonder any words came out.

"I don't have a sister," Jenna screamed. "Who said

you could walk around looking like me? I didn't give you permission. I won't let you do this. I don't like you." Jenna's blade came up. She poised it over the side of Shanna's face. The tip pressed into Shanna's cheek. "I'm going to make sure nobody thinks you look like me ever again," Jenna promised.

Shanna took a deep breath. She wouldn't let Jenna know how frightened she was.

"Wait." Adam Delaney strolled in from the side door. Shanna's heart pounded in her chest. She worked her blade faster. The rope gave a jerk. A few more minutes and Reese would be free. She kept her hands together behind her so no one could see what she was doing. She wanted them both to live. She prayed they had a chance.

****

Reese stiffened at the sound of Adam's voice. He hoped to God Shanna kept quiet. Adam Delaney was not a man to trifle with. His rope got a little slack. Reese flexed his muscles to see if he could break them. They might have a chance if Shanna kept her mouth closed. Reese figured they had roughly the same chance a snowball had in hell.

Adam walked over to stand in front of Shanna. Jenna still held her knife against Shanna's cheek. "Put the blade away," Adam said. He stared at Shanna for long moments then asked, "Who are you?"

"My name is Shanna," Shanna answered.

"The bitch claims she's my sister," Jenna's blade pressed deeper. The tip punctured Shanna's skin. Blood dripped down the side of her face.

"That is enough." Adam took hold of the knife. He had to pry it out of Jenna's hands. "We aren't going to kill her until we find out who she is," Adam said. "Explain who you are. Jenna doesn't have a sister. I was there shortly after her birth. You will have to come up with something else," Adam commanded turning to Shanna. Shanna didn't say anything. Reese held his breath. If she said the wrong thing, she'd be dead before he got out of his ropes.

"We know, the answer, boss," Frenchie said. "We heard them talking before we captured them and turned them over to Whiskey John." Adam nodded; his eyes still on Shanna's face.

"There was a lady with them named Abigail Smythe. She claims she delivered someone named Alice's babies. Alice had two babies and one was in the other room with Abigail when—" Frenchie realized his mistake right before he said the words.

Adam claimed his brother Robert and his wife Alice died in a carriage accident, leaving him with the family business and a newborn baby to care for. No one was aware Adam murdered his brother and his sister-in-law or knew he murdered Mushet for the plans to make tungsten steel. Delaney Steel was the leading manufacturer of tungsten steel. Adam took all the credit for its invention. Frenchie coughed to cover his slip. He had Adam's undivided attention.

"When—what?" Adam asked softly.

"When Robert decided to take his wife and baby on a drive," Frenchie answered.

Adam stared at the man. "Why would he leave the other baby behind?"

Reese looked from Frenchie to Adam. Adam was not pleased the man knew so much. He recognized the look on Adam's face. Frenchie just signed his own death certificate and would soon be having a reunion with the devil.

Frenchie shrugged. "Maybe he didn't know about the other baby, or the Abigail woman stole the baby. Maybe Robert took a carriage ride to try to find his other baby when he had the carriage accident." Frenchie warmed to his idea. "Yeah, it would explain why they were all in the carriage when it wrecked except the other baby and why you didn't know about it."

Adam's gaze turned deadly. He looked back at Shanna and studied her some more. "Where is Abigail now?" he asked.

Reese closed his eyes again. He willed Shanna to keep quiet. Adam Delaney planned on killing them all. Anything Shanna said now would only aid Adam's cause. Reese waited. Shanna said nothing. She was busy cutting his ropes. He could feel her blade working on them. Reese tugged at them again, hoping they would break. Any minute now and he would be free.

****

"So, which one of them bitches blew up my brother?" Mack yelled. He'd been listening to their conversation and if the Delaney bitch hadn't done it, the other one had. He would get vengeance for his brother before he died even if he did it with his dying breath. Everyone ignored Mack, but he wasn't done. He'd seen the Delaney bitch kiss the marshal. It meant they must have a thing together. He bet she wouldn't much like it if she thought her sister had been poaching. She didn't like having a sister, especially one who looked like her. Mack figured he could get the Delaney bitch mad enough to hurt the other one bad. He didn't doubt they were all going to die, but he wanted the bitch who blew up his brother to be the first to go.

"Seems to me the marshal there is the only one who knows those sisters. From what I've seen, he knows 'em both inside and out, if you know what I mean." Mack waited to see what effect his announcement would have.

****

Everything happened at once. Jenna let out a scream of outrage. She lunged to get her knife from Adam. Adam knocked her back and shot Mack between the eyes for annoying him. The rest of the Turley Gang, tipped off on Mack's location by the man who escaped Jenna and her men, now entered the warehouse guns blazing. Bullets flew in every direction as the Delaney Gang dove for cover and returned the gunfire. When Jenna couldn't get her knife from Adam, she pulled a pistol from her belt and dove behind a stack of crates firing wildly.

Reese's binding fell to the floor, and his hands were free. He twisted around, grabbed Shanna, and fell to the floor, rolling as he did so. Her chair smashed to pieces. He wanted to get her out of the line of fire before Adam or Jenna had a chance to kill her. He scooped her up and ran toward a group of barrels. He stuffed Shanna behind them. "Stay here!" he ordered as he made his way over to a fallen man. Reese pried the man's gun from his lifeless hand and dove behind a stack of crates. Bullets hit the crates, and wood fragments split the air.

Adam threw down a spray of bullets for Jenna as she ran toward one of the Turley men who stopped to reload his gun. It looked like the Delaneys might win.

There were more of them than the Turleys, and they were better shots. Reese stopped to calculate how far the back door was from Shanna when a spray of new gunfire rained down on them. Reese looked cautiously out from behind the crates

Omaha police appeared and began taking out both gang's members. Sergeant Baxter popped out from behind a barrel and started shooting. How did Sergeant Baxter know he was here and in need of backup? And how did he convince the local police to come? Adam took aim and shot the second man hanging next to a dead Mack Turley. Then, he carefully worked his way toward the side door.

*****

Shanna crouched behind the barrels, listening to the gunfire. Bullets hit the barrels, and Shanna ducked. Her heart was beating so hard she thought it would bound from her chest. How far was it to the door? She peeked out and spotted Jenna across the way. Jenna was screaming obscenities and shooting officers and Turleys as fast as she could. Shanna stared at her. She couldn't believe she had a sister. Shanna wanted a brother or sister as long as she could remember. Watching Jenna shoot and swear, Shanna realized she had more in common with Rose Tanner than she did her identical twin. She felt nothing for the woman who looked like her. Shanna shook her head at the thought. A bullet hit the barrel beside her. Shanna looked around for Reese. He was crouched behind a bunch of pallets. He lifted his head, looked toward the exit, and then at her. He nodded in the direction of the door. Shanna nodded. He wanted her to make her way out. Jenna screamed, and Shanna looked over at her. Jenna had her eyes on

Reese. She smiled an evil smile and lifted her gun. Reese had his back to Jenna, motioning at Shanna. Shanna didn't stop to think. She reacted. Her knife flew across the open space and lodged in Jenna's throat, silencing her scream. Jenna's gun fired as she fell to the floor, dead. A bellow of rage came from Shanna's right. Adam Delaney covered the distance between them and knocked her to the floor. Shanna couldn't breathe. The roof of the warehouse blurred. The air was knocked from her lungs on impact.

****

Reese turned as Shanna stood and threw her knife. He saw Jenna go down. Fire burned his chest. Adam roared. Reese turned his head in time to see Adam knock Shanna from behind the barrels! Anger coursed through him. The bastard had Shanna and there was nothing he could do. He was too damn far away to do anything but watch. An ache settled in his stomach. A wave of dizziness washed over him. Reese shook it off. Something warm trickled down the front of his chest. Shanna needed him. If the bastard hurt her, he would tear him apart. He kept his gaze trained on Adam and Shanna as he eased toward them. He moved swiftly and silently, intent on gaining as much ground as he could in the least amount of time possible. Adam held his pistol to Shanna's head as he backed toward the side door. Reese sped up. "That's far enough, Calhan! Drop your gun or the girl is dead!"

Chapter 25

Adam Delaney stood in the open holding Shanna in front of him. His pistol was pressed against the side of her head. Reese stopped, but he held his gun for another heartbeat or two. There was nothing stopping Adam from shooting Shanna, whether he dropped his gun or not.

"Don't make me say it again, Calhan, or the girl dies." Adam had control of the situation, and he smiled. He didn't see Sergeant Baxter.

Sergeant Baxter was directly to the right of Reese. He summed up the situation and noted Reese's hesitation. Sergeant Baxter shot Adam Delaney in the head, twice. It was the only thing he could think of to save the girl's life. It made him mad as hell, too. Sergeant Baxter had been after Adam Delaney for the last ten years, waiting and watching for a chance to take the man down. He wanted the bastard to stand trial. He wanted him to have to look into the faces of his victim's families while the noose slipped over his head. He'd wanted the families to watch the man responsible for taking their loved ones, hang. There was little satisfaction in being the one to kill the bastard, but it had to be done. He wouldn't stand by and watch Delaney take one more life. Now he'd be going to a funeral instead of a trial.

****

It was over. Shanna looked down at Adam Delaney. He was the man who shot her father, then killed her mother, taking her newborn sister from her dead mother's arms. He was the man who would have killed her, too, if he'd known about her. He was also the man who minutes before had a gun to her head. Shanna frowned at the blood pooling around him. She folded her trembling arms over her chest. She felt nothing, not even horror at the gory scene before her. This man was her uncle, her father's brother. He was family. He was her family. Why wasn't she hysterical? Why didn't she feel anything?

Reese stumbled toward her. "Shanna?"

She looked up at him, the fog lifted from her mind. She read the concern on his face, and tears filled her eyes. She'd worried they wouldn't make it out alive and worried she wouldn't get his rope off in time. She was afraid they were both going to die. It took everything she had to free herself, then him. She worried she would never see her mother again or Rose. Now it was over, she needed Reese. She needed his strength. She was so happy they were both still alive. Tears filled her eyes and rolled down her cheeks.

"Are you crying for Adam Delaney?" Sergeant Baxter asked in astonishment.

Shanna shook her head, wiping her cheeks with her sleeve. "I'm not sad he's dead. I was going to kill him myself for scaring my mother the way he did."

Sergeant Baxter raised an eyebrow over her comment. He swallowed a chuckle. "A little thing like you would be no threat to Adam Delaney. He would eat you for lunch."

Reese stepped to Shanna's side. He swayed.

"Sergeant Baxter this is Miss Shanna Johnston. Shanna, Sergeant Baxter, my boss from the old days in Chicago when I was a lowly detective."

"I figured she was Miss Johnston by the way you were acting. You never would have slowed down if Adam had a gun to Jenna's head." Sergeant Baxter held a hand toward Shanna.

"How did you know where I was, and that I needed back up?" Reese asked rubbing a hand over his forehead, removing the perspiration. His hand shook. Reese stared at the ground.

Shanna frowned. What was wrong with him? He was acting strange, and she didn't know why. Was he upset she killed Jenna?

"Well, now there's a story by itself. My lad John there," Sergeant Baxter waved at a freckle-faced youth in uniform, cuffing the remaining three members of the Delaney Gang, "was on patrol. He was walking the street when he was attacked by a wild-eyed woman screaming at him to save her daughter."

Reese nodded his encouragement. Shanna listened with half an ear. Her mind still reeled from the events of the last few hours. She gazed from Adam to Jenna and then to the floor. She gained the family she longed for and lost them in the same day. She glanced back at Reese.

He swayed beside her. Shanna frowned with concern. Apprehension filled her. What if he loved Jenna, and now he hated her for killing her?

"It took the lad a bit to get the woman calmed down enough to make sense. John thought it strange a marshal would be attacked by Adam Delaney from Chicago along with the woman's daughter. He related the story to me, and I knew exactly whom he was talking about, and where you'd be. After you sent the telegram, wondering about any connection between Adam Delaney and the Johnstons, I've been in Omaha doing a little detective work. I've been working with the Omaha police chief trying to track the Delaney Gang and make any connection between the two. We've had our eye on this warehouse. We had it pegged as the Delaney stronghold. After John told us the story, we loaded up every available officer and brought them along, just in case." Sergeant Baxter slapped Reese on the shoulder. "Good thing you kept me up to date with those telegrams of yours."

Reese nodded his agreement. "We've got one more problem," Reese said. "I suspect we have one or more employees of the railroad on Adam Delaney's payroll. The explosion on my way to Rock Creek a few months back was set by Jenna and her boys. They knew I was on the train as soon as I bought my ticket. They also knew I'd be in Omaha today. It gave them time to meet us here. They followed me to Shanna's mother's house and got the jump on us."

Sergeant Baxter nodded. "I'll see to it we arrest those responsible."

Reese nodded too and looked toward Shanna. She stared at the ground. She didn't know what to think. If Reese tore into her over Jenna, she wouldn't be able to control herself. She didn't know how she felt about him or about what happened between them. She didn't know how he felt either. Until she sorted it out, she had nothing to say. A drop of bright red blood dripped onto Reese's foot. Shanna stared. Her gaze jumped to Reese's face. He was pale and sweating profusely.

"Reese!" Shanna said. She stepped toward him as he crumbled to the ground.

****

"You headed to Chicago?" Sergeant Baxter asked Shanna.

They stood inside Reese's room at the hospital in Omaha. Reese had a bullet lodged in his chest. The doctors were able to stop the bleeding, but the bullet was close to Reese's heart. None of the doctors in Omaha had the expertise to remove it.

Shanna's hands shook. She hadn't been fast enough. Jenna's bullet hit Reese in the chest before Shanna's knife found its mark. Jenna might get her revenge after all. Shanna was too dazed to cry. She was numb all over. She didn't want to think about life without Reese.

Sergeant Baxter was a godsend. She was grateful he was nearby when Reese collapsed. He caught Reese before he smashed Shanna into the ground. He laid Reese on the ground and called for help. The officers on scene transported Reese to the hospital where he underwent a laborious surgery. Sergeant Baxter stayed beside her the whole time, seeing to her comfort. Hours later when the doctor emerged, Sergeant Baxter stood beside her while they gave Shanna the news. They did what they could to stabilize Reese. There was nothing more they could do but wait. There was a specialist in Chicago who had excellent success removing bullets so close to the heart. The problem was Reese couldn't be moved. Movement would cause the bullet to pierce his heart. The specialist they needed would have to come to Omaha to do the surgery, and he cost a lot of money.

"Why would I go to Chicago?" Shanna asked. "I

can't get the specialist until I figure out how to pay him. I need money."

Sergeant Baxter removed his hat and scratched his head. "Well, now, with Adam Delaney and Jenna dead, you are head of Delaney Steel."

Shanna shrugged. "What good does that do me?" Her mind was on Reese and what losing him would do to her. She wasn't sure she had him anyway. But alive, she had a chance. Dead, there was no hope.

Sergeant Baxter rubbed his chin. "The answer is staring you in the face, Miss Shanna. If you go to Chicago and see the solicitors, you can pay for that specialist. Delaney Steel is worth a lot of money. There are no other Delaneys, just you. It all belongs to you now."

Shanna's heart skipped a beat. Her gaze snapped up to his. "Do you think so?"

Sergeant Baxter nodded. "I know so. One look at you should convince the solicitors you are who you say you are. You might want to take your mother with you, too. She knows the city. Her testimony will come in handy."

Shanna looked uneasily at Sergeant Baxter. "What if they don't believe me?" she asked. Her mind swirled with doubt. She was a nobody. She had nothing. She had no friends or anyone to vouch for her.

"Why wouldn't they?" he asked. "You are the spitting image of Jenna. I'll wire the solicitors and let them know you're coming."

Shanna trembled. She had never been to a big city before. What if she got lost? What if she missed the appointment? The thought of going to see the Delaney solicitors frightened her. They might not like her. They might not want to give her the money she needed to help Reese. Then what would she do? Shanna looked at Reese. He hadn't woken up since his surgery. What if something happened to him while she was gone? What if the bullet moved in her absence and he—?

Sergeant Baxter took her hand. "There's no need to worry, Miss Shanna. I'll stay right here and take care of Reese. I won't let anybody get close to him. If anything happens, I'll get word to you."

"Shanna?" Mary walked into the little curtained off room.

Shanna turned at the sound of her voice. Her whole body began to shake. The room spun around her. "How did you get here, Mama? And how did you know I was here?" Shanna asked incredulously.

"I stopped by the station and one of the sergeant's men brought me here. He told me what happened on the way. How is the marshal?" Mary's eyes went to Reese.

For the first time in years, Shanna lost control. Tears streamed down her face. She flung herself into Mary's arms and wept. All the anguish, all the pain, and all the loneliness poured out of her. Sobs shook her body as her emotions erupted in a violent flood of tears. Mary stood quietly letting Shanna weep.

Sergeant Baxter cleared his throat and updated Mary on Reese's condition. "Reese needs the specialist." Sergeant Baxter looked at Mary. "I was telling Shanna; she will need to go to Chicago."

Mary went deathly pale. "Why would she need to go there?" Her arms clung to her still weeping daughter.

"Shanna is now the head of Delaney Steel," Sergeant Baxter explained. "If she claims the company, she will have the money to pay for the specialist."

"No!" Mary tightened her hold on Shanna. "Shanna can't go to Chicago. She will be in danger! I can't lose her."

"It's quite all right to go, madam." Sergeant Baxter continued. "Adam Delaney is dead. Jenna Delaney is dead. There is no other family. There is no one there to hurt you. All the wealth, all the power, all the people employed by Delaney Steel are Shanna's to command. Shanna is now the boss," he pointed out. "You'll have to convince the solicitors first, of course," the sergeant continued, "but that shouldn't be a problem. One look at her should do it. Once Shanna has control of the Delaney holdings, she can send for the specialist." Sergeant Baxter placed a hand on Mary's shoulder. "I understand your concern, madam. I have to admit, a world without Adam Delaney will take some getting used to."

"Of course," Mary murmured. She hugged Shanna. Her hands trembled, but she nodded her head. "Then we will go."

Shanna didn't want to go to Chicago. She looked at Reese. He was so pale and still. Without the specialist, he would die. Her heart beat furiously in her ears. She turned to Mary, wiping tears from her puffy cheeks.

Mary's face was pale, but a light entered her eyes. "I suppose you're right, sergeant. I've been frightened of Adam for so many years. I can hardly function without worrying. With him gone, there isn't any need to be afraid." She took a deep breath. Her gaze searched Shanna's face. "We can do this. Together, we will go and see the solicitors and get help for the dear marshal."

Shanna nodded. Mary gave up so much to rescue a helpless newborn baby, and Shanna owed her. She owed Mary her life. Now, Mary gave her the courage she needed to do what must be done. "Thank you, Mama. No girl could ask for a better mother."

Shanna turned to Sergeant Baxter, her gaze on Reese's still form.

"I'll be right here, Miss Shanna. Nothing will happen. Go, get him some help," the sergeant said before Shanna could shape the words.

She nodded. Bending, she whispered in Reese's ear, and then she took Mary's arm. Together, they left the room.

Chapter 26

Chicago turned out to be a lot bigger than Shanna expected, and louder. There were so many people coming and going. Everywhere there were carriages, horses, and people walking and talking. The noise was deafening. The streets were narrow and crisscrossed each other. Everyone knew where they were going, except her. It scared the life out of her.

They had an appointment with Delaney Estate solicitors at one o'clock. One of Sergeant Baxter's officers met them at the train station with the news. He had the address and escorted them to their destination in his carriage. The solicitors were only a block and a half from the train station. They arrived outside the prestigious law firm of Penwell and Brinks Esquire five minutes before their scheduled appointment. Mary's hand tightened around Shanna's arm. Shanna gave her a quick smile and led her through the large glass door. Their feet echoed on the gray and white marble tile. Their reflections bounced around on gilded mirrors hanging in the spacious reception area. Mahogany tables stood proudly beneath the gilded mirrors. Marble statues stood in the corners. The walls were maroon velvet, and a magnificent crystal chandelier hung from the white plaster ceiling.

Shanna looked around the opulent room in amazement. Her gaze fell upon a young woman in a severely-cut black jacket and skirt. Her blonde hair was pulled tightly back and pinned atop her head. "May I help you?" the woman asked. Her gaze wandered up and down Shanna as she rounded the impressively carved mahogany reception desk set in the center of the large room.

"We have an appointment at one o'clock," Shanna answered.

The woman's eyes flickered momentarily, and then a practiced smile touched her lips. "This way please." She turned toward a curved oak staircase leading to the upper floor.

Mary took her arm, and they followed the blonde woman. At the top of the stairs, the woman turned right and after a quick knock, opened double doors leading into a conference room. Two men sat at the large table. They were elderly men with graying hair. One had glasses, the other not. Their eyes traveled from one to the other of the visitors, then settled on Shanna.

One gentleman stood up. "I am Mr. Penwell, and this is Mr. Brinks." He extended his hand to Mary, his eyes still on Shanna.

Mr. Brinks pushed his glasses up and extended his hand as well. "Please, sit." Mr. Brinks invited, waving his hand toward the waiting chairs and sat down once more.

They sat.

Mr. Penwell cleared his throat. "We understand you believe yourself to be a blood relative to Mr. Delaney. Do I understand correctly?"

"Yes," Shanna answered. Her throat was dry.

"You are?" Mr. Penwell inquired.

"Miss Shanna Johnston," Shanna said. "This is my

mother, Mary Johnston, er…"

She glanced at Mary anxiously. Mary wasn't her mother. Shanna twisted her hands in her lap. She was so nervous she wasn't making any sense. This had to work. Reese could be dying. He needed the specialist.

"Shanna is the daughter of Robert and Alice Delaney," Mary explained. Her hand rested on Shanna's. Mary gave it a squeeze. "We have come to claim her right to Delaney Steel and holdings."

Mr. Penwell leaned back in his chair. His hands made a steeple. "How can you be Miss Johnston's mother?"

Mary leaned forward. "My name is Abigail Smythe. I was employed by Mr. Robert Delaney as a lady's companion to his wife Alice…" As Mary told her tale to the two solicitors, Shanna stared at the floor. She listened halfheartedly. Her mind was on Reese in Omaha.

When the story concluded, Mary folded her hands in her lap, her eyes on Mr. Penwell. Mr. Penwell exchanged glances with Mr. Brinks. "Forgive us for requiring further proof than the presence of the young lady. Mr. Robert Delaney paid us a visit the day before his disappearance and death. He was quite agitated and believed his brother Adam meant to do him and his family harm. He made known to us his plans to relocate his family in a safe location. He made us swear, before we approached any legal matters regarding the company, we would both examine the evidence to our satisfaction. Mr. Robert warned us his brother Adam could be quite devious. We gave our word we would not be hasty in signing over the company or any family holdings without due diligence on our part."

Mr. Penwell looked at Mary. "Mr. Robert informed me of your employ and the direction he wished to take his family. I am satisfied you are Abigail Smythe. I believe the story you told us here today."

Mr. Brinks stood up. He extended his hand to Shanna. "Congratulations, Miss Delaney, on your good fortune. Mr. Penwell and I will draw up the necessary paperwork for your signature. We will be in touch. Until then, we have a letter of recommendation for you to present at your hotel or any bank in town to acquire credit or funding for any need you may have until we contact you to sign the paperwork."

Mr. Penwell scratched his pen along the top of a piece of parchment. When he finished, both men scrawled their signatures. Mr. Penwell affixed their seal in wax at the bottom. He handed the paper to Shanna. "Give us a couple of days and we will have the paperwork ready for you."

"Thank you, sir," Shanna said. She glanced at the parchment. It worked. She could pay for the help Reese needed. Her hand trembled.

"Should you wish to stay at the family estates, inform Miss Denton downstairs and a conveyance will be arranged to take you there."

Shanna swallowed her nervousness. "Mr. Penwell, I have an urgent need for a specialist." She hurriedly explained the situation.

Mr. Penwell knew the doctor she described. He took another parchment and scrawled across it. Both solicitors signed it and affixed their seal.

"This should get you the help you require," Mr. Penwell said.

Shanna blinked back tears. Reese had to hold on

until she got back. "I must go immediately. The marshal doesn't have much time."

"I understand. There's one other thing."

Shanna's gaze shot up.

"What arrangements would you like us to make for the burials?"

"What choices do I have?" Shanna asked slowly.

Mr. Penwell glanced at Mr. Brinks. "There has been some discussion among the employees about the topic. Some feel like Mr. Adam and Miss Jenna should not be buried in the family cemetery next to Mr. Robert, Miss Alice, and the rest. As head of the Delaney family, Miss Shanna, you will make the choice."

"What other choice would there be?" Shanna asked.

"Well, they could be interred in the city where they died or transported here to the city cemetery if you don't want them interred on the estate in the family cemetery." Mr. Penwell explained.

"They can stay in Omaha. They shouldn't be buried next to the rest of the family," Shanna said.

"Very well," Mr. Penwell stated. "I will walk you down." He escorted them down the stairs and told Miss Denton to call his driver around. Mr. Penwell handed Shanna a note of introduction to give the doctor. He saw them into his own carriage and on their way.

****

Two weeks later, Shanna arrived back in Chicago. A carriage waited at the train station to take them to Delaney Estate. Reese sat opposite her. He was pale and quiet. The operation was successful. The specialist removed the bullet, and the danger was over. Mary sat beside Shanna; her eyes glued to the streets around them. She smiled and murmured to herself, squeezing Shanna's hand.

Shanna was glad Mama was happy. She watched the lines of worry on Mary's face disappear as the days went by. Mary smiled a lot. The terror left her eyes. Shanna glanced at Reese. She didn't know what to do to break the ice. He hadn't said two words to her since waking from his surgery. She didn't know how he felt, and it was driving her crazy. She thought he would at least thank her for saving his life, but he didn't. Going to Chicago scared the life out of her, but she did it anyway. She did it for him because she loved him. When Sergeant Baxter explained how Shanna paid for the specialist that saved his life, Reese grew silent. He hadn't said another word to her.

The carriage slowed and turned through an ornate metal gate with "Delaney" formed across the arch. A long tree-lined cobblestone drive curved its way through the grounds toward the large two-story stone mansion. Shanna gaped in surprise at the acres of manicured lawns and immaculate flowerbeds glimpsed through the shelter of trees. Mary told her stories about the house while they were on the train. Nothing prepared her for the grandeur before her. The carriage pulled to a stop before a heavily ornate front door. A liveried footman hurried down the stone steps to open the carriage door and help the ladies alight. His eyes widened when he caught sight of Shanna's face.

"Shanna, hand the footman your note from the solicitors, he will take it to the butler, and then we will introduce ourselves," Mary said. She saw the fear on the man's face and guessed the man was uncertain about Shanna's identity. They must not know Shanna and Jenna were identical twins.

Shanna handed the footman the letter from the solicitors, and they followed the footman up the stone steps to the front door.

"If you will wait here," the footman said. The footman's gaze riveted on Shanna's face. He swallowed nervously. There would be many adjustments now Adam and Jenna were gone.

The front door opened a few minutes later. A tall gray-haired man in tailored clothing appeared. "Come this way, if you please." He stepped back to allow them to enter. If he was surprised at Shanna's appearance, he gave no indication. They followed him into the richly decorated entry hall. Shanna gasped in surprise. Reese stepped to her side. Shanna didn't look at him. Her gaze was on the magnificent room. The walls were mahogany. Gray marble tile covered the floor and heavy navy velvet draperies hung from the ceiling. They were held back by golden ropes on either side of the floor-to-ceiling windows overlooking Delaney Estates. Ornately carved tables held massive flower arrangements. Gilded candlesticks adorned the walls, as well as beautiful paintings depicting angels frolicking and playing their harps. Marble statues of angels stood on pedestals in the corners. Shanna eyes rounded as she surveyed the room.

The butler looked Shanna over carefully. "Your name, miss?" he asked.

Reese rolled his eyes.

"Shanna Johnston," Shanna said.

"I believe you mean Delaney. Don't you, miss?" the butler said. "Allow me to introduce myself. I am—"

"Giles," Mary said from behind Shanna's shoulder.

Giles turned in surprise. "Upon my word, Miss Abigail! I never thought I would see you again." Giles took Mary's hand warmly in his. Tears brightened his eyes as he looked at Mary.

"You must come sit with me one of these evenings and tell me where you've been all these years. I did wonder what happened to you." Mary nodded her agreement, blushing all the while.

****

Giles clapped his hands together. Servants entered from every direction and stood at attention. Giles introduced Shanna to each one. She had no idea how she would keep all their names straight. She smiled and shook hands all the same.

"Would you care to have a tour of the estate after you freshen up?" Giles asked.

Shanna nodded. Reese needed to lie down. He was too weak to stand very long. Giles led them up the staircase to the second floor. It was as impressive as the entry hall. Giles stopped at the first door on the left. It was an elaborate guest room with gleaming furniture and navy décor.

"I hope this suits your needs," Giles said ushering Reese into the room. "If you need anything pull the rope beside the bed."

Reese nodded, and Giles shut the door. He turned and walked across the hall. He opened another door. This room faced the front of the house. Mary and Shanna followed him into the room. It was the master chamber. A massive bed dominated the room, four carved posts at each corner. The bed so high Shanna decided she would need a stepladder to climb onto the mattress. A large marble fireplace covered almost the entire wall facing the bed. Large arrangements of flowers in tall vases stood on either side of the fireplace. Heavy velvet drapes hung by the windows. The room was decorated in a heavy masculine fashion all navy and maroon. Shanna ran her fingers over the navy brocade coverlet on the bed. The heavy velvet drapes matched it in color. If this were her room, she would lighten it up a bit. Reality whispered in her ear as she looked about. *This is your room. This is your house!*

Giles led her into an adjoining room. The entire room served as a wardrobe with hooks and drawers, hangers and rods. Shanna stood still staring. She'd never seen such a thing in her life. Shanna turned to go, and her eyes fell upon her little travel case. It sat alone on the floor, waiting to be unpacked. The sight caused her to think about how much her life had changed in the last few days. She must find some answers before she decided what to do next. She could go anywhere in the world. Do anything she wanted to do. Yet, here she was. She had to know how Reese felt about her, had to know who he wanted that night by the river. She wanted to know whom he loved. Was it Jenna? Was he angry with her for killing the girl he used to love? She was so confused. She had to decide where she wanted to live and what she wanted to do with her life. And she needed to know if that life included Reese.

Chapter 27

Shanna stood alone in the quiet garden staring at the pattern the moonlight made on the rippling water of the tiered fountain. Everything was different, surreal, and disconcerting. She had been here a week, and it wasn't any easier. Shanna never imagined people lived like this. The house and grounds were massive. There was a dining table large enough to hold thirty guests, servants who served the dinner and saw to every guest's needs, a cook who did nothing but prepare food, and maids who cleaned the rooms and did the laundry. They even had servants who did the dishes and swept the floors.

Shanna felt out of place, like someone from another country, another world. Reese accepted it as if a servant poured wine at his elbow every day. Mary fit in too. Shanna was the only one who was troubled. At dinner, she accidentally knocked over her glass. It tipped over and rolled off the table. Shanna went to grab it, but Giles appeared at her elbow. He shook his head at her. Several maids hurried over and soon every trace of the accident was gone. It wasn't only the servants and the size of the house. Giles showed her into the office, and she got a chance to look over the books. She bit her lip to keep from exclaiming at the dollar amounts she saw. If all of it was hers, she had enough to buy the entire town of Rock Creek and possibly the neighboring town as well.

The realization she owned so much, and she was wealthy beyond all reason, was why she stood here now, staring into the fountain. The soft sound of the water soothed her fears and calmed her nerves. What in the world was she going to do with all of this? She ran her fingertips through the pooled water and sighed. Rose. She needed Rose. She couldn't do this without Rose. Rose would know what to say. She would know what to do with the house, the servants, the money, and the corporation. She missed her friend desperately. Rose always knew what the right thing was.

"Shanna." She turned at the sound of her name.

Reese stood a few feet away, his blond hair gleaming in the moonlight. "We never got a chance to talk, you and me," he said.

"What is there to talk about?" Shanna asked. A full week of silence and suddenly he wanted to talk. She shrugged. Maybe she should get it over with. If he wanted to tell her he only touched her because he thought she was Jenna and then walk away, now was a good time. Her life was all mixed up, and she had no idea how she felt about anything.

****

Reese frowned, put off by her question. It should be obvious. He wanted to talk about the night they spent by the river. He wanted to talk about getting married. He wanted to talk about the way she responded to his kisses.

"I want to talk about us," Reese said.

Shanna turned to look at him. "There's not an *us*. Now that you're well, and there is no danger, there's no reason for you to hang around. As you can see, I have what I need, and I don't need you. So, thank you for escorting me back to Chicago. Have a safe trip back to wherever you're from."

Her dismissal hurt. Reese stared at her in consternation. She didn't mean what she said. *"I don't have what I need,"* he said.

Shanna rolled her eyes. "Okay. So, what is it *you* need? I saved your life at the warehouse, twice. Once when I cut your ropes, and the second time when Jenna shot you. Afterward I went to Chicago, I found a specialist, and saved your life, again. I took care of you while you were in the hospital. I paid for your ticket back to Chicago. What else is there? Do you need money? Another train ticket? A horse? Whatever it is, you can have it, as long as you leave."

Reese took a step closer. "I don't like the conditions you set. Maybe we could negotiate."

"You haven't told me what it is you need yet," Shanna countered.

Reese took another step closer. They were almost nose-to-nose and chest-to-chest. Shanna didn't step back. Reese could see the pulse beating frantically in the side of her neck. So, she wasn't as unaffected by him as she seemed.

"I need you," he whispered as his arms pulled her toward him, and his mouth came down on hers.

****

It was unexpected. She thought he was going to say something else. She opened her mouth to reply, and Reese took advantage of the opportunity. His tongue swept inside to mate with hers. He cradled her head in his hand as his mouth assaulted hers. She whimpered and began to pull away. She knew where this trail led, and she wanted to get one or two things straight before she ended up naked beneath him again.

She pulled back, and he decided to change his approach. His kiss became softer and gentler. He teased her lips and tongue with his while his hands rubbed a lazy pattern on her back and arms. He still held her head cradled in his other hand and tipped her head slightly to gain deeper access to her mouth.

A shiver worked its way through her body. She leaned in and kissed him back. He felt so good, tasted so good, and hopefully this time he wouldn't call her—

Shanna shoved against his chest with all her strength.

Reese lifted his head, his eyes hooded as he stared at her.

"Who am I?" Shanna asked.

Reese raised an eyebrow. "You're one damn sexy woman. Now, come here." He reached for her again, but she took several steps backward evading him.

"No. I'm not coming anywhere near you until you answer the question," Shanna said. She folded her arms over her chest in a defensive gesture and glared at him. This wasn't going any further until she got the answer she was looking for.

Reese dropped his hands. "What do you want to know?" he asked.

Shanna rolled her eyes heavenward. She was getting annoyed, so she repeated the question. "Who am I?" If he said one word about Jenna, she'd go for her knife and cut his heart out.

"Shanna Delaney," Reese answered.

Shanna narrowed her eyes at his innocent expression. Was he trying to trick her? "Who am I when you kiss me?" she asked. "Who was I the night by the river?"

****

Reese frowned. He said the first thing that entered his mind. "Shanna Johnston."

Shanna stared hard at him as she considered his answer. Reese felt like he was standing before the preacher making a confession. He wasn't sure what the judgment would be, and he resisted the urge to squirm.

"Are you sure?" Shanna asked the question quietly, her gaze searching his. This was important. Reese considered the situation and couldn't think of one reason she might be worried about who he thought she was unless—

Reese took a step toward her. She took a step back. Reese stopped. "Shanna, I want you to listen to what I have to say and don't interrupt. Agreed?" He wanted her to listen, really listen this time. He'd tried to explain before and somehow ended up making her mad. He hoped he got it right this time.

"The night by the river—" he began, and Shanna closed her eyes. She would have turned and run away, but Reese caught her arm. "You promised to listen," he reminded her.

Shanna dropped her head and nodded.

"The night by the river, I only meant to kiss you. I never meant for it to go as far as it did. I held your soft body next to mine, and as I tasted your sweetness, I wanted more. I couldn't seem to stop myself from touching and tasting. I wanted you from the first moment I saw you—"

"The first moment when you thought I was Jenna?" she asked bitterly. Reese watched her face as she said the words. So, he was right in thinking she still smarted over his confusion between the two. "The first moment when I saw your sweet face looking up at me, and you cringed. Your cringe was like a punch in the gut. I told myself I didn't care, but I did. I told myself not to care because, yes, for a time I believed you were Jenna."

She would have said something, but he held his hand up to stop her. "You promised to let me talk. Please, Shanna. Let me explain." At her reluctant nod he continued. "But then, you would do the kindest most unselfish things, and it would confuse me and what I knew about Jenna. I believed I knew her, too. At first, I didn't listen when friends and family warned me away from her. Then, I found out she used me the whole time. She used me to get information and used me to get rich at the expense of innocent people. I took it out on you. Allow me to apologize. I am deeply sorry for any hurt I caused in my assumption you were Jenna. Had I known there were two of you, I would have treated you differently. The more I was around you, I found myself drawn to you and your sweetness, but then I would remember what Jenna did, and I would hate you. The night by the river, you were so sweet and so responsive. I had to have you. I couldn't deny myself any longer. I reasoned I was a smarter man than I was before. Although everyone considered you an innocent girl, I told myself I knew better, since we were lovers before."

Shanna winced at his words.

"I reasoned if I took you again, I would get you out of my system for good. I drowned in your sweetness, soaking up everything you gave. I marvel still at the way you gave yourself to me. It was only when I found you to be a virgin, I realized how wrong I'd been about you. My mind went completely blank. I couldn't believe it. *You weren't Jenna!* I lay there trying to comprehend how you could look like her and not be her. You were crying and pushing at me. I didn't want it to end badly. I needed to make up to you the pain I caused. I wanted to make it good for you. Nothing in your life had been good before then, and I wanted to do something to change it."

"So, you made love to me," Shanna said.

"So, I made love to you. When I said I only touched you because I thought you were Jenna, I meant I never would have allowed it to go so far with you before we marry. I would have waited until our wedding night to make you mine." Reese watched her closely. Did she believe him?

"Our wedding night? But we aren't getting married," Shanna said.

"Oh, but we are," Reese contradicted. "It's the honorable thing to do. After all, you gave yourself to me, and you could be carrying my child," he said matter-of-factly.

"So, that's it? You want to marry me because I might be carrying your child?" Fire shot from her eyes.

****

What about love? "I don't need you to take care of me," she yelled. "I am more than capable of taking care of myself. Look around you, Reese. I didn't need your help before. I need it less now. I could have nannies and tutors. Whatever my child needs, I can provide."

Reese took another step toward her. "*My child*. It's my child," he stated, "and I'll do the providing."

Shanna held up her hand. "I'm not going to discuss

this, not now, not ever. I don't need you to marry me out of guilt. You owe me nothing. It's true I did give myself to you, and if there's a child I'm more than capable of taking care of her. I'm relieving you of any responsibility you feel you have toward me. Now go. Please." Shanna turned on her heel and ran toward the house. Her eyes swam with tears. She should have known Reese would try to marry her out of some sense of guilt over what happened. She didn't need him! As soon as her stupid heart got done breaking into a million pieces, she'd show him how much she didn't care!

Chapter 28

"Then what happened?" Rose asked.

"I ran to the house and caught the first train to Omaha," Shanna answered.

"Marshal Reese didn't try to stop you?" Rose asked.

"Of course, he tried to stop me. I told Giles to have him removed from the premises," Shanna said.

Rose's mouth dropped open. "You did what? Why, Shanna?" Rose was incredulous. Obviously, Shanna shouldn't go anywhere alone. She needed Rose to keep her from making colossal mistakes.

"I told Giles to remove Reese from the premises so I could think, in peace. Reese kept sending notes saying he needed to speak. Every surface in the entire house seemed to contain a note from Reese. He sent flowers, too, lots of them. He waited in the corridor for me. I was forced to leave the dining hall by way of the kitchens to avoid him. He even tried to pick the lock on my chamber door, so I posted a servant outside to keep him away."

Rose stared at Shanna dumbfounded. "The man loves you, Shanna. How can you be so cruel?" she asked.

Shanna snorted. "He should have told me then."

"Did you ever consider that might be what he wanted to talk to you about, and you wouldn't let him?"

Rose asked.

"He had a chance the night before, and he didn't say anything about it. His words were that he intended to marry me and provide for me and any child who might be coming," Shanna finished lamely.

"And you don't think he meant it?" Rose asked.

"Oh, he meant it. He thinks he's responsible. All he could talk about was how much he wanted me and how hard a time he had because he thought I was Jenna," Shanna answered

"And when he knew for certain you weren't?" Rose asked.

"He attempted to make it up to me. He tried to love me better," Shanna said.

Rose looked at her friend. Shanna was too emotional to realize what she said. The more Rose questioned her; the more Shanna struggled to convince them both Reese was an unfeeling monster. Rose considered the situation. Shanna obviously hadn't spent any time thinking about her own feelings for Reese. So, maybe it was time she did. "I think you're right," Rose announced. "I think Marshal Reese is a scoundrel. He took advantage of your trusting nature and left you to suffer the consequences on your own. Hanging is too good for him." Rose nodded her head to emphasize the point.

"What are you talking about?" Shanna asked. "I don't have a trusting nature, and Reese didn't take advantage of me."

"Well, I don't care how you word it. The man left you to care for a child all on your own. He doesn't care about you or the baby. All he cares about is himself. Now you'll have to raise the child all on your own because the child's father is a no-account, irresponsible monster. I think you should hire a lawyer and send Reese to prison for what he's done," Rose said.

Shanna stared at her friend in horror. "No! Reese offered to care for the child. He didn't want me to raise it on my own. It made him mad when I suggested it. I don't know why we are arguing about it anyway! There isn't even a baby to raise!" Shanna wailed.

"What did you say exactly?" Rose asked.

"I told him I didn't need him," Shanna answered.

"And you wonder why the man didn't fall to his knees professing everlasting love? Shanna, you've spent the last few minutes telling me Reese wants to make it right. You told me he's trying to accept responsibility, and he is trying to make it up to you. You also told me he apologized for any hurt he caused by thinking you were Jenna, and you told him you didn't need him." Rose let her comments sink in for a minute then asked. "Did you think to tell him you love him, too?" Rose asked softly. For a smart girl Shanna sure was a twat.

"No, I didn't," Shanna answered. Her head dropped.

"Why not?" Rose asked again.

"Because he thought I was Jenna," Shanna said.

"But didn't he apologize and tell you he would have treated you different if he'd known there were two of you?" Rose asked.

Shanna squirmed and nodded.

"So, you're mad at him for not telling you he loves you, after you tell him you don't need him. Then you decide to not forgive him, even though he's apologized, and you don't tell him you love him, either?" Rose shook her head. "Explain to me whose side I'm supposed to be on because I'm starting to favor the marshal."

****

Shanna twisted her hands together. Even Rose thought she was being unkind. Giles sat her down before she left Chicago and attempted to tell her the same thing, as well as Mary. A knock sounded at the door of Rose's bedchamber where the girls were stretched out on Rose's bed talking. Mrs. Tanner's head appeared around the door.

"Someone's here to see you, Shanna." Mrs. Tanner smiled. Shanna looked every bit as lovesick as the marshal in her drawing room.

"She will be right down," Rose said and turned to Shanna.

"He's not going to come for you too many more times, Shanna. He didn't have to come now, and I'm surprised he did after you told Giles to turn him out. If you tell him no again, he might believe you mean it. Then what will you do?" Rose wondered.

"I don't know," Shanna said softly. She'd had Reese following her around for months, and she was used to him being there. There was also her stupid traitorous heart. If Reese went away and it was the last time she ever saw him, she would die. Shanna got slowly to her feet and walked toward the door.

"Give him a chance, Shanna," Rose called after her softly. Reese held all the keys pertaining to Shanna and her happiness. Shanna crept into the drawing room. Reese had his back to her, staring into the fire.

"Reese," Shanna said as she stepped further into the room.

Reese turned to face her, his hands at his side. Shanna looked him over with concern, noting the shadows under his eyes, and the stubble on his chin. He must have ridden his horse all the way here without stopping to sleep. She took a quick step toward him and stopped.

Reese looked her up and down. He stared at her face. "Shanna."

"Will you sit down?" she asked remembering her manners. Two weeks was a long time to not see his handsome face. Shanna tried not to stare.

"I'd rather stand," he said, his eyes watchful. "May I speak?"

"Please," Shanna said. Good Lord they sounded like a couple of old people. Shanna smiled to brighten the stilted air around them. Encouraged by the smile, Reese took a step toward her. He took her hand in his.

"You asked me in Chicago who you were to me when I kissed you. I've puzzled over the question in my mind, and I've concluded you think I was in love with Jenna, and thus you, because I thought you were Jenna. Am I right?"

Shanna nodded her head.

Reese smiled. "I never loved Jenna, Shanna. It is true I was attracted to her when I first met her, but attraction turned to anger, then hatred at the things she did, and how she used me and my job. When I met you, you were everything I believed she was and more, so much more. I love you, Shanna, only you. It's only been you."

****

Reese knelt in front of her and pulled a jewelry box from the pocket of his vest. He opened the box and there sat a beautiful marquis cut diamond ring.

Shanna exclaimed in surprise, her eyes going to his questioningly.

"Will you marry me, Shanna?" Reese looked into her eyes, her beautiful blue eyes and waited, his heart thundering in his chest. He had no idea why she would after the way he treated her.

"Of course, she will," Rose said from behind them. Mrs. Tanner, Mary, and Rose filled the doorway. Mrs. Tanner and Mary dabbed at their eyes with handkerchiefs. Rose jumped up and down with excitement. Reese turned his gaze to Shanna once more. She hadn't answered yet.

"Before I answer, I must tell you I love you. These last two weeks have been the most miserable—" She never got a chance to finish. Reese had her in his arms, his mouth on hers before she could say any more. Mr. Tanner coughed from the door. Reese reluctantly let Shanna go.

"Will you please answer, Shanna? He'll likely bust something if you don't answer the man's question," Mr. Tanner said. He wasn't above eavesdropping either.

"Yes, yes, I will marry you," Shanna said. Her smile lit the entire room. Reese grabbed her once more, twirling her in his arms.

Mr. Tanner watched with amusement. "It's been awhile since I proposed, but I still remember how nervous I was."

****

Mary smiled as she watched the happy couple. She'd done it. Her job was nearly done. Marshal Reese would take care of Shanna from now on. He was a good man. He'd see to Shanna's happiness. She knew it in her heart. There was nothing to fear and no one to hurt either one of them ever again. She wasn't certain how long it would take her mind to adjust to Adam Delaney's death. She lived in fear of him and his gang for the last twenty-five years. Now she could go where she wanted and more importantly, she could visit with Shanna without fear of leading Adam to her. Maybe sometime Shanna would tell her all about her life in Rock Creek. Joseph sent his required telegrams once a month over the years, but she knew they were lies. Shanna was not as well cared for as Joseph depicted. She knew Shanna had a hard time on her own, and she knew Joseph and Sara begrudged Shanna the money she sent for her keep. She confronted her brother over it the second she arrived in Rock Creek. He denied everything. He mentioned the loss of their cabin, and told Mary she would foot the bill they had at the mercantile for lumber. The new cabin was not finished. The lumber sat out in the weather. They had a hard time getting the locals to help. Joseph was too lazy and liquored up to work on it. Mary sighed. It was not a pleasant situation. She squared her shoulders and informed them both, that she would not be paying for anything. Their treatment of Shanna forced her to reconsider the loan. They had one year to repay her in full or the marshal would be back to place them under arrest. Joseph spluttered and threatened her in return. Mary smiled when he was finished and informed him she knew of the beatings he gave Shanna over the years. One more word and she would press charges for abuse. Joseph and Sara had nothing else to say. Mary returned to the hotel fuming. Once she calmed down, she realized her job was finished. Shanna had the handsome marshal to care for her. Her future and freedom lay before her. Mary smiled. Maybe they would start a family as soon as they were wed, and then she would have grandchildren to fill her empty arms. Mary sighed. They would make beautiful babies together, and she couldn't wait to hold them.

****

"Where will you marry?" Rose asked. She wanted to go to Chicago. Shanna needed to show her this house she'd been hearing about. Shanna said it defied the imagination. Rose wondered at the comment. Her imagination worked extremely well so that house had to be something special. She also wanted to see all the servants she had been hearing about, maybe drive around the streets of Chicago and see the sights.

Reese looked at Shanna. "My family is in Chicago, except for a couple of my brothers."

"Brothers?" Rose perked right up. "You have brothers?" she squeaked. Oh yeah, she was going to Chicago, especially if the marshal had brothers.

"You didn't mention any brothers," Shanna said.

Reese looked from Rose to Shanna. "I have three of them. I have a brother in Texas. He's a ranger. His name is Chase. I have another brother way up north; he's a Canadian Mountie. His name is Max. My oldest brother is Connor. He runs the family business from New York," Reese said.

Shanna looked over at Rose and shook her head, but Rose paid her no mind

"Do they look like you?" Rose asked Her mind was on three men who looked exactly like Reese. Rose couldn't believe it. It felt like Christmas, but it was only October! She paid no attention to anything afterward;

her mind was filled with sinful thoughts of three more men, who looked exactly like the marshal.

****

Reese shook his head. "Chase is younger, better looking, and likes to get into trouble. Max is a loner. He's more serious and keeps to himself a lot, and Connor is the best looking and the smartest." Reese looked at Shanna. "My mother and sister live in Chicago. They'd be more than pleased to meet you," he said.

"Then you should marry in Chicago," Mrs. Tanner said. "Every mother wants to watch her son get married."

Mary nodded her head. "The Delaney house and gardens would make the perfect place." She sighed. "Giles will be bursting with pride, and Shanna will make a beautiful bride."

Reese looked questioningly at Shanna. "Where do you want to get married, Shanna? It doesn't matter to me where. The important part is who, and now I have your answer, I'm happy to go down the street and visit the preacher. My mother would like to be there though, I can tell you. She's been trying to marry us off for years, and it will upset her if she doesn't get to watch. The choice is yours, sweetheart."

Shanna's heart jumped at the endearment. "Let's get married in Chicago, then. I would like for your mother to be there, as well as your brothers and sister if they can all make it. We will tell Giles to get the place ready and to make all the arrangements. How much time do you figure we will need so your brothers can be there?" Shanna asked. The last thing she needed was Rose upset about not meeting any of Reese's brothers.

She looked over at Rose and shook her head over Rose's sorry state. Rose would no longer be the sane friend Shanna knew. She could tell by the sighs coming from her direction and the dreamy look in her eyes. Any sound advice would be coming from Mary or Mrs. Tanner. Rose could no longer be trusted.

Reese chuckled. "As soon as I make the announcement I'm getting hitched, the others will come running. They will want to meet the girl who lassoed me and look you over."

Shanna wasn't sure she wanted to be looked over. Maybe if she kept Rose close by, they would look her over too. If one of them took a shine to Rose, they would be forever sisters. Shanna hugged the notion close to her heart.

Chapter 29

They married the first week of November. It snowed the night before. The entire grounds were covered in a blanket of white. Shanna's gown arrived from Paris a week before the appointed date. Giles ordered it the day after Shanna first stepped foot on Delaney estate. It took him minutes to realize this girl was the opposite of her twin sister. Maybe if the marshal hadn't been so confused about his feelings, he would have seen it, too. The first week Shanna was there, Giles knew he was right about Marshal Calhan. He was a good man and would take care of their girl. Giles started the carpenters on a baby cradle, although he wouldn't have confessed to it for anyone, not even the reverend. Then, Shanna ran away to Rock Creek to confide in her dearest friend, Rose Tanner. Giles couldn't wait to meet her. From what he heard; she was utterly delightful. Not long after, Reese followed on his stallion, his sources said. Giles trusted his sources. The information they passed on was always sound. From then on, Giles rolled up his sleeves and began preparing for the wedding in earnest. It wouldn't be long, and he was right. One month later and here they were, planning a wedding. Weddings of this caliber didn't happen overnight, but Giles had everything under control. Good thing he always trusted his gut. After all, he was the best butler around.

Mary and Shanna were astonished when the parcel arrived from Paris. Mary shook out the beautiful lace gown, her eyes wide at the delicate, intricate pattern of the lace. Surely the fairies had a hand in its creation. The dress itself was simply cut with long tight sleeves and a fitted bodice. The skirt was fitted until past the hips and then fell in graceful ripples to Shanna's feet. A five-foot train flowed from the skirt in the back. The dress fit Shanna perfectly, complementing her slim silhouette.

"But how did it arrive so quickly?" Mary wondered.

Giles drew himself up to his full height of five feet eleven inches, his nose high with self-importance. "I ordered it weeks ago, madam. In truth I think it should have arrived sooner. Something must have delayed it."

Mary was confused. "But Reese only asked Shanna to marry him a fortnight ago. How did you know they were getting married?" she asked.

"It's what butlers do, madam. They observe and adjust to fit the circumstances. I observed quite a bit and promptly sent for the dress. I will have you know, I am the best there is." Giles said. Chuckling, Mary had to agree.

****

The couple married in the ballroom. Chairs were set up in rows to seat the two hundred guests attending. Many of the residents of Rock Creek were there, including Daniel Anderson and Delphine Otis. Shanna was never sure how they made it to the guest list since she never invited them. Delphine told everyone her and Shanna were the best of friends. They always had been. Delphine hovered close by whenever she got the chance, her eyes green with envy.

Connor, Max, and Chase all made it to the ceremony. Reese was right. They did come to look her over. They liked her instantly. After a bit of good-natured teasing, they welcomed Shanna to the family and gave brotherly advice on how best to deal with Reese. Shanna hadn't laughed so much in a long time. She liked these brothers. She liked Reese's mother, too. Maggie Calhan was a handsome woman, even at fifty-one. Thin and lithe, she had the figure of a young girl. No one would have supposed her to be the mother of five, four of them boys. Her hair was grayer than blonde, but her eyes were the same shade as her son's. Shanna instantly liked her, and the feeling was mutual.

****

Rose Tanner took one look at all four Calhan men and nearly swooned on the spot. They were all tall, muscular, and handsome as hell. They joked and nudged each other, as they surveyed the dancing after the ceremony. It was easy to see the love and respect they had for each other. Rose stared so hard, Chase Calhan felt her eyes on him and turned her way. Rose's face heated up. Chase looked her up and down with a slow heated look. He had dark brooding eyes which caused all sorts of wicked images to run through her mind. Rose clutched the arm of her chair. She had to get control.

The ranger winked at her. A slow wicked glint entered his eye as if he could see the things she'd been thinking. Rose dropped her gaze and focused on her lungs. She hoped Chase hadn't seen her thoughts, for they still danced in her head, him without his shirt, his bronzed naked chest glistening in the fire light, her hands running slowly over his warm skin, touching, caressing, and feeling. Her breathing quickened involuntarily.

"Would you care to dance?" the deep voice made her jump. She looked up into the warm whiskey colored eyes of Chase Calhan and melted on the spot. Rose swallowed hastily. Her mouth was so dry she struggled with her tongue. She opened her mouth to speak, but no sound emerged. Perspiration broke out on her forehead. Rose tried to stand, but her legs trembled so bad she was afraid they wouldn't hold her up. She stared helplessly up at him. What was she going to do? Here was her chance to get close to one of the most handsome men she'd ever seen, and she was drooling like a half wit, unable to speak. In frustration Rose merely nodded her head. It was all the encouragement the Texas Ranger needed. He had her in his arms leading her across the floor before she knew what happened.

His hard, warm chest pressed against her through the fabric of her dress. She closed her eyes, and pressed closer, her breathing ragged. His hands burned where they touched her waist, squeezing her. Rose looked into his eyes to see if he knew what he was doing to her. He did. His smile was heated and held wicked promises of things to come. Chase leaned forward and whispered in her ear. Rose stumbled at his suggestion, but he held her close against him, keeping her upright. They kept dancing. Chase circled the floor drawing her to the door and led her onto the terrace.

****.

Shanna watched Rose and Chase. They looked good together. Chase didn't seem a bit bothered by

Rose's inability to communicate with him. A smile touched her lips. She had high hopes for those two.

"Are you ready to retire?" Reese stood beside her, whispering the words into her ear, his voice husky with desire. Tonight was their wedding night, and he was impatient to have his beautiful wife alone. They would be spending their first night as husband and wife here. Tomorrow they would be going to Paris and then on to Venice. Shanna recognized the fire in Reese's eyes and blushed. She nodded shyly. She was anxious to be alone with him, too.

Reese kissed her fingers and pulling her arm through his, made his way to the door. His brothers whistled and cheered. They called out suggestions and soon they had everyone laughing. Reese saluted the crowd, and then they were alone. They walked up the stairs to the master chamber. Once they were on their honeymoon, refurbishing would begin. Shanna had it all planned out in mauve and lavender, but for now, it would stay as it was when her father lived here. Shanna hoped wherever her father was, he could see how happy she was at this moment.

Reese closed the master door and walked slowly toward her, removing his topcoat as he walked. It dropped to the floor along with his vest and shirt. He stood before her naked to the waist, his bronzed skin rippling as he moved. Shanna ran her fingers over his chest. He skin was as warm and smooth as melted caramel. She put her mouth against his chest, kissing and licking, tasting the saltiness. Reese groaned and reached for the back of her gown.

"Turn around, Love, let me help you with your gown," he said softly, his hands gentle on her shoulders as he turned her. He made quick work of her laces. The gown slid to the floor silently. Reese untied the knot on her corset, loosening it also, and dropping it to the floor. His lips kissed the back of her neck softly. Shanna turned around to face him. She slid her satin slippers off and reached for her garter.

"Let me." Reese growled. She sat on a brocade chair as he slid first one silk stocking down a shapely leg, and then the other one. He traced her calf and then ran his fingers along the inside of her thigh. He parted her legs and slid his hand up to the apex of her femininity. He felt the moist heat gathering there and groaned. Shanna tried to stand, but Reese pushed her back.

"Let me pleasure you," he said. His fingers rubbed her sensitive parts gently, the silk of her drawers sliding against her heightened skin. Shanna moaned with pleasure, opening her legs wider. Reese stood between her legs, one hand rubbing her softly. With the other one, he caught the end of her chemise, pulling it up. His fingers rubbed and stroked her belly, moving upward. Shanna's nipples hardened; her breasts grew heavy with need. When his fingers finally found her aching breasts, she moaned out loud. He found her straining nipple and rolled it between his thumb and forefinger. Shanna cried out again, arcing toward him. Reese leaned forward, capturing her mouth with his. Heat pooled against his hand, her drawers becoming moist with her desire. Reese reached for the waistband of her drawers, drawing them off her while his tongue stroked the inside of her mouth. Then his fingers were there, touching the secret throbbing center of her arousal. Her entrance was moist with heat. Reese penetrated her with one finger, and Shanna clawed at his arm. His tongue stroked against hers. She whimpered in response. Her arms wrapped tightly around his neck. Her legs opened wider as his hand worked against her, his finger penetrating then withdrawing, then slowly penetrating her again.

****

He slid two fingers into her tight sheath, and she cried out, her hips coming off the chair to meet him. Her cry of desire stoked his passion. "Sweetheart, let me touch you. Let me taste you," he whispered. He grabbed her chemise and pulled it over her head, dropping it on the floor. He stood back and looked at her. Her head was thrown back, her blonde hair spread behind her like a halo. Her face was flushed, her lips pink and swollen from his kisses. Her long, beautiful legs were spread wide, her sex pink and moist. She was completely gloriously naked, and she was his.

Reese picked her up in his arms and moved her to the bed. He drew back the coverlet and placed her on the satin sheets. Her legs dangled over the side. The high bed put her nearly waist high. He reached for her, hooking her knees over his shoulders.

Shanna sat up. "What are you doing?" she asked, confused.

"I'm tasting you," Reese replied. He leaned forward placing his mouth on her sensitive part. A shudder and a moan came from Shanna. Reese spread the lips of her mound and gently licked and sucked on her until she screamed his name. Her hands were full of his hair as she pulled him toward her, crying and writhing and then pushing at him as the pleasure tore at her, again and again. Then she screamed, her body shuddering against him, his name a chant on her lips as her head thrashed side to side. He sucked one more time and then opened his mouth on her entrance, his tongue penetrating her.

She bucked against him. Her hips rocked back and forth against his mouth. He slipped both hands beneath her buttocks holding her as he tasted her molten center. Shanna thought she'd died. She never imagined such incredible ecstasy existed. She was covered in a sheen of perspiration, her body still racked by the tremors Reese created. Then he was naked, next to her, scooting her around so all of her was on the bed. He knelt between her legs, pushing them open with his knees.

Reese knelt over her, his eyes boring into her. "I love you, Shanna," he said, and then he was inside her. Shanna grabbed at his shoulders as the sensation of his invasion shook her still trembling body. She arced against him to take him deeper inside. Reese groaned and surged forward until he was firmly seated inside her. She rocked against him, moaning at the pleasure his manhood gave her. He was so deep inside; he stretched her there. She wrapped her legs about his waist and grabbed his shoulders for support. He pulled out slowly and then slid back inside, moaning at the sensation. Her sheath gripped him with every movement. Shanna cried his name, clawing at his back.

She was so tight, so hot, so wet it was driving him over the edge. He pulled out and then plunged back inside her going faster and harder. Shanna clutched him tight screaming his name. He pumped harder, and faster still, until she screamed with her release, her arms locked around him. Her tremors tipped him over the edge. He plunged into her one last time. He roared as he found his release. It went on and on. Reese shook against her with the force of his tremors. He fell against her, slick with sweat and weak from the aftermath of their lovemaking. Reese rolled off her onto his back, pulling Shanna into his side.

"Did I hurt you?" he asked. His orgasm was nothing like he ever experienced before. It was mind blowing. He wasn't sure if he was too rough with her or not. He rolled to his side so he could see her face. "Love, did I hurt you?" he asked again. Shanna looked up, her eyes bright with emotion. "No. You could never hurt me, not when you love me like you just did." She smiled up at him, too weak to move.

Reese tucked her back against him. "I do love you Shanna, more than you will ever know."

Shanna leaned over and whispered, "I love you," in his ear.

Reese gazed at her. "After I was shot, I remember being in the hospital. I heard Sergeant Baxter and you talking. I was in serious pain. I knew I was dying. I wanted to talk to you, but my eyes wouldn't open, and my mouth wouldn't move. I yelled at you in my mind to wait for me. The blackness closed over me, and your voices got further away. I knew I was going." Reese pulled her closer. "Then I heard your voice. You whispered 'I love you' in my ear. It gave me the strength to fight the darkness. I held onto those three words through all the pain and the darkness. It's the reason I am alive. If I hadn't heard those words, I would have given up."

Shanna blinked back tears. "You were so quiet at the hospital, so withdrawn. After we arrived here, you refused to talk to me. I worried you hated me for killing

Jenna. I worried it was her you loved and not me."

Reese frowned. "You got it all wrong. It's you I love and only you. Every time I tried to explain about Jenna, it made you mad. I didn't want to mess it up again. I reasoned if I had a way to make you feel obligated to marry me, I could convince you to love me. It might take some time, but you'd be mine, and I wouldn't be worried about losing you. I knew how I felt about you. I didn't dare ask you to marry me without a good reason."

Shanna wrinkled her brow and laughed. "Why not?"

Reese gazed into her beautiful eyes. "I ruined your life. I accused you of terrible things and treated you poorly. Then I took your virginity and broke you heart. I made you cry, Shanna. I didn't figure I had a chance. So, I used the only thing I had, your loving nature. I knew you would do the right thing. I used the possibility of a baby to get you to agree."

Shanna chuckled. "That didn't work either."

"No. It made you mad and you ran away again. I nearly went crazy. I didn't know what to do. I can't live without you, Shanna."

"What made you decide to come to Rock Creek?"

"You and Giles. I remembered those three words in my ear. I realized I hadn't told you how I felt about you. I worried over the right way to approach you. I might not get another chance. I couldn't lose you. Then, Giles found me." Reese chuckled. "He informed me you loved me, and he had a wedding under construction. He warned me, I had a week to find you and tell you how I felt, or he was coming after me. His wedding would not be sabotaged by my cowardice to express my feelings to his girl."

"He threatened you?" Shanna asked, laughing.

"He did."

"Thank God for Giles. Remind me to give him a raise," Shanna murmured.

"It will go right to his head. He already thinks he's the best there is."

"He is," Shanna murmured.

Within minutes they were both asleep.

Chapter 30

Nine months later, the large house at Delaney Estate was once more filled with people. They hadn't come to another wedding. They came for the birthing. Shanna lay upstairs in the massive master bed screaming once more. It wasn't for pleasure this time, at all. No, it was with pain as the tide of ever-increasing contractions tore at her body, preparing the way for her babe to enter the world.

A midwife stood at the foot of the bed holding one of Shanna's legs up as the babe's head became visible. Mary stood on the other side of the bed, holding Shanna's other leg, talking in a soft, soothing voice telling Shanna it would soon be over. Twelve hours of labor took their toll on Shanna. She was covered in sweat, weakly lying against the mountain of pillows behind her. Her hair was plastered to her head; her eyes nearing panic as another urge to bear down took control of her. The midwife guided the baby's head as Shanna pushed. Her face turned purple with the effort. Reese stopped pacing and clenched his hands. He didn't dare say a word. The midwife ordered him out of the labor room once already because he threatened to shoot somebody if they didn't help his wife.

It was Shanna who calmed him down. Smiling weakly, she said. "It's all right, dear. Women do this sort of thing all the time. Please be still for my sake, so the midwife lets you stay. It encourages me to see your face."

Reese nodded his agreement. His face paled as his wife grew weaker by the hour.

Suddenly, there was a gush and the midwife held a newborn baby in her arms. The infant gave a cry of outrage at having to leave her warm haven. Reese stared at the tiny little life screaming her discontent. The room began to spin. He was a father! Mary had him by the arm, pushing him into a chair, and shoving his head between his knees.

"Breathe, Reese. It's finally over, you have a beautiful baby girl, and as soon as they get the baby cleaned and wrapped, you can see her." Mary smiled with satisfaction at her newborn granddaughter.

****

Shanna lay worn and spent. Her breathing slowed as she looked down at her baby daughter. The child had a dusting of blonde hair. Shanna smiled. She held her baby close to her heart. Then she stopped, her smile disappeared. "Mama, something is wrong. I need to push."

Mary looked up in alarm. She'd seen this happen once before. She took the infant from Shanna, holding her close as Shanna pushed some more. A second daughter was born a few minutes later, as blonde as her sister. They looked exactly alike. Reese got to his feet and walked unsteadily to the bed. Shanna held a baby in each arm, a wide smile on her face.

"It's apparent I did not overeat as you suggested. I had two daughters growing inside me, instead of one," Shanna said. She looked from one to the other. A worry crossed her face. "What if one of them turns out like—"

"It's not possible," Reese cut in. He didn't want her to even think it.

"It is possible," Shanna said.

Reese shook his head. "The reason your twin was the way she was, is because your uncle raised her. These girls will both grow up kind, gentle, and intelligent like you." He sounded certain.

"How do you know?" Shanna asked.

Reese smiled. "Because you are their mother, and you won't let them do anything different."

Shanna smiled up at her wonderful handsome husband. She'd come to value his strength, his wisdom, and his intuition. Could life get any better than this? At last she had her family. She belonged to this man, and to these daughters. She had them, and they had her. She also had Mama and the staff. She had the Tanners, and soon Rose would be making her own announcement with Chase. Shanna was part of the large Calhan family and savored the times they were all together. She couldn't wait to show her daughters to the family and the family to her daughters.

Reese leaned over and kissed her softly. "Well done, my love."

At last, life was good. In fact, it was perfect.

A word from the author...

I have been married to my best friend for thirty-nine years. I am the mother of ten children, six boys and four girls. My youngest is twelve years, and my oldest is thirty-seven. I have twenty grandchildren. They are my whole world. We laugh, we cry, we celebrate, and we grieve, but we do it all together. No matter what, we have each other's back. That is how it should be. I believe in miracles. I believe in love. I believe in family, and I believe in happily ever after.